Also by M. J. ROSE

Fiction

LYING IN BED
THE DELILAH COMPLEX
THE HALO EFFECT
LIP SERVICE
IN FIDELITY
FLESH TONES
SHEET MUSIC

Nonfiction

HOW TO PUBLISH AND PROMOTE ONLINE
(with Angela Adair-Hoy)

BUZZ YOUR BOOK (with Douglas Clegg)

M. J. ROSE

THE VENUS FIX

MIRA

ISBN-13: 978-0-7783-2317-4
ISBN-10:   0-7783-2317-X

THE VENUS FIX

Printed in Canada

It's about time someone dedicated a book to my dear friend Carol Fitzgerald, a true and tireless book champion.

Carol, for everything you do, this one's for you.

Venus—*Mythol.* The ancient Roman goddess of beauty and love, especially sensual love.

Fix—*slang* (orig. U.S.). A dose of a narcotic drug. Also short for fixation—*Psychol.* In Freudian theory, the arresting of the development of a libidinal component at a pregenital stage, so that psychosexual emotions are "fixed" at that point. Also, loosely, an obsession, an *idée fixe.*

Mine Enemy is growing old—
I have at last Revenge
The Palate of the Hate departs
If any would avenge—
Let him be quick—the Viand flits
It is a faded Meat
Anger as soon as fed is dead
'Tis starving makes it fat
—Emily Dickinson

One

~~~~~~~~~~~~~~~~~~~~

Dearest,

After all these months, I'm willing to concede. Nothing will
make me miss you less. Nothing will ease the razor-sharp
pain that wakes me up every morning and keeps me from
falling asleep at night. Not while those women roam—no,
not quite women, but witch women who go haunting,
casting spells and capturing souls without anyone realizing just how dangerous they are or noticing the evil running in their veins. Evil that glows secret bright in the night
and feeds the junkies who drool, eyes glued to their bare
breasts and wet lips, ears attuned to low moans and dirty
chatter while they stroke, massage, and manipulate themselves to orgasm and then languish in some fugue state
until they crash back, back, back to earth.

There are twenty-three days left until your birthday,
and to show you how much I love you, I promise, by then
all five of these women will have been punished.

What I'm going to do won't bring back my appetite or
my curiosity or my energy. It won't do a damn thing for
me. That doesn't matter. Because this I do for you.

Thursday
Twenty-two days remaining

Two

Damn, it was freezing. He'd opened the window to chase away the smell of beer and grass and sex, but then he'd fallen asleep, and now it was so cold he didn't even want to stick his head out from under the covers to see if she was still there. But Timothy wanted to come again more than he wanted anything else, so he did it, he pushed the blanket down just enough to peek out.

In his darkened bedroom she was the only thing that he could see. Still there. Still naked. Her lovely breasts with their pink-tipped nipples pointing up.

His erection stirred.

Timothy was awake now, the dreams replaced with a fresh fantasy of what the next minutes would bring. She was golden. That was the best way to describe her: the tawny color of her skin, the long blond curls, and the feeling inside of him that burned like a sun when he was in her glow. And all he had to do was lie back and let her magic work on him.

None of the girls at school were this experienced.

Or this gorgeous.

Or this willing.

Penny was sitting in the big red armchair where he'd left her—her legs spread, playing with a dildo, smiling at him. But it was one weird smile. He leaned forward. Nope, she didn't look right. She was shaking a little and her mouth was sort of contorted into a sick clown's grimace. Then her head fell forward, her back heaved, and she vomited.

Timothy had fooled around with a lot of different crap, but this was weird. What kind of pervert would think this was hot?

Usually Penny was coy and sweet and sexy. Sure, she was a little kinky sometimes with the crazy-shaped dildos she used, but she wasn't moving any of those magic wands in and out of her now.

"Penny," he whispered. "What are you doing?"

Her answer was an agonized groan. Low and feeble. Like the sound a wounded animal might make. Nothing like the exciting sounds she'd made when she was riding the lubricated pink plastic dildo and coming right along with him.

Maybe she wasn't acting. Maybe she really was sick. Food poisoning made you sick like that. He'd had food poisoning once. She looked sick, didn't she? Her skin was slicked with sweat, her hair was flattened to the sides of her face, and her eyes looked glassy and feverish.

She looked like she needed help. Now. Fast. But what could he do?

Grabbing the blanket off the bed, he wrapped it around his naked waist and started for his bedroom door. Then he stopped—there was no one home. His parents were out. Jeez, what was he thinking? Thank God they were out because Penny, sick or not, was way off limits.

He looked back at her to make sure. Yes, she was still moving in that slow-motion, sick way, her moan now a low constant sound that made him want to put his hands up to his ears and block it out.

He grabbed the phone.

He'd call for help. But who? The police? An ambulance? Amanda? Would she know what to do? No, she might tell her mother. He couldn't risk that. Besides, what if he was wrong? What if this was a game? What if Penny was acting out some perversion by request? He knew she did that sometimes.

He glanced back at her, at her small hands gripping the arms of the chair, at her feet, so fragile and inconsequential, at the worn carpet he'd never noticed before. Everything looked sort of pathetic now—the meager furniture, the really small television—except for the view out the window. He'd never noticed any of this before. He'd always been too busy, under her spell. But not now. Not anymore.

Pick your head up, Penny. Look at me. Tell me what's going on. What should I do?

She threw up again.

He dialed 911.

"State your emergency, please."

At the same time he heard the voice, the screen went black. He ran to the monitor and stared at it, seeing only his own ghostly image staring back.

Penny was gone.

What the hell?

He hit the back button to see if the problem was his computer or hers. The site he'd been to before hers popped up. He hit the forward key.

Her site was gone.

"Hello?" shouted the voice on the other end of the phone. "Hello?"

A dozen thoughts hit him all at once. They were going to ask him who he was, and he was going to have to tell them, and then his parents would find out he'd broken the rules again, and God only knew what they would do to him this time. He had been going to all those stupid therapy sessions at school and his parents were finally easing up on him, but if they found out about this…what would happen then? Besides, maybe he was wrong. Maybe Penny had only been acting out some stupid game.

"Hello?"

"Hello," Timothy finally answered.

"Can you tell me what the emergency is?"

"It's not…I don't think. What if it's not an emergency?"

"We have a car on the way to your house. Are you hurt?"

"No. It was a mistake, it's not an emergency."

"Are you all right?"

"Yes. It's not me. I thought someone…I thought someone was breaking in…but it wasn't… I was asleep."

"The police are on their way. They should be there in less than thirty seconds." The operator's voice eased and softened.

Timothy heard the intercom buzz in the kitchen, hung up, ran out of his room and down the hall, the panic rising like bile in his stomach.

He pressed the button.

"Yes?"

"Timothy, the police are here," the doorman announced. "They said it was an emergency. I'm sending them up."

"No," he shouted at the doorman. "No. Let me talk to them."

There was a pause. Then: "Timothy Marcus? This is Officer Keally. Is there something wrong up there?"

"No."

"Are you sure? You called 911."

"Yeah, but by mistake. I was asleep, dreaming, thought I saw…heard something, but it wasn't real."

"Are you sure you don't want us to come up and check things out?"

Timothy actually hesitated. Should he tell them and face

the consequences? Deal with whatever his parents would do to him? He had seen something weird on the computer, hadn't he? She was sick, wasn't she?

Or had some weird fucker convinced Penny to act out his perverted scenario?

"I'm sure," he said into the intercom.

Monday
Eighteen days remaining

Three

It was going to start to snow again, soon. I could smell it. Snow had always been magical to me. Something that, until I was ten, I thought I owned because my last name is Snow. Morgan Snow.

The sky was gray and the trees were dusted white and my breath came out in visible puffs. I had been mesmerized by that when I was a child, and like me, my daughter, Dulcie, had found it equally absorbing.

"Ghost breath," she'd say, then suck in a great gulp of air and blow it out again. "Do you believe in ghosts, Mommy?"

I did, but not in a way that my then eight-year-old would have understood. How could I have explained that the ghost of my mother lived inside of her? And that there were also the ghosts of the secrets that my patients told me that could, in the midst of a moment of my own pleasure, surface—interrupting and demanding acknowledgment. That it was in between all those moments that I hoped it would all be okay, that we'd all be okay.

At the corner of Sixty-sixth Street, I stopped for a red light. A woman in a black fur coat shifted impatiently from her right foot to her left. "I hate this weather," she said. Not quite to me, but not to herself, either. I nodded, and then the light changed.

We crossed and went in opposite directions.

The Northeast was suffering a severe cold spell but I didn't mind. I liked to bundle up in layers of sweaters and fleece-lined boots, wrap a big scarf around my head, and walk the mile from my apartment on Eightieth Street and Madison to my office.

At Sixty-fifth, I turned the corner and trudged toward Park Avenue. Side streets don't get as much traffic as the major avenues so the snow never melts as quickly. The early twentieth-century limestone maisonette where I work was halfway down the block. The building's facade is elegant: Ionic columns support an overhang that shelters the patients while they wait to be buzzed through the wrought-iron door into the most progressive sex clinic in the nation—the Butterfield Institute.

In the country, the snow stays pristine and is so clean you can reach down, scoop some up in your hands and eat it. But in the city, the exhaust from the thousands of cars, buses and trucks turns it gray within hours.

Near the gutter, on the sidewalk in front of the institute, there were filthy mounds of snow smeared with black soot, but close to the building, where I was standing, it was still white, and would be for at least a few more hours.

Four

M y ten o'clock had just left and I was about to make a
phone call when the patient I knew only as "Bob" walked in,
early and unannounced.

"I had an awful weekend," he said in a tense voice as he
strode across the threshold.

Bob, who normally had ramrod-straight posture, looked
weighed down. Behind him Allison, the receptionist, explained that she had tried to stop him from barging in but that
he refused to wait once she'd told him that my last patient had
already left.

I was sitting in the oversize chair that faces the couch
where my patients either sit or lie down. I glanced at the clock
to my right.

"Your appointment isn't until eleven o'clock," I said to
Bob, and then told Allison she could go.

While I waited for him to sit down, I drank some tea from
the mug I was holding. Jung at Heart, it read. Green letters
on a white background. It was one of a set of six that Dulcie
had made for me, each emblazoned with a psychoanalytic
pun. It amazed me how many patients saw me using one of

those mugs week after week, and then one day suddenly said, *How funny—when did you get that?*

That was an important moment. It meant we were making progress, that my patient was noticing his or her surroundings, and was no longer absorbed just with the self. Bob had not reached that point.

He hadn't even progressed to the point where he would tell me his real name. I'd had patients who wanted to protect their privacy before, though never anyone as secretive as Bob, who was bright and charming, intense and secretive, and desperately in need of my help.

"These fifteen minutes between sessions are my only breaks. It's not okay to just barge in."

Bob wasn't at the point where he could think about anyone but himself. "I'm very upset about my wife. No matter what, I love her. I just can't stand this." Usually he folded his jacket carefully, but as he talked he dropped it on the edge of the couch, and when it fell to the floor he didn't notice.

"What happened over the weekend?"

Bob was in his early fifties, about six feet tall, and had the build of someone who worked out religiously. His suits were always pressed and his shoes were shined. Incongruously, a blue New York Yankees baseball cap always covered his head. His black owl-rimmed glasses had tinted lenses that hid his eyes.

I didn't know if his efforts to disguise himself were working or if he simply wasn't as well known as he thought he was, but I did know he was paranoid about being seen at the Butterfield Institute. Over and over, he reminded me how bad it would be for his career—and his wife's—if his "issue," as he referred to it, was to be discovered.

He didn't pay his bills by check or through his insurance company. Rather, twice a month, ten minutes before Bob arrived, he was preceded by a man named Terry Meziac, who wore a business suit and carried a briefcase and gave me an envelope containing crisp hundred-dollar bills, and then swept my office for bugs.

He never found any. I never expected him to. But since his third visit, when I noticed the gun in his waistband, I had occasionally wondered if, as the receiver of Bob's confessions, there was a chance that my own life was in danger.

In ancient Egypt, the architects of the pyramids, the only men who knew the entrances and exits through the stone puzzles, were killed once the monuments were completed, so the secrets died with them.

I wasn't that disturbed by the gun. I dated a detective. I lived in Manhattan. A lot of powerful people had bodyguards. What did disturb me was that Bob was so paranoid about being in therapy. He even used our hidden entrance, which links to the basement of the building next to ours. We don't generally encourage our patients to take advantage of it because it causes logistical nightmares for Allison, who has to keep track of all the appointments and make sure no two people show up next door at the same time. In the previous six years, only one other patient had asked to use it.

We keep secrets at the Butterfield Institute. Hold them tight and protect them the way we protect our own children. That is what we promise our patients, what we swear to, what we stake our reputations on. Because our currency is secrets, nothing on the outside of the building proclaims its status as a prestigious sex therapy clinic. But still patients sometimes worry that they will be seen walking through the wrought-iron-and-milk-glass doors.

Three, four minutes had gone by and Bob remained quiet. Only his fingers, tapping a code on the leather of the sofa, broke the silence in the room. I judged his level of anxiety by the tempo of the tapping. Today was one of the worst in the three months since he'd been seeing me.

"I don't know how to save my wife and myself, too. And I have to save her." His voice softened.

"Why is it up to you to save her? Can't she save herself?"

"Yes, yes, but I'm the one that put her in this hell."

"We've talked about you taking all the blame."

He frowned. Bob had never allowed me to even suggest anything disparaging about his wife. She was above reproach. She was an angel. She was innocent.

"She's not the one surfing the Internet, jerking off to pretty little girls who whisper dirty words to me in the middle of the afternoon. Maybe…" he said, and then stopped again. Outside my second-floor window a car horn honked.

"Yes?"

"Maybe I need to find another therapist."

This didn't come as a surprise. Often a frustrated patient imagines another doctor will be the solution.

"We can talk about that. But first, tell me what's going on at home."

"My wife is having…she's gone into some sort of new crisis. It's not just a depression anymore, it's a meltdown. And it's completely my fault. She's erratic. Volatile. Angry one minute, crying the next. I can't stand it. I'll do anything to stop it. To make her happy." He hesitated. "If I can. I'll do anything I can."

"I know you think it's your fault, but—"

"I don't *think* it is, Dr. Snow. I know it is."

"Explain that to me."

"Do I need to spell it out?"

Spelling it out was Bob's code that he'd broken his fast and gone online again. Since he'd been seeing me, the longest he'd been able to go without a fix was five days, and he'd done that twice. The previous Wednesday, he said he was ready to try to quit again and had already abstained for two nights.

"No. You don't have to spell it out if you don't want to, but I'd like to hear what happened."

"Bad boy that I am, I went online. I tried not to. I hadn't for two days. Just like I told you last Wednesday morning. But Thursday…I don't know…I was home, by myself. I went online to read my e-mail and…I clicked over…no big deal…just for a few minutes. Anyway, I didn't hear her come home. I was so deep into the fantasy and the goddamn fucking pleasure that I didn't hear her, and she walked in on me. She fucking saw me at the computer. I hadn't heard her. I wasn't paying attention."

Bob stood up, walked to the window and put his hands against the glass, as if he might push it out and escape.

"Can anyone see in? Is this glass treated?"

"No, it's not."

Quickly, he turned around. For a second he looked as if he didn't know what he was supposed to do next. Stand? Sit? Leave?

"Bob, you need to come sit back down, or lie down."

He nodded and did as I'd asked.

Silently again on the couch, he clasped his hands in his lap and then stared at his white-gold wedding band.

"Bob, when you talk about going online, you refer to yourself as a bad boy. Tell me how it feels to be bad?"

"Horrible. Despicable. Out of control. How else would it feel?"

"Well, the expression on your face when you said it made me think being bad was exciting. Thrilling, maybe. Is that possible?"

He seemed startled. "No. That's crazy. Why would I like breaking rules? Rules, laws, are what separate us from savages."

He was disassociating. It wasn't the first time. His posture had become more rigid. His hands relaxed. He spoke as if he were addressing a group of people, rather than just me, somewhere other than here in my office. I had to bring him back.

"How do you feel about your wife finding out about you going online?"

"I didn't want her to know. I'm not a sadist. You know that, don't you?" He looked directly at me, imploring me. This was when he reached me, when his childlike need to be acknowledged broke through the professional veneer.

"No, you're not a sadist. But let's get back to the question. Is that the only reason you didn't want her to know?"

"Isn't it enough?"

"Yes. But I'm not sure it's the only reason. Think for a minute, Bob. Why didn't you want her to know?"

"Why can't you tell me? I don't understand what would be so detrimental to the therapy for you to make a suggestion here and there. Use an example about another patient—without names, of course—to illustrate a point?"

This was something Bob often did, interrupting the therapy to try to understand the theory behind it. Occasionally it was a deadly tactic, but often I knew it was a deep-seated need to understand the precepts of the process. He was highly intelligent, and I'd found that if I answered him, he became more responsive.

"In this case I don't have an answer. But something makes me think that even if you aren't conscious of it, there's another reason. I need you to find it."

He sat. Thought. Seemed to accept my rationale.

"Okay. Now. Why didn't you want your wife to know?"

His brow furrowed and then relaxed. He'd thought of something.

"Tell me."

"Her knowing ruins everything."

I nodded but didn't speak. I waited. I knew there was more. After ten years of being a therapist you learn when the end of a sentence signals more to come, or when the patient has closed up again and you need to find another way in.

"It's not mine anymore. Even if it's hell, it's been my hell. Something that she wasn't part of. Now that she knows, she can lie in bed and imagine me watching my pathetic little Web-cam girls, with my dick in my hand and she can laugh at me and my dependency."

"Why do you think she'd laugh at you? Has she laughed at you before?"

"No." Sharp. Decisive.

"Then why now?"

He shook his head.

"Anything that comes to mind."

He shook his head again. We'd get back to that. Or I'd find another way in.

"What happened after she saw what you were doing?"

"She smiled at me." Now he shook his head as if he was trying to shake away the image. "It was crazy. A crazy smile. Like she'd really lost her mind for a second. She just kept smiling. It was horrible. But the worst part was that even though I wanted to get up and hold her and promise her that I'd never do it again, I didn't. I just sat there."

Something was happening to Bob. His eyes were not as intense. His muscles were relaxing into a professional mask again.

"It couldn't be more ironic," he said in a more imperious, less-emotional voice.

"What couldn't be?"

"Me. Going online—" He stopped midsentence.

I gave him a few seconds to continue. Then a few seconds

longer. We were at a critical juncture. I knew how careful I had to be to push but not too far.

"Did you say anything to her?"

"I tried to talk to her. I told her it was not a big deal. That I'd just stumbled on the Web site. I lied."

There it was. That odd elation in his voice when he said he'd lied. I felt a rush of adrenaline. It doesn't always happen that a set of circumstances occurs in your patient's life at exactly the right time in his or her therapy to create an opening like this.

"Bob, how did you feel when you were lying?"

"Terrible."

He didn't. I knew he was lying. I could hear it in his voice, see it in the way he clasped his hands suddenly, hiding the wedding ring with the fingers of the other hand.

"Really? Terrible?"

"Yes. Lying is horrible. To lie to your wife…"

"Yes, but just because it's horrible doesn't mean it has to feel terrible."

He was nodding. He knew. Was he going to tell me?

"It didn't feel terrible, did it?"

He shook his head.

I lowered my voice. "How did it feel, Bob?"

He shut his eyes. He couldn't do it. That didn't matter. I knew he had consciously thought it. We'd get there. He was so close to understanding that he'd felt real pleasure.

"Did she believe you?"

"No. And she told me she didn't. She asked me how often, and I lied again. I told her I mostly did it when she was out of town. I didn't want to hurt her. It was killing me to hurt her. I love her." It was a plea for me to stop, but I wouldn't. Quickly now, before he could think about it, I asked again. "How did you feel lying to her?"

"Elated." Once the word was out of his mouth he seemed confused by it.

I let out my breath. We'd just jumped a new hurdle.

"Why?"

"Why did it feel good?"

I nodded.

"I don't know. Can't you tell me? I tortured her and got pleasure from it? What kind of sick fuck does that make me? I broke every single rule and I didn't care. I don't understand."

He rarely used the work *fuck*. He was using it a lot today. "You don't have to understand everything now. You just need to be open to feeling it."

He couldn't tolerate his feelings, though. Even before he said a word, I knew he was stepping back. His expression and posture changed again.

"It is really very obscene." His sounded as if he were observing the scene from a great distance. "My wife was standing in front of my computer, staring at a woman who was thrusting a dildo in and out of herself in time to some stupid rock song. When I reached out to shut it off, she yelled at me to leave it. For some insane reason I did. She stood there like a soldier and took it. Like she was being sentenced. I couldn't stand it. Me. I was doing this to her. To my wife."

I ignored the non sequitur and tried to follow where he was leading. "What happened then?"

"She leaned in, over my shoulder, and in a very low voice, she said, *'Bob, you don't think you fooled me, do you? I've known about what you do in here for weeks. For weeks and weeks and weeks, and I'm going to kill you for this.'"*

Five

Detective Noah Jordain, of the NYPD Special Victims Unit, leaned against the Jefferson Parish courthouse. His cell phone was wedged between his ear and shoulder while he sipped a cup of real New Orleans coffee and waited for his partner, Mark Perez, to get back on the phone.

Watching the street traffic, he squinted against the sun's brightness, put the cup down on the stone ledge of the building, pulled his sunglasses out of his pocket, and put them on.

Coming back to New Orleans, his hometown, had always been bittersweet, but since the hurricane it was also surrealistic. How could so much have changed? So much still be left to do? And yet feel the city's spirit so alive?

Across the road a light-skinned man wearing jeans, a short-sleeved white shirt and sunglasses walked down the block for the second time since Jordain had been standing there. Something about the way he swaggered alerted the detective.

It was most likely nothing, but he couldn't be too sure. The Hatterly trial had made a lot of people angry five years earlier, and now that the defendant's lawyers had won an appeal, those same people were getting angry all over again. Much of it was directed at Jordain, whose incriminating testimony had been critical to the prosecution before and would be again.

To be more precise, which Jordain always was, the papers were reporting that he'd been the nail in Louis Hatterly's coffin. Everyone expected that same nail to be driven back in again.

Meanwhile, in Manhattan, Perez got back on the line and continued describing the brand-new nightmare where he'd left off. "All over the country, 911 operators started getting calls. According to the guys watching the Web cast, one minute she was playing with herself, the next she was sick. That lasted for about a quarter of an hour. Some of them were more specific about what *sick* meant, some less, but it sounded pretty brutal. Then she dropped offline."

"How many calls were there?"

"Over 150. Jersey City operators took twenty-two. Dallas took thirteen. Syracuse, twelve. Eighteen in New York. You want me to keep going?"

"I don't know, you want to keep going?"

"Not unless you have a while," Perez quipped. "The calls started on Thursday night. Most of them were logged by Friday a.m. A few are still dribbling in."

"Four days later?"

"Guilty consciences."

"If calls were taken all over the country, we're handling this out of New York why?"

"A few of the guys described the top of a building they could see out of her window. Three of the New Yorkers identified it as the Met Life tower."

"And it took us until today to get this because…?"

"You don't really want to go into that now. You'd much prefer I keep filling you in on the more important information. It's just bureaucratic crap that will raise your blood pressure, and you have to go on the stand in a few minutes. Instead, I'm going to tell you that no one has any idea who the girl is or where she is or anything about her except for the URL where the guys went to see her little show."

"You getting details?" Jordain asked.

It was his most oft-repeated phrase and there were cops both in New Orleans—where he'd worked until five years ago—and in New York who called him Detective Details.

"The URL is registered to a porn site registered to a holding company, which is owned by another holding company, which is owned by a corporation in China, and communicating with them is taking some work. It's all going to come back to some guy sitting in an office right here in Manhattan or L.A. or New Jersey. You know it is. But we have to circle the world first."

"Is there anything that suggests foul play? Could the woman have just been sick? Or could it be suicide?"

"The descriptions of how the illness was presented suggest poison. Self-inflicted is possible, but unlikely. Add that to the sex angle and we hit the jackpot. Besides, they know that we have absolutely nothing else to do."

"Funny, funny man. Okay. I'll be finished here by two and should be on a five o'clock—" Jordain broke off. The stranger in the cap was walking down the street again, now for the third time. "I'll call you and see if you need me to come in."

"No need tonight. We don't have enough."

"Yet."

The man crossed over and was heading toward him. Jordain's hand moved to his waist and rested on his gun. It was an unconscious move.

Nothing happened, though. The man sauntered by, not even glancing at him. But while Jordain had been paying attention to the man in the glasses, he hadn't noticed the woman who was now standing right in front of him.

"You aren't ever wrong, are you, Detective?" Mrs. Hatterly, the defendant's mother, was in her sixties, with white hair pulled back off a face that was deeply etched. Her eyes were red-rimmed and she was trembling. She stood so close to him that he could smell her sweet perfume.

"Perez, gotta go." Jordain snapped the phone shut. "I'm sorry for everything you've had to go through, Mrs. Hatterly." His New Orleans drawl made the word *sorry* stretch all the way out.

"What I've had to go through is nothing. It's my son who is suffering. Because of you. Because you are so sure you're right. Don't you realize that your being right is what got my son convicted—"

A young man came over and put his hand on the woman's arm. "Mom, let's go inside."

But Mrs. Hatterly wasn't done with Jordain yet. "You're so sure. But what if you are wrong? Haven't you ever been wrong? Haven't you—"

Her son pulled her away just before her angry fists reached Jordain's chest.

He sighed. Other cops claimed they got used to people's pain, and he envied them for that. But becoming hardened took its toll in other ways.

He watched until she was gone from sight, and then he, too, headed toward the courtroom.

It took some effort. And not because it was so hot out and the air was so heavy. He loved that air. No, that wasn't why. This case had been bad enough the first time. Having to go through it all again was bringing back ghosts, because during the last trial, his father, Detective André Jordain, had died.

Jordain had been back to New Orleans often since moving to New York. He'd been to the cemetery where his dad was buried. But this was different.

He couldn't stop the memories from washing over him. The defendant's mother had shook him up, and whenever he was unnerved, the dam he'd erected to keep the past from seeping into the present leaked.

Jordain passed through the cool lobby and proceeded to the courtroom. He stopped in the hallway and looked in. Five years earlier, Jordain had been on that stand when his lieutenant had walked in and stood, as if at attention, at the back of the room. Noah had wondered why he was there. But he didn't find out until after he had finished his testimony: His father had died.

He stared at the spot where he'd been when he'd heard. The ghosts were demanding their time.

Six

At noon, Nina Butterfield popped her head into my office. She was dressed in a three-quarter-length, copper-colored fur coat that matched her hair, and was holding up a pair of ice skates, swinging them in the air.

"You want to take a break?" she asked, her amber eyes sparkling.

I did but, preoccupied with Bob, told her I didn't think I should.

"You never need to get out more than when you don't think you should. I know these things. I'm a therapist. Now, come on. I cleared your schedule with Allison. She said you're free." It sounded like a suggestion but it wasn't. More often than not, she knew what was best for me. More often than not I recognized that.

At least twice a week Nina and I went out together at lunchtime. Sometimes to eat, but usually to walk, either in Central Park, which was only two blocks west of the institute, or wherever we wound up, exploring stores that we'd never noticed before, taking in exhibitions at museums or shows at art galleries. In the winter, when strolling in the street wasn't as enticing, we went ice-skating.

Outside, we pulled on our gloves and buttoned up our coats. Someone else might have turned back because of the snow and gray sky. Not Nina. She was fearless about venturing out into a potential storm.

She'd taught me how to skate when I was an eight-year-old without a mother and she was a childless divorcée who hadn't yet realized she'd inherited me. Then years later, she'd taught my daughter.

"Dulcie hasn't been skating at all yet," I told her as we walked into the park and headed west toward the rink. Since my daughter had been appearing in The Secret Garden all of our old routines had changed.

"I'd imagine with six performances a week on Broadway, she's overwhelmed."

"Do you really think it's a good idea that a thirteen-year-old works so hard? She's missing out on so much."

"Is she happy, Morgan?" She sighed.

"She seems happy," I said, and heard the wistfulness in my own voice.

"You'd know if she wasn't."

Since she was a baby, I'd sensed Dulcie's emotional and psychic temperature even if we both weren't in the same room, or the same building as each other. Miles away, I'd get a sudden pain in my stomach or hand or back, only to find out when I arrived home that she'd been sick, cut herself or fallen. When something wonderful happened, I'd feel a sudden lightness for no reason. It had been going on so long that none of us found it odd.

Nina glanced over at me. She had it too—that sense when something was wrong with me—but in her case, it was exceptional insight as a therapist.

"Are things back to normal?"

Weeks earlier, my daughter and I had an argument about

her being offered a three-week part in a television series. She'd wanted to do it and I'd been adamant that appearing in a play six times a week was more than enough work for her We fought. And then, of course, she brought her father into it. I'd already talked to Mitch, and he had backed me up on the decision. Nevertheless, when I'd gone to pick her up from his apartment that weekend, she'd refused to come home with me. She said she knew that if I'd said yes, her father would have said yes, too. That he was more fair. That he wanted her to have a career. That I wanted to hold her back. And finally—the coup de grace—that she wanted to live with him.

Legally, at the age of thirteen, she had the right to make that decision, and there was nothing I could do.

She'd stayed at her father's for almost four weeks, until we worked out a cease-fire.

"The drama queen seems to have forgiven me. But I'm still furious at her emotional-blackmail techniques. She's too damn intuitive."

"What's holding on to the anger about?"

"You know that?"

"Probably. Do you?"

We laughed. "There's nothing worse than two therapists having a conversation. Especially two who have known each other forever. Yes, oh master, I know. As long as I focus on the anger I don't have to focus on how scared I was that she wasn't coming back. I know it's not about her. It's some crazy thing where I've confused her and my mother in my head. But the loneliness was real. And it stung."

"And—"

I interrupted Nina. We'd had this conversation before and I knew where she was headed. "I know she's not going to fol-low in my mother's footsteps: a star at sixteen, lost by twenty, dead at twenty-nine. I know Dulcie isn't my mother. She might have her talent, but she's had a secure and healthy childhood. She's had Mitch and me as parents."

"I love it when you do all my work for me." Nina smiled.

We'd arrived at the Wollman Rink. Inside, we got a locker and put on our skates. Then side by side, we glided across the ice in time to a Schubert waltz. Probably due to the light snow, Nina and I had the whole rink to ourselves for the first twenty minutes, until an explosion of laughter and shouting preceded a group of twenty or thirty kids. All the private schools in the area used the park as an escape from indoor gymnasiums.

A flash of a shocking-pink parka crossed my path. A turquoise scarf fell on the ice. A boy in a heavy black sweater, one cherry-red glove and one forest-green glove sped by and scooped up the scarf without stopping.

Along with Nina, I watched them with delight, and then I noticed two of the boys smirking as one of the girls spilled onto the ice, her legs spreading wide as she spun out.

Four boys took off from one end of the rink, racing one another, their blades sending shavings up into the air. It looked like an updated Norman Rockwell until one elbowed another viciously as he skated too close, and the kid went crashing into the handrail.

Two girls took each other's arms and danced across the rink. Sweet friends, until they came up behind a third girl and started whispering about her, clearly making fun of her and the way she was skating.

We don't treat kids at the institute, but a few months earlier, as a favor to a friend of Nina's—the principal of one of the city's prestigious private schools—I'd taken on a once-a-week group session with eight fifteen- to eighteen-year-old boys who were seriously addicted to Internet porn, as well as four girls who were involved with them and affected by it.

Seeing these kids skating, seeing the subtle messages beneath their easy exuberance, reminded me of how I felt in the room with my group: knowing there was something worse than their problems with pornography going on deep beneath the surface of what they showed me, anxious to get to it.

Just as Nina and I were leaving the rink, the snow started to fall heavily. These were not the soft flakes that had been floating down before but a heavy, wet snow that caught in my eyelashes and made it hard to see.

There are landmarks throughout the park, but the easiest ones to use to orient yourself are above the treeline. At the end of the nineteenth century, Frederick Law Olmsted had designed the park's hills and valleys so that, no matter where you stood, you couldn't see any of the city in the sky. More than a hundred years later, there were buildings on all four sides, their spires and roofs standing tall, and you could always tell where you were by looking up.

But this snow was so dense that not only couldn't we recognize any landmarks within the park, we couldn't see into the distance to get our bearings. Peering into vague whiteness, Nina and I set off.

No problem. Up ahead was a fork. We knew to take a right. Straight. Another right.

Then nothing looked familiar. It should have—we'd walked this route so many times—but nothing was visible other than soft mounds of white.

"We should be coming to a left," Nina said after a few minutes.

But we didn't. Somehow we'd gotten turned around. For two New Yorkers, it was a strange experience. We were lost in our own backyard.

Nina pointed to an overpass. "Do you know which footbridge that is?"

"Not a clue." I peeled my glove back and peered down at my watch. The face was clear only for a second before flakes obscured it. We'd been walking long enough that we should have been at a park exit if we'd gone in the right direction.

We both had patients waiting for us. We had to find a way out.

It was silly to panic. The city was all around us. There were people and taxis and traffic and noise and stores and lights and sidewalks just hundreds of yards in any direction, but we were circling inside a storm. Every tree, rock, pond and bridge had become part of an unfamiliar landscape. We just had to trust that since we'd done this so many times before, our instincts would lead us home.

But what if we really were lost? Could we be lost in Central Park?

Square breathing, I thought. The way Nina had taught me long ago. *Breathe in, one, two, three, four. Breathe out, one, two, three, four.* Nina must have heard my inhaling and exhaling. She glanced over. "We can't be lost for long if we just keep going in the same direction. It's kind of fun, isn't it? Not knowing where you're going for once?"

Before I could answer, she said, "No it isn't, not for you."

Seven

It wasn't a blizzard, at least not yet, but it was bad enough that a lot of people were shutting down their offices early. Kira Rushkoff, a senior partner at Forrest, Lane and Graffe, had walked fifteen blocks in the snow without anything on her head before she found an empty taxi.

A half hour later she arrived home. Upstairs, she didn't remember to take off her coat or her dripping boots. She didn't turn on any lights or make herself a cup of the English breakfast tea she liked so much.

In her husband's dark study, she sat down at his desk in front of the computer. Alan never shut it off. The screen saver twinkled with stars in the cosmos. Tentatively, as if she didn't know whether she was reaching into a treasure chest or a snake's nest, she put her hands on the keys.

She hit the *H* key but it could have been any key. The screen saver disappeared, replaced by the desktop. The brighter glow made the diamonds in her wedding band glint hypnotically, and she stared at the silver-white bright shine for a second, distracted.

Each time she had done this, she'd felt the same overwhelming exhaustion at first. A feeling so heavy her shoulders sagged under its weight. That this was morally wrong should have mattered to her. At least as a concept. Only four months earlier, she would have found her actions abhorrent. Was it possible that she had become this person, living this life, doing these things, in only sixteen weeks?

Her fingers typed out his password.

It was an accident that she knew it. She'd barely been paying attention that night. They'd been here, talking, and he'd wanted to show her an e-mail from one of his students, so he'd typed out the seven letters. She'd hardly been aware that she was watching his fingers move on the keyboard, but when the time came that she decided to go searching for the truth, the password was there in her mind, teasing her with its irony.

J-u-s-t-i-c-e.

All around her, leather-bound legal volumes with gilt lettering on their spines stood at attention on their shelves, mocking her actions. Alan had seen to that. He had chosen as his little hobby—the single most insulting pastime he could have, considering who she was and what she did and how she felt about it.

Yes, she defended porn kings and smut dealers because there was no greater test for the First Amendment. Each and every time she won a case, she got satisfaction that she was tightening the screws on the protective glass over the Constitution.

The last big civil case—between her client, a pornography king, and well-known feminist Stella Dobson—had garnered more media attention than she'd ever had before. Even though public opinion was with Dobson, the law was clearly on Kira's side. She'd won.

But at what cost? she asked as she lay in bed at night, staring at the ceiling, not able to sleep, seeing the faces of the women she betrayed—feminists and trailblazers and reformers. Women like her own mother, who struggled so her daughter could go to law school. Women who'd made a difference, like Judy Wilson, Emma Michaels. Like Dobson herself. All women she knew and admired, versus these men who were in it for the dollar. Not for principles. She talked to, met with, worked with, defended and saved the hides of businessmen who brokered in some of the most disgusting images she'd ever seen. And it was justified because she was proving and protecting inalienable rights. Except…

She couldn't think about that now. She had work to do before Alan came home. He couldn't find her invading his privacy. *Even though he's done worse to you,* the strident voice in her head whispered. The voice talked to her all the time now and said there were no more excuses and there was no more time for weakness. There was too much to do.

The computer made a slight humming noise, like a bee circling overhead. The keys clicked in a rhythm that was slightly off kilter. It was easy enough to check where Alan had been the night before. Since he didn't suspect she had access to his computer, he didn't empty his cache, and the last twenty Web sites he had visited were right there for her perusal.

Three different women.

He'd spent the night with three women.

When she was lying in their bed by herself.

Kira had promised herself that all she was going to do was collect the Web addresses and the names of the women Alan had seen. She was not going to go look at them, but like a reformed smoker lighting up, Kira hit the key that pulled back the curtain and showed her the still photo of the last woman Alan had watched perform last night via her Web cam.

This was a new one. She was blond. Green eyes. Clear skin. Young. They were all young. She read the description of what this one did.

To date, Kira had watched every one of the women that Alan had visited. Studied their moves. Examined the way they looked at the camera and acted out their little sexual plays. She'd watched a brunette strip down, slowly, letting one piece of silk clothing after another drift to the floor, watched how the woman used her hands to touch herself. If anything, she'd been a little demure. Kira hated herself, but as long as Alan was addicted to having some kind of virtual fuck session with these women, she was addicted to looking at them, burning their images into her mind, hating them.

To the right of the computer, on Alan's desk, was a framed photo of Kira posing for him on a beach twenty years earlier, when they had first started dating. She was wearing a two-piece suit and standing in the water, the waves lapping at her ankles, one hand on her hip, the other blowing him a kiss.

Dearest, it said in her handwriting, *Dearest, I will love you always.* That was the picture that Alan could see, that was the inscription he could read while he was jerking off to these strange women's bodies.

She picked it up. She wanted to protect it. To put it in a drawer in her bedroom, between soft cashmere sweaters, where it would be hidden. Laying it facedown next to her, she planned to take it with her when she left. But then Alan might notice, and she'd have to come up with a reason for taking it, along with a reason for being in his office in the first place. She wasn't ready for that yet. It was too soon to make him suspicious. But when the time was right, he'd know everything.

Gingerly, she put the photo back in its place on the desktop and got up. At the door, she lingered. She'd loved this room. His study. His lair. Alan looked so handsome in here, sitting at the big oak desk, or in the leather armchair. He was relaxed in this room, surrounded by his books, the photos of their life and their families on the mantel. She wanted to run her hands over the back of his chair and cry.

Crying, she told herself, was not going to help. Crying was what women did who had no life apart from their husbands and their children. Who had no self-respect. She was a success.

Alan's weakness was not due to any fault in her.

But the tears came.

He was the one with the fissure running through his soul. With the sickness. With the problem.

Not her.

She had not sent him out of their bed or rejected him or stopped wanting to make love to him. That had been all his doing. He had lost interest in her. So long ago, it seemed now. She remembered exactly what it had been like to be with Alan. What they were like in the beginning, when he couldn't keep his hands off her. When she would wake up in the middle of the night to find his arms wrapped around her, holding her close to him, his knee pushing her legs apart, his erection pressing into her hip.

She slammed the door on her way out, not hearing the crash of the frame as it fell onto the wooden floor and shattered.

Eight

The plane had landed two hours late due to the weather, and the cab didn't drop Noah at Broadway and Eleventh Street until ten that night. Upstairs, he threw his suitcase on the floor and dropped his coat on a Stickley chair. He wanted to call Morgan, but first he had to get the day out of his system. He poured two ounces of Maker's Mark into a crystal tumbler and sat down at the baby grand piano.

For a detective, he had a lot of fine things. Smiling, he ran his hand lovingly over the piano's black-lacquer top. Even though he'd only published a few dozen songs over the years, they'd sold well and afforded him some extras. His apartment was beyond the reach of a detective's salary, as were the antiques and artwork. These things were indulgences, but he appreciated each and every one of them. Like the whiskey, they smoothed away some of the rougher edges of his job.

Noah took a drink, put the glass down and started to play. It took almost fifteen minutes for him to slip into the zone where he was no longer conscious of his fingers flying over the keys, or the day he'd had, or the problems waiting for him at the precinct house. There was just music. And he was sailing on it.

Being a detective was part of him. It was what his dad did. What he always wanted to do. But he played piano from inside. He needed it for balance, for beauty. For the sliver of soul he still had intact. That's what the music had salvaged.

The music.

It had always come through for him the way nothing else had. When his father died, when his long-term relationship had broken up, when a case burned its images into his head and held him captive in its gruesomeness, only the music offered consolation.

It had been too long since he'd felt the first thrill of the birth of a new jazz piece. He needed to hear one now, so he stayed at it long after the whiskey was gone, longer than he should have, considering how many hours he'd been awake.

The sounds that rose up soothed him even when they made his listeners want to weep, but there was no one there to hear him that night. That mattered. But not that much. The music mattered more. It was his faith. As long as he could write it, and as long as a few people showed up to listen to him play it on Saturday nights at the jazz bar around the corner, he could take the darkness when it came.

Inside of him, that darkness churned. Until he'd met Morgan he'd never tried to explain it to anyone. But she'd understood. Because she was insightful and listened to him with her heart as hard as she listened with her head. She did everything like that.

But it was more than that. Morgan had understood because she had that same darkness inside of her.

Morgan.

He pounded the keys.

Morgan.

Morgan of the fathomless brown eyes brimming with compassion. Morgan of the skin that felt too soft for his callused fingers. He closed his eyes. Notes poured out. He could almost feel her head on his chest, her tears wetting his skin.

You let me cry and it doesn't scare you, she'd said to him once. *And that's practically some kind of miracle. If only I believed in miracles.*

It was the same for him, too. Because of their professions, they were both confronted with proof of too much depravity. Evidence of too much evil shoved in their faces, twenty-four hours a day. They had no choice but to focus on it. You couldn't just shake off the darkness when you got home. Couldn't just drown it in a drink, though God knows how many of his fellow officers tried.

He liked the idea that what he was writing would be Morgan's song. Then he smiled at the utter romanticism of the thought.

Noah worked on it for a while longer, wanting to get it down and smoothed out before he saw her again.

They hadn't gotten off to a good start when they'd first met. They clashed as much as they connected. And now they didn't see each other often enough. Unlike so many people who fell into being together all the time, they hadn't. The old-fashioned pacing was foreign to him, reminding him of a time and place he'd never experienced. It made him that much more aware of how tenuous their connection still was.

The song was complicated: an enigma for a few bars that turned suddenly, revealing a hint of sensuality. It was uneasy. Edgy. And exciting.

Parts of Morgan were closed down so tight that he didn't know if he'd ever be able to pry them open. For the present, he wasn't trying. When she felt too exposed, she disappeared and he had to start over. He didn't want to grow tired of doing that and so this time he was hoping he could wait her out. Perez kidded him that the more complicated a case, the more hopeless, the more it obsessed him and captivated him. The more tenacious he became.

It was true. Not just with work. Other women, less complicated women, hadn't held his interest. But still…

Jordain began his search for a riff that would lead him past the transition. He was picturing Morgan waking up in his bed, each time still slightly astonished that she was there.

They'd known each other eight months, separated into two periods. Four weeks last June, followed by a three-month break, then together again in the October. Since then they'd seen each other regularly, usually once a week. Her first priority was her teenage daughter. Her second was her job. Then there was his schedule. After those three things, there wasn't all that much time left. It was simple to explain.

And yet.

He played the riff again.

And yet.

Morgan remained just out of reach for a reason.

His phone rang. Once. Twice. His fingers hovered over the keys. Damn how he wished he didn't have to get up and answer it.

"Jordain," he said tersely into the receiver.

"So, can you see the Met Life tower from your window?" Perez asked.

"No, I can't. What's up?"

"Well, I'm only about six blocks away from you and I can see it just fine."

Nine

The apartment, on 17th Street between Eighth and Ninth avenues, was just one room, twelve sorry feet wide by fourteen pathetic feet long. The only thing that saved it from being unlivable, Jordain thought, was the magical view out the window, where the tower of the Met Life building sparkled like a beacon.

There was a bathroom but no separate kitchen. Everything—bed, table, small refrigerator, smaller stove, still smaller sink—was crammed in. But it was astoundingly clean. Spotless tub and toilet. Not even a stray hair in the sink.

That made the stench all the more horrific. It made the sight of the young woman, folded up on herself, fallen out of her chair, all the sadder.

Jordain watched the forensic team preparing the body for removal.

"How old?" he asked the medical examiner who was leaning over the girl.

"Twenty-three."

"She looks younger."

"Yeah," the ME agreed.

Jordain looked away from the woman's bloated face to the shocking pink plastic dildo on the floor beside her left foot, the color of the sex toy too bright for the solemn occasion. He looked up at the wall and at the paintings. Three canvases, each of a nighttime Manhattan skyline. They weren't bad.

"You read the descriptions of the symptoms she exhibited?"

The ME nodded.

"Any educated guesses as to what it might have been?"

Sam Gordon looked up. "Noah, give me some time. Don't make me guess what happened until I at least run some tests."

"But your instincts are so right on that I thought—"

Gordon held up his hand. "Buttering me up won't get me to speculate. I need some time."

"Time. Yeah. Sure, you take your time. After all, it's not your fault it took so fucking long to find her." Jordain's voice was full of recrimination.

Across the room, Perez looked up. "Hey, it happened. Calm down."

Jordain shook his head. "It shouldn't have."

Officer Tana Butler, who was standing at the woman's desk dusting her computer for prints, heard Jordain's complaint and turned around to explain. "The calls were too scattered, boss. They came from all over the country into local police stations and no one noticed the pattern for the first forty-eight hours."

"I heard."

"Then finding the company that owns the company that owns the porn site wasn't easy. Did you know that a subpoena issued in New York City, even to a company that does business as New York Girls and employs some New York girls, doesn't mean much to a group of guys working out of a parent company in Shanghai called Global Communications?"

"Excuses," Jordain muttered as he watched the forensic

team lift the body. He'd seen this ritual enough times that he should be inured to it. But on occasion something would get to him. Like the lock of hair that had fallen across the young woman's forehead as they put her into the bag. He wanted to brush it back, get it out of her eyes.

Butler was still quoting statistics. "Approximately five thousand men logged on to Penny's Web site during the last hour of her shift. That doesn't mean they all saw the end of her performance. Some of them no doubt left their computers because of phone calls or wives coming home, or because they just weren't in the mood. There's no way to know how many men might have still been watching during the last fifteen minutes, when she actually got sick. But certainly, men were signing on at various points throughout her performance. She's usually on for at least an hour and a half. She got sick after forty-five minutes."

"These guys were sitting in front of their screens, their eyes glued to Penny's bare breasts, wide eyes and wet lips, and they listened to her moans and dirty chatter and watched her get sick and didn't do anything about it? What did they think?"

"Well some of them thought she was getting a flu or had food poisoning," Butler said.

"Or that it was a kinky new game she was playing," Perez said.

"I still don't understand why it took so long for us to find her," Jordain said. "From the report, within the first twenty-four hours, fifty calls had been made. Within forty-eight hours there were hundreds. I know the calls meant nothing without the woman's name and address. But she was online, for Christ's sake. Wasn't there a way to trace her connection?"

"Sure. If her connection had stayed live," Butler answered.

"I didn't hear about that. What happened?" Jordain asked.

Butler plugged the power cord back into the laptop. A red light came on. "It looks like her battery died."

So it had taken five days from the time the first phone call had been logged to find the woman whose screen name was Penny Whistle, and whose ad claimed that she'd "Wet your Whistle, so good." That had been one hour and twenty-four minutes ago. At that point, the police had realized that Penny was the same woman whose parents had reported her missing thirty-six hours earlier—just a dozen hours short of what the NYPD requires before starting work on a missing persons case.

"Is there any chance she could have been saved if someone had gotten to her in time?" Jordain asked just before they took the body away.

Gordon, who was at the door, turned, looked back and shook his head. "I won't know that until I know what killed her. Besides what good is knowing?"

No one needed to answer.

"And there is absolutely no sign of anyone breaking in?" Jordain asked even though he knew the answer.

"And no sign that anyone was here with her," Perez said.

Jordain couldn't stop staring at her, asking her questions in his head.

Did you kill yourself? Or did you get sick? It couldn't have been that sudden. Why didn't you call someone before it got too bad? Didn't you realize how sick you were? Or did someone do this to you?

Jordain shook his head. At no one. Or at her ghost, who couldn't answer, anyway. They'd find out eventually. As if it would matter to her. As if it would matter to anyone who loved her.

If she hadn't died from an illness or an accident—if someone had done this to her—then at least they might be able to protect another life. That was what you had to focus on. His father had always said it. And Jordain knew it was true. *"Your job isn't to punish, it's to protect."*

Perez nodded at the laptop Butler was dusting. "There's got to be information on there that can help us."

Jordain looked over at Butler, and as he did he noticed a small, finely painted, porcelain robin on the floor behind the chair.

"Did you see that?" he asked her.

She hadn't. Jordain walked over and inspected it. A simple painted porcelain bird. A lovely thing, except for a chip in one wing. Had that happened when it fell? The bird had his head cocked and there was a sparkle in his black eye. Had someone given Debra—her real name was Debra, and the least he could do was call her by her name—this bird? Had it meant something to her?

It didn't matter. It didn't mean anything to anyone anymore.

Ten

Dearest,

In the dark, there is one candle lit and the smell of the wax is a promise. I have four more candles on the table, ready to light. One candle for each woman—if you can call that a woman. I call her a witch who dreams evil and shows it to any man who wants to see, who offers up her own blood to quench their addictions and watches as their eyes glaze over and their fat fingers itch and they give in and give up to the plastic fantastic sham. These who call themselves women take bites out of the people they pretend to please, leaving poison on the skin. The pollution of innocence and filth in the name of freedom. No more. No more. No more. Nomorenomore. Nomorenomorenomore.

Last week wasn't the first time I watched your little friend. Did I tell you that? I'd watched her a half a dozen times before, but what choice did I have? I had to see what she did, what her "act" was, didn't I? How else could I have approached her or known where her weak spot would be?

She peddled, and she lied, and she plied, and she seduced with a falsity that seemed so obvious to me it's a wonder that anyone falls for it. Can't men see she is just playing with them? Didn't you realize the damage, the ravage, the travesty that is enacted, pulled off, executed by these women who are not women but are instead this other thing?

There was nothing innocent about the way she died except that she didn't suspect it and that was my own sweet surprise. She just performed as usual, twisting her little toy up high into her vagina without guessing that there was anything different about it. Not an idea in her head that it would be her last night and that her minions, her army, her horde out there, alone in the dark, watching her, imagining that she was performing lust just for them, were seeing her for the last time. For the last time might be one of the saddest phrases I've ever written, don't you think? For the last time…no, not there, I will not go there and not play that misery game where I try to remember the last time I felt your arms around me. You do not remember something you do not expect to lose. Lose. Life. Lost life. Her life lost. It wasn't an easy end for her, you know, it wasn't a sweet sleep death or a drifting but a jerking, painful sickening full of shit and stink and vomit and sweat death. Toward the end there was none of that vile purple lipstick left on her lips. And her hair wasn't all wavy and soft and pretty anymore. She was not that lovely woman who was not a woman anymore, anyway. Not lovely. Lovely. Love.

You see how much I love you, don't you? This worst thing I could do is the best thing I will ever do—prove to you what you are to me. I don't feel any relief or happiness, but there is satisfaction and there is biblical justice and there is rightness. I don't care if I am ever forgiven for this. Until you have lost someone you love you can't understand how crippling emotional pain can be. And, oh, how I love you.

I didn't think I was going to be able to watch her die, and certainly it wasn't easy for me. It made me remember too much. But when the time came, I had to do it, because this I did for you.

Tuesday
Seventeen days remaining

Eleven

Her eyes sparkled and there were snowflakes melting in her thick lashes. You always noticed her eyes first. They were a very light green, the color of a new spring leaf. But it was the way she looked at you, from under those lashes, in a surprisingly innocent and sensual way, that you remembered. It was incongruous. But then so much about Blythe was.

"God, it's freezing outside," she said as she dropped her leather backpack on the floor. Around her shoulders and flowing behind was an old-fashioned, green velvet cape. She unhooked it and took it off, revealing a pair of black trousers, a white tuxedo shirt and what looked like a real leopard vest, but I couldn't be sure. A devotée of eclectic vintage clothing stores, Blythe put outfits together the way an artist mixes colors.

After draping her cape on the coat stand in the corner of my office, she sat down on the couch. Her movements were lithe and lovely.

"Is it okay if we don't talk about my patients today? I need some help. I had a serious setback this week—it's really affecting me badly," Blythe said. Her voice was soft and sounded the way a rose petal feels. The sensuality subtle but unmistakable.

Blythe was a getting her Ph.D. in psychology at Columbia University and was specializing in sex therapy. It was not an unusual choice given her own problems. All too often we find that therapists are best at helping those whose problems somehow mirror their own. All psychologists starting out are supervised. Nina had liked Blythe enough to hire her to work in the clinic—a free service we run for a dozen or so patients who can't pay our prices—and asked Simon Weiss, one of my closest friends and the senior therapist at the institute, to be her supervisor.

Simon had met with her once.

The next day he asked me out to lunch. After one session, he recognized that he was not the right therapist for Blythe. He was a forty-year-old man with a shaky marriage, and, despite his best efforts, he found Blythe provocative. When I saw her, I wasn't surprised. After I heard what her issues were, I understood completely.

"What happened?" I asked.

Blythe squeezed her right hand with her left and her skin went white under the pressure. What she was doing was clearly painful. She repeated the action, and every time she did, I fought the urge to reach out and separate her hands.

"Blythe, it's not going to help to punish yourself."

"Punish?"

I nodded at her hands. She looked down. "I didn't even know I was doing that."

"What's wrong?"

"I feel so helpless. I'll be fine and then something will happen, just out of the blue, and I'll feel like I'm in its grip all over again. I'll want to go back online."

"What happened this time?"

"A really well-known feminist e-mailed me. Someone I've looked up to my whole life. She's writing a book about women who become sex workers in order to put themselves through school—how they cope with it, what it does to their social lives, how it changes or doesn't affect their self-esteem. She wants to interview me for the book."

"How did she find you? I thought you weren't doing Webcam performances anymore."

"I haven't for five, six months. Apparently she saw me back then. My profile said I was a student. She'd kept my e-mail address, she said. The site gave out addresses that were forwarded to our personal e-mail. Anyway, she gave me her phone number and asked me to call."

"How do you feel about that?"

Blythe clasped her hands together again, this time even more tightly. "I'm not sure. There are all kinds of reasons I want to do it. And all sorts of reasons I don't. Just…just talking about talking about it…going back into that mind-set just a little while…" She shook her head and her blond curls fell in her face. She didn't push them away. Why not? Her hair was clearly in her eyes. It should have bothered her.

"Blythe, when you were online, how did it feel to know that all those men were looking at you?"

"I wore a mask." She clasped and then unclasped her hands again.

"A mask? Why? Didn't you want them to see you?"

She lowered her head.

"Blythe?"

"I didn't want to be recognized. There probably wasn't much chance of that, but sometimes there are coincidences. Can you imagine if one of my professors…or another student—" She broke off and sat there looking down at her hands.

Blythe reminded me of the pre-Raphaelite painting on the cover of a book I had read about adolescent girls. The painter depicted Hamlet's poor drowned Ophelia in a river, her hands by her sides, her hair floating around her shoulders; the only color in her pale face was her still-red lips.

"Do you still have the mask?"

She nodded.

"Have you worn it since you stopped going online?"

"Not until last night. I took it out after I spoke to her. Took it out and put it on and looked in the mirror for a long time and tried to see myself the way all those men must have seen me. After a few seconds, it was like I was looking at a stranger. As if I'd separated from myself."

She curled her fingers into tight fists and frowned.

"What are you thinking? You look upset."

Anger twisted her mouth.

"What is it?"

"What's wrong with how I look?"

"Nothing."

"You said I look upset. What does that mean? How does my face look?" Blythe's anger excited me. We were getting somewhere.

"You seem to be upset about something. I can see it on your face." I repeated the words that I thought had sparked her reaction.

She shook her head. *"What's wrong with your face? What's wrong with your eyes? Why do you look different?"* She was saying it all in a fake singsong voice and was clearly in distress.

"Blythe, what are you thinking about?"

Another moment of silence. She bit her bottom lip, held it between her teeth for a moment, then finally took a breath and made her confession. "When I was born, I had cataracts on my eyes. Did I tell you that?"

"No."

"It's pretty rare, but it happens. I had three surgeries before I was ten years old. I had to wear glasses. Normally glasses aren't the worst thing. A few other kids had glasses. But regular ones. Mine were the thickest, most horrible glasses you ever saw. But that wasn't all. It was my eyes. They looked weird." She took a long pause. "It was awful. You know how kids are. If there had been another girl with a worse affliction, she would have been the one they picked on. But it was a small class and I was the only one with any kind of physical deformity. So I became the outcast. The one who was never invited to the popular girls' parties. Always the last one picked for teams." Her eyes teared up.

I'd never seen her cry before and was surprised how much younger she suddenly seemed. Something inside of me lurched.

"When I was fourteen I got corrective contacts," Blythe continued. "You need to really see my eyes. To understand."

I wasn't expecting what happened next. I thought she was going to describe it to me, but instead she lowered her head and plucked the contact lens out of her right eye.

Then she looked up at me.

Her left eye, the one with the lens still covering it, was green, intense and lovely, but the iris of her right eye was twice as large as normal and the black wasn't a pure circle but seeped into the outer ring of green, spoiling it. She focused on me but her eye didn't appear to be seeing me at all. I couldn't find her, couldn't connect to her.

Yes, it was noticeable. I wouldn't have gone so far as to describe it as a deformity, but to a young girl it must have seemed like one.

Blythe didn't let me look at her naked eye for long. She popped the painted lens back as if it was painful to let me see her. It hid the flaw.

"Everything changed once I got these corrective lenses. For

the first time, when I looked in the mirror I saw someone I recognized, and she was suddenly pretty, Dr. Snow. Boys noticed me. No one teased me anymore. One day I was a freak, the next I was as normal as everyone else."

She settled back on the couch. "After all those years of being ashamed of how I looked, I can't even describe what it was like not to have anyone stare at me anymore."

"Is there a connection between that and you going online? Inviting men to look at you?"

"Isn't that obvious?"

"Yes, but I need you to articulate it."

"My exhibitionism is a fuck-you to everyone who ever looked at me crooked. It was proof to me that I wasn't a freak anymore. Each time I went online and stood there in front of my computer and stared into the camera as if it was a lover's eyes, I was testing reality, saying to myself, it's true, I'm good enough to look at."

She used both hands to pull her hair up off her neck, twist it up, and then let go of it again.

"But you wore a mask."

"It's just like that." Blythe pointed to the glass box that sat on my bookshelf. Inside was an iridescent blue butterfly, seemingly suspended in midair—one of the many butterfly artifacts I had. I'd been collecting them for years. Even the small terrace off my office was planted with bushes and flowers to attract butterflies in the summer.

"My butterfly comes from Venice and is made of silk with a string that ties around the back." She put her hands up to her face, her fingers splayed so that her eyes peeked through. "It comes down to my mouth. There are two holes in the wings. The only thing you can see of me, through the mask, is my eyes."

Twelve

Detective Perez walked into the office he shared with Noah Jordain to find his partner just starting to make a fresh pot of what everyone else in the department referred to as "Jordain's mud," but which Perez had come to enjoy.

The office was standard fare, badly in need of a new coat of paint and a lot of new furniture, but the window looked out onto the street rather than a back alley or a brick wall like the rest of them.

"You are not going to believe this," Perez said as he sat down, put a wrinkled piece of paper on his desk and tried to smooth it out.

"Try me, anyway," Jordain said as he added a scoop of chicory to the freshly ground coffee.

"Debra Kamel was poisoned," Perez stated matter-of-factly.

"Okay." The second syllable was elongated by his southern accent. "We thought that was a possibility. What's the surprise? The kind of poison? Does Gordon think it was self-administered?"

"The poison is called atropine," Perez read. "It's one of a family of anticholinergic drugs—often referred to as the belladonna alkaloids…easily absorbed from mucous membranes, skin, intestinal tract or lungs." He looked up. "But in this case we're talking the membranes. These drugs can be toxic, Gordon said, even in an otherwise safe dose. For instance, an individual who is having his eyes dilated at the ophthalmologist's could end up in the cardiac unit. It's happened."

"Eyes dilated? You've lost me. What does this have to do with her eyes?"

"It doesn't, I'm just giving you some background. That's one of the basic uses of atropine. It also causes heart attacks. Oh, and get this—belladonna was historically used as a sexual stimulant."

"You threw that in for what, a little irony?"

"You might think so, but I was thinking that if someone else did this to her maybe it was someone who had a bad sense of humor and used these alkaloids on her specifically because they've been known as stimulants going way back in time."

"Okay. So is that what happened to her? The toxic reaction was cardiac arrest?"

"You know that's cooked, don't you?" Perez nodded at the coffee.

"Forgot about it, I was so engrossed by your story." Jordain turned, poured out two cups and handed one to his partner.

Perez took a sip, then continued.

"Basically what happened probably started with symptoms like dry mouth, high fever…" He consulted the sheet of paper again. "Blurred vision, dilated pupils, vasodilation, rapid heartbeat, excitement, dizziness, delirium, confusion, hallucination, then death resulting from circulatory and respiratory failure."

"How long?"

Perez read on. "Onset of action is rapid from fifteen minutes to two hours, with death in one hour to one day, depending on lots of factors—route of exposure, dose, sensitivity, health."

"If we go by what time the first call was logged in Sarasota, Florida, to what time Gordon thinks she died, we're looking at between two-and-a-half and three hours max from onset. So what dosage are we talking about?"

"The fatal dose of atropine for that time period is—" Perez scanned the sheet of paper "—fifteen milligrams, which is five drops of concentrated extract."

Jordain was surprised to find his cup of coffee was already empty. He got up and refilled it. "And I suppose this stuff is shockingly easy to come by?"

"You aren't going to believe how easy."

"Try me."

"It's used in dozens of medicines. Anti-Parkinson drugs, gastrointestinal antispasmodics, urinary tract antispasmodics, ophthalmology, colic, motion sickness, dry secretions, pre- and post-op. It treats bradycardia and is the antidote to organophosphate insecticides. Atropine is also the antidote for cholinergic nerve gases. One interesting note is that, in the Gulf War, much more toxicity was reported from inappropriate use of the atropine syringes found in soldiers' emergency kits than from actual nerve-gas attack." He paused, looked up from the piece of paper and shook his head. "But get this. The easiest way to get the damn stuff is from prescription eye-drops. Anyone working in any hospital can grab a handful of vials and slip them into a pocket or purse. No one would notice them missing. A typical stock bin holds about two hundred and fifty vials, and it's not even considered dangerous. It treats inflammation and is a basic in any eye exam."

Jordain started to ask his next question when the phone rang. He let it go until the third ring, then grabbed it, said his name, listened, said a brief yes, and then hung up. "Follow-up on the Bullard case. Nothing that can't wait. I was about to ask if there are other places as easy to get it as a hospital."

"Yup." He checked the sheet. "Army supply units would have it. Any doctor might prescribe it. The prescription eye drops would most likely go by the brand name Homatropine or Isopto Atropine, which of course you could get from an online pharmaceutical site. Know what else? You can buy the stuff from any shop or Web site selling Wiccan supplies. They use it to introduce hallucinations. Butler checked and found three atropine injectors for sale at eBay."

"Paper trail," Jordain muttered.

"There's an even easier way to get it. You can grow it yourself. Or take a field trip with a little pocket knife to one of the dozens of medical gardens attached to so many museums and schools. Quite a few have a poison garden and—"

"Damn it, Perez, I got it. You can get the stuff anywhere and everywhere. I can get the stuff. Butler can get it. It's a no-brainer. It's probably even growing in Central Park."

"Probably."

"Great, so, we know the *what*. Do we know anything about the how? Do you know the details?"

"That's the part you aren't going to believe."

Jordain's expression went from serious to impatient, tinged with slight annoyance.

"The poison entered her system through mucous membranes. Specifically through the membranes in her vaginal wall." He paused.

Jordain made a hurry-up motion with this hand.

"The atropine was mixed into the lubricant she slathered on her dildo."

Thirteen

I opened the door to the English lab at five twenty-five to find three members of the group sitting there in the shadows. Hugh was scrolling through a PDA. Barry seemed to be sleeping with his head on his arms, which were folded on the desktop. Amanda also had her eyes closed, but she had headphones on and from the sway of her shoulders she was clearly engrossed in the music she was listening to.

The original group consisted of eight boys who ranged in age from fifteen to eighteen. They'd been meeting with me late every Tuesday afternoon since early November after the Park East School on Manhattan's Upper East Side. Six weeks later, the principal had recommended four girls join the group. Each of them, with the exception of Amanda, had been sexually involved either with one of the boys in the group or with one of their friends. The three of them were adapting well. They were even helping the boys to open up a little.

But Amanda sat in each session not participating—fidgeting, anxious, waiting for something, ready to jump up and bolt at any second. Since she was the only teenager who had asked to join the group her actions and silence worried me.

I switched on the light and walked into the classroom.

Hugh looked up, Barry continued sleeping. Amanda started and opened her eyes.

"You might want to wake Barry up," I said to Hugh as I took off my coat. "Then the three of you can help me put the chairs in a circle."

Amanda looked down at her finger. There was a small, fresh cut on her left thumb, an angry half moon of dark, dried blood. She was touching it lightly with the forefinger of her right hand. The shape was familiar to me—it was the shape a chisel made when it slipped on the wood or marble you were sculpting.

"You shouldn't move chairs with that. Does it hurt?" I asked her.

"It did."

"How did you do it?"

"In art class."

It was the most she'd said in three weeks.

"Sculpture?"

She seemed slightly surprised.

"Do you like art class?" I asked.

She shrugged, the kind of shrug that meant yes, not no.

"I'd like to see your work. I'm something of an amateur sculptor."

"I don't show my stuff to people. Ever."

Too much emotion in the sentence, but I was thrilled to have heard it. "Sometimes I do. Because if I keep it secret, it gets too important."

She was staring at me.

While the boys formed the circle, the rest of the group straggled in. Timothy, who was one of the brightest but also most disturbed kids, walked in talking on his cell phone. When he saw me, he ended the call.

Amanda's eyes followed him across the room. She seemed to settle down a little now that he was here. When he glanced over and saw her, he gave her an almost imperceptible smile. They had a bond, but what kind of bond I didn't yet understand.

I asked Timothy to help with the last few chairs, and he grudgingly threw his coat and knapsack on the floor and went to work. Jeremy came in with Charlie. Both clean-cut and well groomed, they always arrived and left together. More than anyone else, they participated in these sessions, and I kept hoping they'd influence the rest of the kids, who were there in body only.

A few seconds later Jodi arrived, a Goth with a long black coat that swept up the dirt on the floor. Every week she came in elaborate clothes and makeup. Ellen and Merry came in right behind her. Jodi's opposites, these two smiled, were poised and were always dressed in clothes that would have seemed ridiculously expensive on grown women.

Altogether they were a cross-section: a Goth, a brain, two preppies, a retro hippie, an art student, a musician, two fashionistas. But they did share an interest that was seriously affecting their lives: the boys were severely addicted to Internet porn, and fearless when it came to ignoring the rules against going to X-rated sites while in school. None of them had been caught in the act, but there had been enough evidence of their travels to put them in jeopardy. Therapy with me was the only thing keeping them from expulsion.

The girls had been affected by the boys' addiction. Their self-esteem had been brutalized, and they had been flagrantly acting out, hoping to get the boys to pay more attention to them. Their parents and teachers were worried.

And then there was Amanda.

We started that Tuesday night only five minutes late, which was better than usual. Right away it was clear that everyone was jittery, especially Timothy, who literally couldn't sit still.

Hugh kept casting glances at him as if making sure he was all right. Amanda kept looking over at him, too, but as if she knew he wasn't okay. Jeremy was tapping his foot on the floor in a precise rhythm and Charlie was biting his nails.

When Timothy clicked his pen for the fifth time in a row, I asked him to tell me what was going on.

He shrugged.

Charlie cleared his throat.

Jeremy turned and looked out of the window so that I couldn't see his face.

Amanda opened her bag and fished around in it for a few seconds, brought out a Band-Aid and proceeded to put it over the cut.

"Timothy?" I asked again.

He didn't respond.

The Goth girl, Jodi, leaned over and whispered to him. It sounded to me as if she'd said *tell her,* but I wasn't sure, so I asked her to repeat what she'd said so we all could hear it.

"It was nothing."

"Timothy, do you want to tell us what Jodi said?"

He shrugged.

"I think she said 'tell her.' Is that right?" I pushed.

Timothy still didn't answer.

"Jodi, is that what you said?"

She looked at me but didn't respond. Living with a teenager myself, I knew that more often than not, no answer was code for the affirmative. But why wouldn't she answer? What was she scared of?

"Tell me what, Timothy? You're not going to get in trouble, but let's get it out in the open."

"I was online, okay?"

I ignored the sarcasm. "Good, thanks for telling me. Did you try to call anyone before you went online?"

We'd set up a buddy system, and each kid was supposed to call and at least discuss his urge to go into a chat room or porn site before giving in to it. To date, we hadn't had much success. In other addiction-therapy programs the act of stopping to make the call worked well and I was still hoping it would have some effect here if I could get the kids to make the calls. The problem was these boys couldn't understand what was wrong with what they were doing other than that adults were telling them they shouldn't be doing it.

"No, I didn't try to call anyone." Timothy sounded irritated.

"Did you even think about calling?"

"What happened…wasn't about me getting off. It was about what I saw."

"What did you see?"

He was, once again, silent.

Amanda was playing with the edge of the Band-Aid she'd just affixed.

"Timothy, what did Jodi think you should tell me?"

"I saw something freaky online, okay? It was bad. Now, can we drop it?"

"Bad?"

"Oh, Jesus. No matter what anyone says, you have another question," Hugh said impatiently.

"None of you have to answer any of my questions. Most of the time, you don't. I know some of you guys don't want to be here. In fact, I know you'd rather be anywhere else. But it's nonnegotiable. Hugh, why do you think you're here?"

"Because we go online."

"Just go online?"

"No."

"Then why?"

"We go online too much. You think, everyone thinks, that we have no control."

"When you are sitting there and you haven't clicked the mouse yet, but you've typed in the URL of the porn site, what are you thinking about?"

He shrugged.

"It's not a test, it's just a question. Think about sitting there. The screen is on your homework, but the Web address of a porn site is typed in…. You don't have to click over…you don't have to give in… What are you thinking?"

"It's not about giving in," Hugh said. "It's just there. It's so easy. Why shouldn't I go? Who the hell am I hurting? That's what I just don't get about this. Who cares so much?"

I looked around the room, waiting to see if anyone was going to respond.

Ellen was watching him. They'd gone out. She was frowning. Pressing her lips together. Wanting to say something, holding back. "Ellen? Is there something you want to say?"

"If you can control it, how come you don't?"

He didn't answer.

Amanda lifted the corner of the Band-Aid and then pressed it back down. It was Barry who blurted out a response, his voice strident. "I'm not hurting anyone. None of us are. I like watching who's online and there's nothing wrong with it."

He'd said *hurting anyone.*

Amanda continued her picking at the outer edges of the adhesive strip, lifting, pressing down, lifting.

"I know you're not hurting anyone, Barry. I know none of you is intentionally hurting anyone." I looked around the room, trying to make eye contact with each of them. Merry inched forward in her chair.

"I can't…it's hard to…I mean, I don't want to have to do that stuff all the time to get someone to like me."

"Do you mean sexual stuff?" I asked.

She nodded.

"Does it hurt, Merry?"

"Well, not like someone cut me. But even with what I did, it was still better to look at those girls than me. I don't know. That sorta sucks."

No one responded.

"You're not hurting anyone, are you, Timothy?"

He didn't respond.

"Do you think you've ever hurt anyone by going online?"

"Maybe," he blurted out.

"How?"

"I didn't do anything."

His answer made no sense to me, but I didn't want to stop and make him explain himself and risk damming him up.

"What should you have done?"

"I couldn't. If I told anyone what I saw they'd know I'd gone online. Three strikes and I'm out. That's my father's fucking stupid rule. Shit. If you tell them now, I'll be thrown out of here."

"But I won't. We have a deal in here, right? You can talk about whatever you want and I keep it confidential. I promised you all that in our first session and I haven't broken that promise."

Someone to Timothy's left murmured something, but I ignored it.

"Timothy, what did you see?"

"No." He said it too quickly.

The rest of them knew what he'd seen. They'd talked about it before the group, I sensed.

"Leave him alone," Hugh said loudly.

"Why?"

Hugh, Timothy and Barry invariably looked out for one another in our sessions, defending one another if they felt I was being too tough on one of them. This time, both of the others were quiet.

"Why do you feel the need to protect Timothy from me?" I asked, pushing Hugh harder than I normally would.

Now Barry leaned forward; he clenched his hands together. "Leave him alone. He's been going crazy."

"I don't want to leave him alone, I want to help."

"It's too late to help." It was Amanda. "Again."

"Why? What do you mean 'again'?"

She turned to Timothy and they exchanged a pained glance. "Amanda?"

Her fingers hadn't stopped fussing with the Band-Aid.

"Do you think it would help Timothy if he told us what he saw?" I asked her.

"It doesn't matter." Her finger stopped playing with the Band-Aid. "Not anymore. No one can help."

"You know, this is stupid," Ellen said. "These guys don't want us to help them. They don't want anything from us. Except blowjobs. And even then, they keep watching the girls online. Right while we're doing it to them. You might as well be dead…." She was hissing now.

Amanda's eyes widened, frightened, pained. Her fingers worked the edge of the strip of plastic.

"Amanda, what is it?"

She shook her head back and forth. "Nothing." And then with one fast jerk, she pulled off the adhesive, baring the line of dried blood.

Fourteen

Five hours later, my daughter was sitting at the island in the middle of the kitchen while I went through the refrigerator looking for something ready-made that I couldn't ruin.

Having a late-night snack after Dulcie got home from the theater had replaced having dinner together. Now we talked over the day while she tried to come down after the performance.

"Hot chocolate or hot cider?" I asked.

"Hot chocolate. Definitely."

I took out the milk and grabbed the powdered mix from the cabinet.

"Can't we make it the real way?" She meant the way Nina taught her—melting quality chocolate and then adding enough milk to give it the right consistency.

She was already pulling out the double boiler. When I had remodeled the kitchen, I updated all the pots, pans and utensils. Everything was state-of-the-art. The appliances had stainless fronts, the floor and splashboard were white tiles with black diamond accents, and the countertops were granite. It was all very elegant. A chef's dream. Except I wasn't a chef.

Far from it. In fact, I could barely manage to broil a chicken and hardly used a double boiler.

That's the problem with being a Martha-wannabe but not having any intuitive homemaker skills. Sure, everything gleamed in my kitchen. You just stepped inside and imagined fresh pies cooling on a rack and homemade tomato sauce simmering on the stove. In reality, I ruined tuna fish out of a can with too much lemon juice, and overcooked frozen food.

Dulcie, on the other hand, was gifted in the kitchen, a talent she'd inherited from her paternal grandmother, and which her aunt Nina encouraged. Since the play had opened, I'd missed having her in the kitchen, egging me on, teasing me and saving dinner on more than one occasion.

"I don't have any chocolate. You'll have to settle for powdered chocolate," I said, putting the tin on the counter. Dulcie took the milk out of the fridge and went over to the stove, where she poured it in a saucepan and turned on the burner.

"That's my job," I protested.

"You'll burn it, Mom, you know you will."

While she stirred, I sliced two apples and opened a package of Pepperidge Farm Milanos. Even though they were Dulcie's favorite cookies, I wished I were one of those mothers who bake for their kids.

"So," I said once we were back at the island with our steaming mugs, "how was your day?"

Ever since she was little, it's been our tradition at dinner to talk about what had happened that day, but with caveats. For everything that had gone wrong or that you complained about, there had to be one thing that had gone right or that had made you happy. Always a balance.

Dulcie took another cookie and chewed it, thinking. "Well, I don't like our new teacher. At *all*." Major emphasis on the word "all." My little drama queen.

"Why?"

"She wants us to read a book called *War and Peace*. Do you have any idea how big a book it is? I'll be fourteen before I finish it."

I laughed. "No, it won't take that long. The hardest part is keeping track of all the Russian names, but you're good with languages."

She rolled her eyes.

"It's been years since I read it. How about I get a copy and we read it at the same time? Then we can talk about it together."

She sort of shrugged an okay, but clearly I was more interested in the mother-daughter reading concept than she was. "So what was good today?"

She gave me her slightly shy look from under partially lowered lids. It was an expression she'd fall back on when she didn't want to brag but still was proud of herself. "Six curtain calls."

"That's wonderful."

She broke into a smile. "Isn't it?"

I smiled back.

"And you, Dr. Sin, how was your day?" she asked.

My daughter had never come right out and said she was embarrassed by what I do for a living, but she didn't need to after the day, three years ago, when she introduced me to her friend's mother as a heart doctor. The moniker Dr. Sin had been coined one night when we'd been arguing about her curfew and she'd accused me of not trusting her.

"Why are you so worried I'm going to fool around or something? You're Dr. Sin. You're supposed to understand about this stuff."

She rarely called me Dr. Sin when anyone else was around, but she did it often enough at home for it to annoy me.

"Should we start with what was wrong today?" she asked me. "Or what was right?"

I drank some of my cocoa to buy myself some time. All I could think of was how badly the group-therapy session had gone that night and how worried I was that those kids were in more trouble than I could help them with. Since I couldn't tell her that, I told her that nothing bad had happened and that the good thing had been going ice-skating with Nina at lunchtime.

"Yeah, well, I believe you that you had fun skating. But I don't believe that nothing bad happened." She stared at my face: my little gnome with electric blue eyes and dark curly hair and an impish smile playing on her baby-pink lips. "You've got the listening look, Mom."

"The listening look" was another of Dulcie's sayings. She claimed that sometimes, even though I was home and focused on what was going on with her, I got an expression on my face as if I was still hearing what my patients had said that day. "It's like you can't stop listening to them. Like if you do, it will be your fault if anything bad happens to them."

I used to get up and check in the mirror when she told me she saw the look, but I couldn't recognize it the way Dulcie could. She was always right, though, when she called it, and she was right that night.

Fifteen

Timothy sat in his room, at his desk, staring at his computer, supposedly reading a friend's movie blog. The ambient glow from the screen was the only light in the room. For the past fifteen minutes, he'd been nursing a beer and was teasing himself with the idea of going online. He was swollen just thinking about it, but he was trying to hold off. Dr. Snow had talked about control. He had control. He knew he did. He had it with all sorts of things; he could have it with this. Especially now. After what he'd seen last week. It was so disgusting. It was still bothering him. How sick had that girl been? What had happened to her? When he'd told Amanda about her, she'd gotten all quiet. Freaked out. He knew why. Knew he never should have said anything.

He took another gulp of the beer. He'd just go online for a few minutes. No one would know. His parents were out—again—and the apartment was quiet and still.

Through the window he could see the snow falling, falling as if the heavens had an endless supply of the white flakes.

Dr. Snow said he should call someone when he felt like this. It was eleven-thirty and there was no one he wanted to talk to, and nothing he wanted to do except go online, find some girl and have her get him off. Maybe he'd find a chick who was into tea-bagging. His erection stiffened. He typed in the porn site's address, but that was as far as he could get.

The image of Penny from last week, writhing in pain, stopped him. He'd dreamt about her every damn night and woken up drenched in sweat, because even in the dream, he didn't do a thing to help her.

What had happened to her?

He needed to see that she was fine and back at work, didn't he? That was a reason to go online: to make sure Penny was fine, even though the small secret voice in his head was telling him something bad had happened. He was afraid she had died.

If she had, she would be the second woman he'd known who had died. That's what Amanda had said to him. Reminding him. As if he needed anyone to remind him.

He put his head in his hands and tried to picture Simone. It was getting tougher to remember. The images had lost their edges. Her face had become less distinct. She was fading. That scared him, too. Is that what happened to you after you died? You just faded away until no one remembered anything about you anymore? He could remember the girl on the Internet from Thursday night better than Simone. But Simone had been flesh and blood and he had touched her. He had smelled her skin and felt her lips on his cock.

He tried to shake off her ghost, but he couldn't. She wouldn't go away.

Sometimes he fixated on her like this and got himself all worked up over what had happened. His heart would start to race and he'd feel nauseous and panicky. He didn't want to feel all that shit tonight. There was nothing he could do about Simone. It was too late.

Timothy clicked on the hard-drive icon, and then the document file icon. Next he clicked on the term-paper file. Inside of that he clicked on the American History file. And within that he clicked on the folder called "Presidents." Inside were a dozen JPEGs, labeled GW1, GW2, GW3, GW4. And there was one MPEG. He moved the cursor over it and let it hover there.

No one knew he still had this. He'd lied and told Amanda he hadn't kept it, and she'd believed him. Since last spring, he hadn't opened it, afraid that if he did it would alert some spyware somewhere, and his headmaster and his parents and the girls' parents and every college he had applied to would know that he was watching it.

That was ridiculous. He was a computer geek. He knew as much as anyone else about how the Net worked. There was no such thing as what he was imagining. But still, he couldn't do it.

He wanted to click on the MPEG damn bad. He knew what he'd see if he hit the key. They'd fill his screen. The two of them naked, touching each other, the one pale, the other darker. He knew the way they'd lean toward each other to kiss and…

His erection strained against his jeans.

How could he? What kind of animal was he that he could still get a hard-on even now that she was dead? But he needed to come. Besides, it wasn't his fault. He hadn't asked them to make the movie. That was their idea—to entice him and show him how sexy they were and how much they were willing to do for him. And Hugh. And Barry. For all of them.

His head was fighting with his cock.

Hit the key, watch it.

Don't watch it.

Don't touch yourself.

I have to.

I have to.

Their images appeared on the screen. He fast-forwarded to

the kiss, to where he couldn't see their faces. He didn't want to see their faces. Just the fucking kiss.

There it was. A long, slow kiss. A kiss that went on and on. He was transfixed. Under its spell. Lost in the sensation it aroused. He didn't even know he was stroking himself. He was too far gone. The pressure was building.

When he came, exploding into his own hand, the clip was still running. He hit the stop button quickly. He hadn't even gotten through sixty seconds of it.

Wednesday
Sixteen days remaining

Sixteen

～∽⌒ↄↄ⌒∽～

Bob was early for his second appointment of the week, but Allison kept him waiting as per my instructions. When she finally let him in, he just stood glaring at me.

"It's worse. Everything is worse," he barked.

"I think you should sit down."

"What difference does it make? Sitting? Lying? It won't change anything. My wife doesn't talk to me anymore, and when I'm out, she's in my office snooping around. I found papers on my desk out of order, a framed photograph broken on the floor."

"What was it a photograph of?"

He looked at me as if I were speaking in tongues. "Of her. On some trip."

"What trip?"

He thought for a moment. Frowned. "Our honeymoon."

I nodded.

"Have you talked to her about being in your office?"

"I've tried. But she just shakes her head and leaves whatever room we're in."

He walked to the French doors that led to my tiny balcony

and stood there with his back to me. Beyond him, the solid gray sky was unrelenting. Bob opened one of the doors and a fresh blast of freezing air, mixed with some snow, flew in.

"Bob, can you close the door?" I got up, ready to rush over, ready for anything, but Bob shut it himself and started to talk to me.

"There is a story in the newspaper this morning about a young woman who was found dead in her apartment. She'd been there for days before anyone found her."

He turned and faced me.

I nodded. He was talking about the case Noah had been brought in on. Noah had called me the night before and told me about it, though not much detail; he was still at work and was only taking a short break to fill me in.

"The young woman…" Bob hesitated. "There was a picture of her…"

In silence, he returned to the couch, sat down, clasped his hands together and leaned forward. The lines in his forehead looked as if a sculptor had deepened them over the weekend.

"According to the newspaper, her name was Debra. I knew her as Penny. Do you understand?"

Bob had a habit of doing this to me, trying to get me to do the hard work for him. "No, I'm not sure I do."

"She was someone I watched, Dr. Snow. On her Web cam. I can't even count how many times I saw her. And now…" He was speaking softly, and I had to lean forward to catch every word.

"There were people watching her on the night she died, the article said. Men who actually saw her getting sick online—" He broke off again. Shook his head. Closed his eyes.

"Were you watching her?"

Thirty seconds went by. Forty. Sixty. Then: "There were

people actually sitting there, online, watching her, not even realizing that she was dying." Bob didn't sound upset so much as astonished.

"What bothers you about that?"

He shook his head.

"Have you ever seen your wife ill like that?"

"Of course."

"What did you do for her?"

"I took her to the doctor. I gave her medicine. Food. Whatever."

"How did you know what she needed?"

"What do you mean? It's what anyone who's sick would need. What I would need."

"How does it feel when you're sick and your wife brings you what you need?"

"I don't get sick."

"Never? No flu? No cold?"

"Sure, but that's not serious."

"Okay, but still. Tell me. How did it make you feel, the last time you were under the weather and your wife brought you soup, or tissues?"

"I wouldn't let her stay home from work to wait on me. I'm a grown man."

"What about at night, when she came home?"

He thought about this.

"Didn't she bring you anything? Not even a glass of water? Cough medicine?"

"She has enough to do. I don't need her ministering to me like some hausfrau. I'm not needy like that."

"But it's part of a relationship. Part of being intimate."

He shook his head. "It's unnecessary. I'm fine on my own."

"That must be lonely."

He looked confused. "What do you mean?"

"Not to need her, not to be able to lean on her."

Because of his tinted glasses, I didn't realize that his eyes had filled with tears until he reached up and wiped one away. Embarrassed, he cleared his throat, as if he hadn't had an emotional reaction at all. "Of course I can lean on her."

We both knew he was lying. To himself as much as to me.

And then, as if it was too much for him to bear, as if the lie chased him away, Bob stood up, and walked out of my office. Without a word of explanation. With so many questions still unanswered.

Seventeen

─❧❧❧─

That afternoon when Officer Butler got back to the station house, she read the note on her keyboard and immediately did as it asked: she proceeded directly to Jordain and Perez's shared office. When she got there, they were both on the phone.

Perez motioned for her to sit. After a few seconds, Butler realized they were on a conference call, talking to someone about the candidate search going on for a forensic psychologist to replace Fred Randall, who'd retired to teach at the police academy.

While they discussed their reasons for rejecting the latest candidate, Butler inspected the scarred wooden table where she sat. Nothing in the room was in worse shape than the table, but Jordain refused to have it replaced. "It gives the room some character," he always said when anyone complained.

She liked that about him. As demanding as he was to work for, he had an artistic streak that she admired. She admired him as a detective, too, but there weren't many officers who played the piano, cooked Cajun feasts, and cared about things like character in a table.

Her boyfriend teased her that she had a crush on him, but

it wasn't true. Jordain was too dark. He didn't joke around enough for her to like him that way. But as a boss, he was fine.

"Okay, let's hear what you have," Jordain said in a voice that was calming, as if he knew that she needed a little encouragement.

She opened a file and began her report. "Of course, suicide seems unlikely, but to rule it out—no one in her family, or any of her friends, thought she was depressed. They'd all seen her recently and often. She had a lot of good girlfriends, was close to her widowed mom and her younger sister, and her teachers had very good things to say about her."

"Teachers?" Jordain interrupted. "You went back that far?"

"No. She was still a student. An art student, getting her masters at Pratt, in Brooklyn. Only one of her friends knew about the Web-cam work. Said she had plans to stop in another few months, when she'd paid off the last of her loans." Butler watched Perez jot down a few words on a yellow pad with a tooth-marked pencil. It was the only kind of writing instrument he ever used, and the only paper he ever wrote on.

"Were those her paintings?" Jordain asked.

Butler thought there was a deeper level of sadness in his eyes since he'd found out what she studied. "Yes."

"They weren't that bad."

Butler nodded, not surprised he'd noticed the details.

"Her mom said Debra had sold two of her paintings recently, and that a Chelsea gallery was interested in taking her on. She said she was sure that by mid-summer Debra would be supporting herself from her art."

"Her mother knew about the Web cam?"

Butler looked straight into Jordain's eyes. "No, it was bad enough telling her that her daughter was dead…" She shook her head.

Jordain gave Butler a minute. He knew she was a professional and would get through this. It happened to them all. Every once in a while someone just got to you. It could be a little thing—a locket hanging around an elderly woman's neck with a faded baby picture inside. The connection could help the cases, made you work harder, even when you didn't think you *could* work any harder.

"Nothing to suggest that the Web-cam work was depressing her?" Perez asked.

Butler shook her head. "The friend who knew about it said there were no signs of that. If anything, quite the opposite. Since Debra was getting ready to quit, she had been happier than she had been in a long time."

"What about a guy? There's usually a guy. At least that's what women tell me all the time. It's all our fault." Perez laughed.

"There was a guy. Until about six months ago. She broke up with him. He was freeloading, but Maxi—that's Debra's friend—said she was fine about the breakup. She'd dated some since then, but no one special. Her painting seems to have been more important to her than just about anything else."

"Sounds good," Perez muttered, and then jotted down some more notes. "But that doesn't mean it is. It wouldn't be the first time someone said she was a friend and knew the inside scoop when she really didn't know squat. So I wouldn't rule out suicide yet."

"That's a pretty complicated way to kill yourself," Butler said.

"Not if you wanted to make a statement. Not if the very job you were doing was making you hate yourself," Perez responded. "You'd do it so that everyone out there in cyberland could watch you slather lubricant on your dildo and play with it, then die a disgusting death online."

"But she wasn't depressed," Butler argued.

"Enough guessing. Let's talk details. Was there any atropine in the apartment? Any recent visits to a hospital? Prescriptions on record for any eyedrops?" Jordain asked.

Butler shook her head.

"Nothing?"

"Nope."

"I think it's unlikely an artist would choose to die that way," Jordain said. "In front of a camera? Recording a hideous death? A visual person wouldn't have wanted to be seen that way."

Butler nodded.

"So that leaves us with an accident or a murder. What about the lubricant? Any way the factory could have screwed up the formula?" Jordain asked.

"No. It's just a simple water-soluble glycerine-based product. The factory doesn't use atropine. At all. Ever," Perez answered.

"So what do we have? A lunatic who is tampering with products? Does that mean we can expect more of these in the next few days?"

"How 'bout it, Butler? You sure there's no one in her life who wanted her killed?" Perez asked.

She shook her head. "I'll keep looking, talking to people. I've only been on this for two days, but she looks like what she was…a sweet kid who wanted to be a painter."

"And who just happened to make her living doing Internet porn," Perez finished.

"That doesn't mean she wasn't a sweet kid who wanted to be a painter." Butler's voice was slightly tense. "She just wasn't that complicated. Jeez. She was twenty-three. A smart kid from a normal neighborhood on Staten Island. No drugs. No abortions. No big problems with her parents. She had good friends whom she'd known for a long time. Even the boyfriend. Nothing stellar, but clean."

"Okay then," Jordain said as he scribbled something down.

"What do I hear in your voice?" Perez asked.

"We're going to need to get a court order."

"For what?" Butler asked.

"I know it could be product-tampering and that Debra just happened to buy the wrong tube of jelly, but there are thousands...tens of thousands...hell, maybe there are hundreds of thousands of men who have been watching her and drooling over her the past four years. I think we're going to have to investigate her online swains. Her e-mail address is right on her site. Anyone could have contacted her. I don't want this to be true because it's going to turn the next couple of days into a full-time nightmare, but that's where we go from here."

Perez was nodding. Butler rubbed her forehead, as if she was getting a headache.

"We're going to need to read her e-mail, listen to her phone messages, go over her phone records, and then cross-check everything with the porn company's records. They're not going to like showing them to us. But I'm betting that one of her admirers sent Debra that lubricant and asked her to use it for him. On camera. So he could watch."

Eighteen

~~~~~~~~~~~~~~~~~~~~~~~~~~

On my way home that night, I stopped at E.A.T, the too-chic takeout/bakery/restaurant around the corner from our apartment, and picked up some tomato-basil soup and a seven-grain roll. It was more expensive than it should have been, but I was tired, and the last thing I wanted to do was cook.

Upstairs, I turned on the news, sat down on the couch in the living room and ate my dinner.

After the first two political stories, the anchor spent three minutes on the case Noah had told me about on Monday night: the young woman in Chelsea who had died on Saturday night while doing a Web cast. After that, he segued into a sidebar about Internet pornography, including information about how popular it was among teenagers.

I ate the last bite of the roll and finished the last spoonful of the soup. I was home, off duty, I had to leave the office and stop thinking. After changing into jeans and a sweatshirt, I turned off the TV, turned on the CD player and retreated to my tiny sculpture studio—really just a table and a cabinet for my tools in the corner of the den. My work is amateurish, but it's how I disappear. The sounds of the mallet drown out the patients' voices inside my head. Carving was the only thing I'd ever found that made me forget about the people who laid their confusions and their sorrows at my feet.

I swiveled the piece around and inspected it from all sides. The pale blue marble I'd been roughing out for the past few weeks was finally starting to take shape. One more night or two and the wing I had envisioned bursting out of this stone would be clearly visible.

Using the mallet, I tapped the wooden base of the chisel, and the blade dislodged the first infinitesimally small sliver of stone. Another tap. Another chip flew. Another tap. Another chip. There was solace in being in control of the shape in a way I could control nothing else. Even if I was barely competent, each piece served its purpose. I worked for almost two hours before I left to pick up Dulcie from the theater.

When I walked into her dressing room at ten-fifteen that night, Dulcie hadn't yet started to take off her makeup, and was just removing the wig she wore to play Mary Lennox.

She smiled and stopped long enough to let me give her a kiss.

"How was the play tonight?"

"It was good."

"Yeah? Anything new?"

"Maybe."

"Out with it."

A knock on the door interrupted us. Did she look relieved?

"Yes?" I called out.

"It's Raul, can I come in?" Raul Seeger was the play's director.

"Sure."

Dulcie watched him in the mirror. When she saw that I was looking at her, she turned away.

When she'd first started rehearsals, she'd developed a crush on Raul, but I'd thought she was over that. Now I wasn't so sure. I stole another surreptitious look at her: She was wiping off her eye makeup. Very slowly. Too slowly.

"Morgan, there was a scout here tonight," Raul said. "He was very impressed with Dulcie's performance."

I looked back at my daughter. Now she kept her eyes straight ahead as she continued to clean her face with the thick cold cream.

Even from where I stood, across the room, I could smell the oily scent of the makeup remover. My olfactory sense is overly developed so that smells other people hardly notice can make me nauseous or give me intense pleasure. I keep rolls of peppermints in all my bags and pockets, so if a smell becomes overwhelming, I can pop one into my mouth and the aroma will neutralize everything else. I once helped save a patient's life by recognizing an obscure scent. Every once in a while, a whiff of a fragrance can throw me deep into the past. For a few seconds, I wasn't in Dulcie's dressing room anymore but was a seven-year-old lying in my mother's bed, late at night, way past my bedtime, watching her taking off her makeup.

She always let me sleep with her during the year that we lived in a tenement on the Lower East Side, where she was hiding from my father. I'd wake up when she came into the bedroom to get undressed, and I'd watch her from under half-closed eyes.

Unless she came home with a man.

Those nights she'd come and get me, wrap me up in blankets, and tuck me in on the living room couch, with an old black-and-white movie to lull me back to sleep and to keep any stray sounds from reaching my ears.

"A scout for what?"

"His name is Hank Riser. He's doing a television series loosely based on the play and is looking for his lead."

I glanced back at Dulcie for the third or fourth time in less than five minutes. Now her attention was openly on Raul, and she was nodding ever so slightly.

"He wants to fly Dulcie out to L.A. at the end of the month to test for the pilot. As much as I don't want to lose her, I don't want to stand in her way, either. This is a great opportunity, Morgan." He held out the scout's card.

I didn't take it.

"We went through this two months ago. Dulcie's working too hard on this play to add anything to her plate."

"This isn't adding TV. She'd have to quit the play. They've got a commitment for thirteen episodes. It would be full-time."

I shook my head. "No. I'm not sure I like that idea."

My understatement was lost on Raul. It even surprised me that I was capable of sounding so rational and calm about something that set off an emotional avalanche inside me. My pulse started to race and my jaw muscles tightened. I didn't bother to look at Dulcie again, no longer sure how I'd react to her. She'd known what was coming. She'd known how I'd respond. We'd been through this over something much simpler. If I'd said no to three weeks of TV work, why would I agree to thirteen weeks of it?

Raul hadn't taken back the card, still extended toward me. So quickly that I wasn't prepared for it, Dulcie was up and out of her chair, and she'd grabbed it.

"I'm completely excited," she said. "It would be amazing. To do a whole season of a TV show!" All this had been directed more to Raul than to me.

I watched my thirteen-year-old daughter as she casually tucked away the small white paper rectangle, without letting on that she might as well have been pocketing a bomb.

We got into the town car that the theater provided for us every night. It wasn't a limo, nothing that fancy, just a black four-door sedan that waited at the theater exit to take Dulcie and me home—or Dulcie and her father, depending on which of us she was staying with.

"Mom, this is something that matters to me."

The car moved away from the curb and headed east. I had no intention of having a serious conversation until we were home. Not the feedback she wanted, Dulcie turned away from me and stared out the window. Her overly dramatic response would have made me laugh if we'd been talking about something else. But this was where we clashed and what all our battles were fought over.

We were catching all the lights and making good time, and the closer we got to the apartment, the more my resolve increased. Beside me, I knew Dulcie's did, too. My kinetic connection with my daughter was in rare form and I was picking up on what she was feeling. No one has ever meant as much to me as Dulcie. There is nothing I wouldn't do for her, and I would happily sacrifice whatever it took to ensure her happiness.

But I was not, under any circumstances, going to allow my baby to audition for a TV series. She knew that. Yet she had taken the card anyway.

My daughter was thirteen.

As a therapist, I knew what the teenage years were going to be like in today's society, but there is a difference between knowing it professionally and living it as a mother. And the reality was testing me. Daily, it seemed.

As soon as we stepped into the foyer, before I had a chance to speak, Dulcie turned on me, and in a more adult voice than I'd heard from her before said: "You're not going to say no to this because of something that happened to my grandmother fifty years ago. I gave in over the other part because it was no big deal. But this is a big deal. I want to do it, Mom, and it would be grossly unfair of you to try and stop me again. If you do, I'll do it anyway."

Nineteen

❧⟋❦⟍❧

Dulcie had gone to sleep, or at least had said that was what she was going to do. I'd poured myself a glass of merlot and sat on the couch in the den channel-surfing, trying to find something on TV to distract me, but there was nothing. Leaving the television on mute, I perused the bookshelves. I kept one shelf of new novels that I hadn't yet read, but nothing tempted me. All I wanted was to go into my daughter's bedroom, sit by her side, rub her back, and have her smile up at me, totally trusting and loving, the way she'd done all her life.

Until now.

I finally took a book out—one I knew by feel, even before seeing the worn leather binding.

I sat down on the couch and opened it gingerly. The upper-right edge was frayed and the bottom left corner was torn. In the middle the first page was a single photograph. A black-and-white studio shot of a two-month-old baby girl. Beneath it was a date, written in ink that had faded just enough to make it look as if it were slowly disappearing.

May 16, 1944

I turned to the next page. There were rows of pictures, all

of the same child, month after month, as she began to get older, each one dated in the same flowery handwriting.

My grandmother had been meticulous about this album of her only daughter. When I was a little girl, I'd been fascinated by it, and used to love to stare at the pictures of my mother and try to find her face, the beautiful face that I knew by heart, in the photographs of the child.

By the time she was six months old, her eyebrows were strong and perfectly arched, the same shape they would be for the rest of her life. And the blue eyes were already as round and brilliant as they were when they looked at me years later. The proof that this baby was actually my mother had somehow been important to me. That she had been small and now was grown reassured me.

It wasn't until she was ten that my mother's lips began to resemble those that had kissed me every night. At twelve, her cheekbones started to show. By the time she was sixteen the resemblance was locked in.

That was the year my mother became one of *The Lost Girls*—a television series about the misadventures of two orphaned teenagers, taken in by a schoolteacher couple.

The show was an instant hit, and my mother became a star at an age when she was too young to cope. It both made her and destroyed her because the show went off the air when she was nineteen and she hadn't been successful at anything thereafter. Her acting never graduated to the next level; her marriage to my father, a few years later, didn't work; eventually she became addicted to pills and alcohol. My father tried to get her help, but she bolted, taking me with her, hiding out in a miserable apartment on the Lower East Side.

We only lasted a year.

A few times she stopped drinking. For five or six days, she'd quit bringing home the men who scared me, start to smile more and even cook dinner. Those days were the best. But she never stayed sober long. Finally one night she took too many pills, washed them down with too much vodka and fell into a coma. At eight years old, I was the one who found her and called my father and asked him to come and save her.

He couldn't. But he took me home with him and tried to save me. His second wife tried to help him, but it was Nina Butterfield, my mother's oldest friend, who truly rescued me, who gave me the sheltering arms and unconditional love that kept me going.

I ran my finger over my mother's long, wavy hair in a photograph taken when she was eighteen. She was lovely, with soft curls and those electric-blue eyes that looked so much like my daughter's that sometimes I am still overwhelmed by missing my mother when gazing into my daughter's face.

In that picture, at the height of her success, my mother looked like a real Hollywood actress. I wish I had known her then, at her happiest, when the bell-toned laugh that I had heard only infrequently was the sound she made the most often.

What was I looking for that night in the den? Something that would help me explain to Dulcie why, out of everything in the world, I could not allow her to follow in my own mother's footsteps.

When the phone rang, I was almost relieved to put the album down and return to the present.

"Morgan?"

The voice was low and the syllables pulled like taffy. It was Noah Jordain.

"What are you doing?" he asked in that slow, southern drawl that brought to mind his fingers on my skin.

"Sitting here feeling sorry for myself."

"Ruin another meal?"

"Very nice, very nice. No. I had some take-out soup. I bet

you had something exotic you just whipped up for yourself in a minute and a half."

"No, darling, not me, not tonight. I just got home. This is one crazy case. But I don't want to talk about that now. I miss you."

The words chilled and warmed me at the same time. He did this to me all the time. Affected me in a way that no one—not even my ex-husband—ever had.

"Morgan?"

"I'm here."

"You got awfully quiet there. What were you thinking?"

"What awful things you see and I hear every day."

"By hearing, by listening, you help people."

"I know."

"You sound too sad. What's wrong?"

I told him about Dulcie's invitation to audition for the TV series. I knew he'd understand. He'd watched us go through this the last time.

"I don't like to automatically take your side, but she's definitely too young to go off to Hollywood."

"Thanks. The problem is how do I convince her of that?"

"Not sure you can."

"So how long do I have to suffer her stony silence and nasty looks this time? You know how bad it was last time. I want her to fight it out with me, but she's so stubborn. So much like my mother. She just freezes me out."

"Need help thawing?" Noah asked.

I laughed.

"You know, it's been almost three weeks since I've laid eyes on you."

Something about the way his voice moved over the words "laid eyes on you" made me tremble. I felt a pull so strong it was almost painful, and then the sharp stab of fear followed. It always did. The red flag. The alarm. The warning. I wasn't used to wanting someone. Or opening up. It made me vulnerable in a way I didn't like.

I pushed myself to respond. "I miss you, too, Noah." I heard the words louder in my ears than I'd uttered them.

"That's good to hear, darling. That means you'll say yes to what I'm going to ask you."

"Yes."

"You surprise me, Morgan, you know that? You don't even know what I'm going to ask."

"No, but I wanted to see what it would feel like to do that. Just take a chance. So, what did I agree to?"

"Spending this weekend with me if Dulcie is going to be at her father's."

"Well, you're in luck. Or I am. Mitch is picking her up from the theater on Friday night and she's not coming home until Monday. What are we doing?"

"You surprised me, I'll surprise you. I'll tell you on Friday night. But it's still two days till then. What am I going to do in the meantime?" His voice was playful. "What if we just stay on the phone for the next three hours. Talk until we fall asleep, and then sleep with the phones by our faces," he said.

"Men do not say things like that. You are entirely too romantic. It makes me suspicious."

"It does not. It makes you giddy. I can tell from your voice. And men do say things like that. At least this one does."

I was about to respond when I heard his cell phone ringing in the background. "Damn it, hold on."

A call on his cell phone was almost always bad news, since he didn't use it personally.

"That's Perez. I'm sorry, Morgan, but I have to go. If I can, I'll call you back later."

"Take care of yourself," I said, not quite sure he heard me as he hung up his phone.

Twenty

Dearest,

I miss you the most at night. Sometimes missing you is a soft ache, but tonight it is like sharp spikes pushed into every joint of my body. Except now I have a goal that keeps me going—knowing that I am doing what has to be done. All five of them will be punished by your birthday. Sixteen days left. Sixteen. Sweet sixteen days. That allows me no room for mistakes, which is why I have to be invisible everywhere I go, in everything I do, even while I'm on the Internet. Invisible me. Visible women. Too visible. Too visible with all of themselves. There were other terrors, other weaknesses, other gross abuses and influences before the Internet, I know there was porn in magazines and X-rated movies and live theaters where women stripped down and danced naked while men sat behind glass walls in little booths and jerked off to prostitutes who cost money.

But these women are not limited to time and place: they fly, they spread their wings and more than their wings, and they are in front of ten thousand, twenty thousand, fifty thousand eyes at once, in living rooms and bedrooms and offices, all at the same time, talking, seducing, acting out, safe with their distance and yet dangerous with their reality.

Sometimes I sit in front of your computer and watch them and try to figure out exactly what it is about these others, these women, that makes them so addictive. I sit at your desk, fingers on the keys of your computer, and try to understand, and eventually the effort leads me back to you.

I miss you and I love you. How could you ever wonder about that? You. You. All I had and all that mattered—that ever mattered—was you. Did I tell you that? Did I tell you that I recorded Penny getting sick but have not watched it again? I don't have the nerve. I have watched enough of her on that screen, playing with herself, the pain kicking in, taking her by surprise. Taking her by surprise the way you took me by surprise, and with pain that kicked in and kicks in. That is why she lost her place in her crude sex play, why she was naked and her body glistened with the perspiration that dripped down her neck like tears, down her breasts and her stomach until it reached her pubic hair, where it disappeared, why she was dizzy and her eyes couldn't focus. She didn't even know what to do to help herself by the time she doubled over and her skin had turned chalk white. Her nipples were erect and they stayed erect, by the way, the whole time she was sick, so that it even seemed like the drug had turned her on.

After it was over, I sat there for a long time and felt as if everything that separates us had disappeared and we were together again. Only then, only when she was dying, did I feel alive and know that you know that I love you, and that I am proving it—that Penny died for our love and so will the next woman. This I do for you.

Friday
Fourteen days remaining

Twenty-One

I had gone to talk to Nina at my ten forty-five break only to find out she was attending a funeral. So it wasn't until that afternoon that I caught her in her office, pouring herself a cup of hot, steaming ginger-and-honey tea, a concoction she made at home every day and brought with her in a big thermos. She offered me some, which I took, and then I sat down on her camel-colored leather couch and asked her who'd died.

"Didn't I tell you yesterday?"

I shook my head.

"I must have been in denial. Nobody does denial better than a shrink."

We laughed. It was true, even if it was a cliché.

Josh Cohen, a professor at Columbia Law School, who had been sick with Alzheimer's for years, had passed away. For his friends and family, it had been like losing him twice: first when his mind faded away and he didn't know them anymore, again when his body had given out. Nina was very close friends with Josh's wife, Claire, who was also a therapist. She commented on the size of the crowd.

"All the important legal minds in the city, along with all

the shrinks. There's a joke in there somewhere but I can't think of it now. Strange bedfellows, that's it. Stacey O'Connell and I were sitting right behind a couple she's been counseling for two years. I saw three lawyers I've worked with. Two of them saw me but went out of their way to avoid me. Kira Rushkoff wound up sitting behind Stella Dobson, and Stacey and I were worried Stella was going to notice."

"Why?"

"Kira Rushkoff was the lawyer who won the privacy invasion lawsuit against Stella."

"That's right," I said. "I forgot that. Do you know about Stella's new book?"

"No, I didn't get a chance to talk to her. How do *you* know about it?"

"Small city. Small world. She's approached Blythe. She wants to interview her."

Nina gave me a very confused look. "She wants to interview a sex therapist? Surely she would have called me. We've known each other for years."

"No, she doesn't want to interview her as a sex therapist. I don't think she has any idea that Blythe works here. She wants to interview her about her Web-cam work. She probably doesn't even know Blythe's name. Online she's called Psyche, after the Greek goddess."

"I hope her past doesn't wind up being a problem for her with patients one day," Nina mused.

"It shouldn't," I said, thinking of the mask, certain I was right.

Saturday
Thirteen days remaining

Twenty-Two

The ride in from the airport led me to expect far more hurricane devastation than I found in the French Quarter. "It's enchanting," I said as the taxi drove down the tree-lined street, past the row of ornate town houses with their iron balustrades and architecture that belonged to another era. My window was down, and the warm air blowing in felt exotic after the freezing temperatures in New York. "It's not like any other city, is it?"

Noah smiled. "No, it isn't. It's crazy and lazy and has a rhythm, taste and texture all its own. But I don't want to tell you what it's like. That's why you're here. To find out for yourself." He squeezed my hand.

Noah had picked me up that morning after calling the night before and telling me to be ready at seven-thirty and to pack for two days in mid-seventy-degree weather. It wasn't until we got to the airport that I found out we were going to New Orleans. He was due in court there on Monday and thought we'd spend the weekend together; I'd go back Sunday evening, and he'd stay on.

We got out of the taxi on a small side street, which looked

as if nothing had changed there for more than a hundred years, and walked into the Saint Dennis hotel.

We'd stepped into what, to my untrained eye, looked like a perfectly restored mansion from the late 1800s. The lobby had tall potted palms, velvet settees and high windows with organza curtains that pooled onto the polished parquet floors. The scent of lush flowers perfumed the air. I stood still and breathed in for a few seconds.

"It's magnolia," Noah told me. I smiled because he knew what I was doing.

The concierge rang for a bellman, who took us in a mirrored elevator up to the third floor. Our room was decorated as authentically as the lobby, and while Noah tipped the bellman, I took a quick inventory. The king-size bed was covered with a heavy lavender damask spread, an antique writing desk stood in the corner and lovely prints of belle epoque New Orleans street scenes hung on the walls. A huge bouquet of freesia, roses and iris rested on the fireplace, gracing the room with its perfume. But it was the small balcony—with its wrought-iron railing, wicker chairs, ivy-covered trellis, pots of geraniums and enchanting view—that charmed me.

Three floors below us was a small courtyard, overgrown with lush, leafy trees, the flower beds studded with dark purple, lavender and blue blossoms. Occasional bursts of yellow. There was a stone fountain of an angel, with water spilling out of the shell she held.

I stood there with the water splashing in the stone basin and a lilting jazz tune coming from somewhere, enjoying the scent of humid green air and a breeze that was as warm and gentle as Noah's touch when he came up from behind and wrapped his arms around me. We stood like that for a moment, and then he dropped his arms.

"Let's take a walk. I can't wait to show you New Orleans."

On the plane, sitting beside him while he slept, I'd imagined that we'd fall onto the bed as soon as we'd closed the door behind us. I'd imagined the room—how wide the bed, how soft the pillows, how fresh-smelling the sheets. We would close the shutters but leave the windows open so that the light wouldn't be too harsh, and so the fresh air could tumble over us. In my mind, while the plane sailed over the clouds, Noah and I undressed quickly, and in the cool, shaded room pressed up against each other, fitting our bodies together, not losing a beat, our breath quickening, wiping out everything else.

As much as I wanted to, I couldn't wish fantasy into fact, and as much as I wanted him to stay with me on the balcony, I didn't say anything. I was actually shy. And then I was angry with myself for feeling that way, and for allowing the fantasy to take root in my head and disappoint me when it didn't come true. This wasn't like me. At least, wasn't like me before I'd met Noah.

It didn't matter. The moment had passed. Noah was waiting for me, ready to show me his hometown.

He searched my face in the elevator.

"What are you doing?"

"Looking for some clue as to how you're feeling."

"You're trying to gauge my mood from the way I'm looking at you, from how I'm holding my hands, from the slant of my eyes. You're using the tools I use on my patients, judging their words against their actions and mental equilibrium. That's not fair."

"Why not? You do it all the time."

I laughed. He was right. "Okay then, so tell me, how am I?"

"You're going to be fine, darlin'. I promise."

Twenty-Three

It was a work night. ZaZa sat at the glass table in the dining area of her loft, with a glass of cheap white wine that really wasn't half bad, and waited for Tania. She was jumpy because she wanted to see her so very badly. For more than a year, every Saturday, Tania Hutchison would show up around midnight. They'd drink some wine, light a joint, and after they were relaxed, they'd get undressed and go at it.

She looked at her watch. Why was Tania late? ZaZa got up, put the bottle of wine back in the fridge and sat down at the table again.

She'd decided. She was going to tell her. Finally. She'd kept the secret way too long. Months earlier, this had stopped being just a way to pick up some extra cash, to supplement the pathetic salary she made as a waitress while trying to get work as an actress.

Like too many other women, ZaZa had come to New York with stars in her eyes, and three years later had only managed to get some work as an extra in a dozen commercials. Every few months, she would decide to pack it in, move away, get a normal job, and yet something made her stay. She hated waitressing. Hated the studio loft in the crappy building in Hell's Kitchen. Even with all the painting and decorating, it still looked like shit. She hated the hope she felt every time she went on an audition, and then the greater hope she felt every time she got a callback, and then the torture of waiting for the phone call that she'd gotten the part. The phone call that never came.

At first she'd resisted when Barbara, a fellow actress, had told her about this job. But ZaZa needed some new clothes, a good haircut and decent highlights. If she didn't look good, she definitely wouldn't get any work. So she'd said she'd try it. After all, how bad could it be—it was acting, wasn't it? And she and Barbara were both actresses. They'd done scenes together in class. They'd gotten friendly, gone out for coffee, talked about their boyfriends when they had them, and their lack thereof when they didn't. They'd become friends, not just fellow thespians.

ZaZa jumped. Damn. The buzzer was too loud. She'd complained to the landlord about it a dozen times already. Every time he saw her in the halls, he wiped his hands on his already dirty jeans, leered at her—not enough to upset her but just enough to creep her out and make her wonder if he'd seen her on the Internet—and promised that as soon as he finished fixing the floor in 4-B or repainting 6-A, he'd fix the buzzer. But it never happened.

Tania brought a freezing cold whoosh of air with her. As she unwrapped her scarf and her hair fell back into place, ZaZa pretended she wasn't watching her, but she was. Tania's nose was a little longer than was considered beautiful, and her jaw was too strong, but that just made her more striking.

The two women did not kiss hello, but they seemed genuinely glad to see each other. While Tania took off her coat, ZaZa poured her a glass of wine.

When, after almost two years, Barbara had finally given up hunting for work as an actress and moved out of New York, ZaZa had recruited her new partner. She'd met Tania doing extra work and they'd gotten friendly, going to auditions together. After a few weeks, ZaZa felt that their friendship was good enough to withstand the suggestion, so she took on Barbara's role and broached the subject of the gig. First, Tania laughed. Then she asked to see what ZaZa did online. They'd sat in front of ZaZa's computer, with two glasses of wine, and when ZaZa hit the play button, Tania leaned in.

She didn't say anything while the footage ran. She didn't get up, or move back, or squirm. The longer she watched, the more hopeful ZaZa became. When the scene was over, Tania stood up and told ZaZa she needed to think about it. A week later she called and said yes, she would do it, because she needed the money. All the stress in the sentence was on the word *money*.

That had been more than a year ago.

This would be the fifty-third time they'd stripped down and played at being lovers for the sake of the thousands of men who were out there in the black nowhere watching. ZaZa didn't like to think about them. No, she *couldn't* think about them. Couldn't picture them, couldn't wonder at what they were doing—it would poison her performance. Instead, each time they got together, ZaZa and Tania spent the first hour or so drinking wine and improvising the story they would use that night. ZaZa played at the scenarios as if she were on Broadway.

It was a test of their acting skills, Tania had said.

ZaZa had agreed. "It's great practice for us. As good as any class I've ever been in."

"So who should we be tonight?" Tania asked once she'd had some wine and warmed up.

ZaZa had bought a used paperback of Sappho poems and read two of them aloud.

"I love those. Let's use them," Tania said.

"You don't think it might go over our audience's heads?"

"As long as we give them virtual head with the scene, they won't care, now, will they?" Tania had laughed, stood up and started to unbutton the black cardigan she was wearing.

"Don't," ZaZa put out her hand to stop her friend. "Let me do it. They'll like that."

And then they turned on the camera.

Twenty-Four

For dinner, Noah took me to a small restaurant that wasn't in any of the guidebooks but was packed. He introduced me to Bella, the owner, who was in her sixties and had big blond hair and earrings that dangled down to her shoulders. Despite the crowd waiting at the small bar, we'd gotten a table immediately, along with a basket of hot corn sticks, dripping with butter, and a plate of spicy pickled okra that I wasn't sure I wanted to taste. Once I had, I couldn't stop eating them.

I let Noah order for me—crab étouffé atop a plate of dirty rice—and then ate more than I should have. The wine was crisp and cold, a welcome respite from the food that was setting my mouth afire.

Afterward, we walked over to Blues Palace, an unassuming club. After the band had played a few songs, the sax player noticed Noah in the audience and called him up onto the stage, insisting he play with them. He looked at me and I nodded. Once on stage, he sat down at the piano and his fingers took off.

Until I met Noah, I'd never listened to music just for the music; it had always been in the background. But I'd discovered that if you give yourself up to it and really listen, your body begins to resonate with the notes, and you hear it inside of you as a sensation as much as a sound.

Noah improvised for more than an hour and we got back to the hotel a little after one in the morning. There was enough moonglow coming through the open window for us to see each other. Without speaking, he reached out, put his hands around my waist and pulled me toward him. I felt as if I were moving in slow motion. First there was his face, with his soft blue eyes looking at me, and then it was closer to mine. I could feel his breath on my cheeks while his fingers gripped me, digging through my sweater and into my skin, the pressure contrasting with the gentle expression on his face. And then there was nothing but the blackness inside my own eyes and the sensation of his lips compelling mine to open. Lips moving in a way that makes nerve endings burst. Lips moving in a way that sends shivers up the back of your neck. Lips that cover your mouth and tease you alive. Lips that do not stop even as one kiss moves into the next, and the next one after that.

The rest of my body felt the kiss as if every pore of my skin was experiencing the same sensation and reacting the same way. It doesn't make sense now, but that was exactly how it felt. As if his fingers were suddenly kissing my waist, and our thighs were kissing each other, and my breasts, beneath my sweater, were kissing his chest, and my shoulder bones were kissing his arms.

His lips kept returning to mine even as he moved me toward the bed and laid me down and pinned my arms to my sides. For one moment, he raised himself up on his elbows and hovered over me, smiling, watching me, before swooping down and taking a kiss away from me, and then giving me one back.

"Don't move," Noah whispered in that slow drawl. "Don't

move. I want to undress you." And then he unbuttoned the first button of my shirt and put his lips on my collarbone and kissed me there.

Twenty-Five

❧⚬❧

ZaZa took her time taking off Tania's sweater. She let her fingers linger on each button, making every moment last an achingly long time. That was what she was supposed to do. It was also what she wanted to do. No matter what, the night would not last long enough. They never did anymore. But she wouldn't think about that. She wouldn't think about anything, because that would make her sad. She would just take the pleasure where she could get it. That her partner in this game didn't feel anything back wasn't what she needed to think about now. That she was in love with a woman, that she couldn't get enough of the woman and her skin and her mouth and her hair and her pussy, didn't matter now. What it meant didn't matter now. What it said about her wasn't important. She wasn't going to put labels on this; it was an acting job. Except ZaZa knew she wasn't acting, she was feeling all of this emotion. She'd stopped doing it for the camera and the money a long time ago.

Tania stood, unmoving, while ZaZa pushed the sweater off her shoulders, down her arms, to her waist. She breathed in sharply when she'd exposed the other woman's breasts. Then Tania undressed ZaZa.

Seconds later, ZaZa felt lips kissing her neck—small fluttering motions that progressed from her collarbone up, up, up to behind her ear, where a tongue reached out and licked her skin on the spot that made her twitch and squirm and emit a small moan.

The tongue slid back and forth and then moved in a tiny circle around and around and around until ZaZa couldn't have told you where she was or who was touching her. It was pure sensation and there was nothing attached to it.

She wouldn't have minded if Tania never moved away from that spot, but she did, and her skin felt abandoned. The spot was jealous when the tongue and the lips started moving back down her neck.

Tania moved to pull ZaZa's pants down, and the air on her bare skin was cold. She shivered.

"Never mind," Tania whispered, "I'll warm you. I'll warm you until you don't feel anything but your own heat." She leaned across her, silky hair brushing ZaZa's bare stomach, and reached for the bottle of oil.

ZaZa smiled. Nothing felt as good as Tania's hands massaging the fragrant oil into every inch of skin on her body. She closed her eyes and waited for the warmth to enter her pores.

Twenty-Six

※━◦⟲⟲◦━※

Noah trailed his fingers down my throat and across my chest. I closed my eyes and focused on the feeling. Or, rather, tried to focus on the feeling.

When you are a sex therapist people assume one of two things: that you are an intensely sexual person and interested in sexuality almost to the exclusion of other emotions, or that you have sexual problems of your own and are on the other side of the couch to try to convince yourself you're fine.

But that's not how it works for most of us. We become therapists first, and then choose to specialize in sex therapy later, because it fascinates us for a wide variety of reasons, many of which we don't always consciously know. But for me, it was because Nina Butterfield was the most constant role model I had in my life and she was a sex therapist. So even before I understood what it meant, I wanted to do what she did.

"I am a doctor who helps heal people's hearts," she'd told me when I was little. And when my own daughter first asked what I did, that's what I told her, too.

In my life, I have never been preoccupied with sex and have never thought of myself as highly sexed or a sensualist. I've met women who are, I've treated them, and I know how we differ. Sure, I'd enjoyed sex with the man I was married to, but I'd never noticed when we went through dry spells the way he did.

But now, with Noah, I was different.

His fingers trailed down my sides and made circles on my stomach. He lingered there, in the dark, spending whole minutes sensitizing a two-inch circle of ordinary skin that I had never been aware of. His fingers moved so slowly that I became conscious of the texture of his fingertips, slightly rough and callused. The intensity of the touch was magnified a hundred times. Looking at a snowflake through a magnifying glass, you see myriad crystals creating a unique and complicated design that the naked eye is incapable of recognizing. So it was with his one finger on that spot of skin. It was not a single movement that elicited a single reaction, but a constantly changing evocation of impressions that not only affected that area but sent electric warnings shooting through me.

Noah was melting me.

It was like this each time we were together. I always started off half frozen and he had to work me into relaxation.

"There's nothing to think about but my fingers, Morgan. Nothing but my fingers and your skin." His voice was as mesmerizing as the movement. The pressure was building to pain. I writhed.

"What do you want?" he murmured.

"More."

"What else do you want?"

I shook my head.

"Tell me."

I shook it again.

He put his lips up to my ear. "Let go, Morgan. Let go. Stop thinking." The rhythm of his words was hypnotic, and the more he repeated them the less I heard them, the closer I got to disappearing into the feelings. "Let go, Morgan, let go." The fingers moved into a wider circle. Around and around. I was seeing the circles as hot-blue neon lines going around and around, each crossing the other, exposing layers of nerve endings, shooting the same hot blue through my skin into an inner core, where they became lightning bolts of hotter blue and searing red, circles and then lines that traveled up my arms and down my legs, always coming back to settle deep in my womb, which sucked them in and still wanted more.

Twenty-Seven

ZaZa moaned under Tania's fingers as she stroked her from her shoulders down her back, down her spine, down around the cheeks of her buttocks, and then, with the same warm oil, made the reverse trip back up.

Now it was her turn. ZaZa grabbed the oil, poured it into her hands and then rubbed Tania's breasts. Around and around.

They took turns with the oil and the massage. Back and forth.

ZaZa used more oil to travel up and down the length of Tania's legs. Tania came around ZaZa from behind and massaged her breasts again. Held them in her hands and gently and reverently drew her fingers around her nipples. At the same time, she pushed her pubis into ZaZa's ass.

ZaZa pushed back, the pressure was building. Her breasts were on fire.

And then she pulled away and turned around. Tania sat back on her haunches, watching and waiting to see what ZaZa was going to do next, both of them instinctively careful to stay at an angle to the camera so that neither of them would obscure too much of the other.

ZaZa was thinking about how much she loved this woman. How much she wanted to keep touching her everywhere and have Tania touch her back, and how complicated it was because she'd never wanted to be with a woman before and now there was no man she wanted to be with as much.

Tania reached out and rubbed ZaZa's hard, small clit.

ZaZa threw her head back and closed her eyes and felt her insides throb. *Rub me faster,* she wanted to scream out, but she knew—she had been doing this gig for so long it was second nature to her—she couldn't rush it yet. There was a pace and a rhythm; she had to stay with it.

But would it really matter if she got off fast once first? Maybe they—the anonymous "they" who never had faces or names—would like more than one orgasm.

Reaching out, ZaZa put her hands on top of Tania's, which were already playing between her thighs, and encouraged her partner to rub her harder and faster.

Then she placed her own hands between Tania's thighs. She knew the other woman wouldn't mind the change in the routine, and would be happy to oblige.

ZaZa put one oiled finger inside of Tania. Tania put one oiled finger inside of ZaZa. Two women mimicking each other's movements.

Twenty-Eight

~~~◦⟲⟳◦~~~

When I came, it was sharp and intense and hard-won. Noah had been waiting for it, holding back until he felt my body stiffen, and then he let go, moaning into my ear. The same ear he had been gently and patiently whispering into—a breeze of words that had, in the end, been the same mantra that urged me into an orgasm.

When he rolled off me he didn't disengage completely, but left our sides touching and our legs crossed. Once he'd caught his breath, he reached out and played with my hair.

"I can't stop," he said. "I'm exhausted but I can't keep my hands off you."

"I'm flattered." I kissed him lightly on his lips.

After I pulled away, I saw him open his mouth and then shut it, as if he had been about to say something and changed his mind. Sometimes I wished I wasn't so damn observant. I didn't want to be an expert at sensing and noticing and understanding other people's emotional states when I was involved. I closed my eyes.

"I'm not going to give up on you, you know," he said.

"What does that mean?"

"You don't know?"

I opened my eyes and looked at him. "I have no idea." And I didn't. His words had caught me by surprise.

"Are you as afraid of us as you seem to be?"

"You know, Detective Jordain, it's not in the slightest bit sexy for you to lie here and psychoanalyze me."

"*Au contraire,* my dear. It's utterly sexy. Two of us, naked and glistening with lovemaking, and me figuring out your very complicated brain. There's nothing I'd rather be doing."

I laughed. He leaned over and kissed me. Not a light and teasing kiss as mine had been a minute before, but a long kiss, with his lips pressed tight against mine, letting it last and linger, taking my breath away. He knew that, too.

"You're completely relaxed now, aren't you?"

"Hmm."

"Good. Just lie there now. There's more I want to do to you."

With his hands on me, the way he was holding me, I couldn't have thought about anything else if I'd wanted to.

Twenty-Nine

$\sim\!\!\!\circ\!\!\!\circ\!\!\!\circ\!\!\!\sim$

Tania was gasping for breath and ZaZa smiled at the intensity of the orgasm she'd given her, increasing the pressure of her fingers on Tania's clitoris. She wasn't going to stop. As soon as her partner's breathing slowed and her orgasm ended she was going to start on her again, and then again. She was going to amaze her. And then, later, when the camera was off, she was going to tell Tania how she really felt about her.

Focusing, listening to the other woman's breathing, ZaZa waited to hear the intensity slow down. Damn, this was lasting a long time. She waited. Still there was no slowing down. Something was wrong.

Maybe Tania wasn't gasping in the throes of an orgasm. Maybe she was gulping for air.

"What is it?" ZaZa whispered, not wanting to break the mood for all the men who were watching, but concerned about her friend.

When Tania slumped over and continued the rasping, ZaZa really began to worry. Clearly this was not a sexually-induced reaction, but before she could do anything, she felt the first wave of nausea overtake her. It hit her hard. Failing to hold it back, she vomited uncontrollably, right there on her own bed. Her head suddenly ached, too. Bad. She couldn't breathe. Christ. Everything was blurry, confusing. She tried to say something. To tell Tania she was sick, too, but she was so dizzy. She could see Tania at the end of the bed, curled up in a ball, shaking, and she wanted to reach out to her, but she couldn't figure out how to move in that direction. Nothing was where it should be, everything was skewed.

"I'm really sick," Tania whispered.

ZaZa couldn't even answer. She just stared at her with eyes that felt as if they were on fire.

"You're sick, too," Tania said. She tried to get up but couldn't find her balance.

ZaZa was willing her to get up. She had never felt so bad in her life. She needed some water. Some air. She needed to be able to breathe. More than water, she needed help. Tania needed help, too. ZaZa could see that.

Finally, using the back of a chair and then the edge of a table, Tania managed to make it to the desk where the computer was. Where the phone was.

ZaZa tried to talk, to tell her to tell them to hurry, but all that came out was a low and raspy moan. She couldn't form the words, but she could still see what was happening.

She watched Tania pick up the phone. She was so sick, but she was thinking about how at that moment, Tania had broken the computer connection and ZaZa's broadcast had gone dead in thousands of homes, hotel rooms and offices. She'd also tipped over a glass of wine that spilled onto the keyboard and shorted out the motherboard. One way or another, that Web cast was fated to go dark.

Right before ZaZa passed out, she saw Tania manage to dial 911.

Sunday
Twelve days remaining

Thirty

The phone rang, jarring me awake. I could barely open my eyes, and I reached for my cell phone where I always left it when I was away from my daughter, on the bedside table. But before I could find it—while I was still groping in the dark—I heard Noah talking. It was his phone.

I lay there listening to the one-sided conversation, unable to fill in the gaps but making wild guesses at what was going on.

"What time?"

Pause.

"What hospital?"

Pause.

"How are they?"

Pause.

"Which one?" One last pause. "Okay. I'll be there in a few hours. I can turn around and fly back here for Monday."

I heard the click as he shut the phone and the thud as he put it back on his nightstand. As he lay back, his breath was rapid and his body was tense.

"Noah? What happened?"

"Did you hear that? I'm sorry it woke you."

"No, it's fine. What is it, though? What happened?"

"Looks like another poisoning."

I sat up in bed and leaned on my elbow. In the ambient early morning light, I could see that Noah's features were drawn.

"I'm going to have to go back to New York this morning," he said.

"I'll come with you."

"You know, you could stay. Your ticket isn't until tonight and there's a lot that—"

"No, I don't want to be here without you. We can come back and you can show me the rest of your city. Tell me about the woman. Is she dead?"

"Women. There were two of them. One has a chance, the other…they don't think so."

"What happened?"

"Crazy. This is so crazy." He rubbed his eyes and ran his hand through his tousled hair.

"Christ, I'm sorry, Morgan. We finally have a whole weekend together and now this."

"It's okay, just tell me what happened."

"Men watching the Web cast saw them getting sick and started calling it in…dozens of them…just like the last time… it might have taken forever to find again but one of the women managed to call 911 before she passed out. The ambulance got there in four minutes."

He rubbed his eyes again.

"Would you like me to order up some coffee? It's already six o'clock. The menu said room service started an hour ago."

"Yes, coffee. And food, too. I'll call the airlines and try to get us out of here." He picked up his cell but just stared at it. "Two women. One's twenty-two, the other one is twenty-three. And God knows how many men, just watching it happen."

Thirty-One

*

Dearest,

Two more candles burning makes three lights altogether, and tonight the smell of the wick is just a little bitter and the scent of the wax is just a little sweet. I pass my finger over the flame, feel the heat, and it shocks me. That I can feel anything shocks me. The women with their naked arms and legs, with their hungry eyes and mouths, they felt heat and passion and pain and they felt sick. And I watched them, even smiling while I watched them, and was someone unfamiliar to myself. I was a stranger in my own skin. They burned with pasted-on passion, but my passion was real, it is a need even I can tell is desperate, a need for revenge that has entered into the cracks of my psyche like some slippery ooze, filling, then expanding, turning those cracks into ever-widening chasms.

I had room for no one but you. Why didn't you understand that? I had love for no one but you. I'm talking about real love, of course, and I do know what real love is. I would slit my own throat and drown in my own blood to prove to you how real that love is. How could you not know that?

The secret of what happened to you has turned me into someone that you would not recognize. Inside of me, where I loved people—you most of all—and cared about what happened to them, I am now hollow.

Three of them have been punished and there are only two left. Are my efforts, working like sandpaper and rub, rub, rubbing at my skin, getting past the top surface, to the muscle, to the bone, to the deep center where I used to be, doing any good?

I have found the edges of my mind and I have touched the corners of my own hell. It is a small room, and on every wall there are mirrors, but when I look into them, I do not see myself reflected back, but you.

I never saw myself in your eyes staring back at me, but now I see your eyes, accusing me.

You were wrong, you know, you didn't understand—you *were* all I had and all I *ever* wanted.

One woman died last night and the other lingers on in a hospital, in critical condition, according to the news. I watched them touching each other. Slathering on massage oil—oil I had sent them—acting out their disgusting scenario for the hundreds of thousands of hungry eyes. I watched them touch each other with sure fingers, not for the sensations it gave them but for the titillation they gave others.

You wrote that I didn't know how to love, that it wasn't you I loved, but some idea of you. How could you ever think that? I would cut my hands off at the wrists and my feet off at the ankles to tell you how much I loved you.

Last night I proved it again. I watched and then I held my breath, and they vomited and flushed bright red and broke out in sweats and fell to the floor. This, I whispered to the computer screen, this is what you get for doing what you do. This, I whispered, as the blond one crawled on the floor to reach for the phone, trying to save her own life, mocking our lives, mocking what happened to our lives, this I do for you.

Monday
Eleven days remaining

Thirty-Two

❧❧❧

Bob was on time for his appointment but he looked even more tired than he had the week before. He lay down on the couch and flexed and unflexed his fingers. While I waited for him to start speaking, I drank some of the bitter, lukewarm coffee in my mug.

The coffee had been so much better in New Orleans.

The sun broke through the clouds, and for a few seconds my office was filled with light. Maybe the snow outside would start to melt. New York City had gone for more than a week without a single full hour of sunlight.

New Orleans seemed very far away.

"My wife has been using my computer again," Bob said. "She's been snooping around and going to all the sites I visit."

"Did she tell you that?"

"Of course not. She forgot to erase the cache of where she'd been while I was at work. Her whole little trip was right there for me to see. She left tracks."

"Did you confront her?"

"I didn't have a chance. She confronted me. You know I've been unfaithful to her in the past. I had a few affairs over the years. It seemed to me that this was so much more acceptable. So much safer. Less threatening. I don't know these women. Don't talk to them. They just stimulate me. And they're there whenever I want them. Beautiful, sexy women who don't want anything from me."

"Nothing?"

He looked at me. "What do they want from me?"

"You can't think of anything?"

"No."

"What do you give them?"

"Nothing. They aren't real."

"Bob, they are real."

"I just meant that they aren't actually interacting with me. We don't have a relationship. They are anonymous to me, I to them. I pay them to—" He broke off.

"Go on."

He shook his head. "I don't know. What was I saying?"

"Bob, what do they want from you?"

He laughed bitterly. "Better my money than what women usually want."

He'd gotten there. Good.

"What do they usually want?"

"They want to get inside your head. They want to own you. And to be the only woman that you think about. As if there could ever be only one woman that I think about."

"But there's a difference between thinking about someone and acting out your sexual urges, isn't there?"

"There is, but that's what the Internet is good for. I'm only thinking about these women. I'm not with them."

"But you're not with your wife, either, are you?"

"No."

"Why, Bob? Why aren't you having sex with your wife?"

"Because she's the same. I know everything she is going

to do and everything she is going to want. I know how she is going to make me work on her for anywhere from twelve to fifteen minutes before she can come, and then once she has, she'll be willing to let me have my turn."

We had talked about this before. Several times, in fact, Bob had described the dry and tedious sex life he didn't enjoy with his wife. But to date, he hadn't broken through and connected to his anger at his wife's lack of interest. He hadn't gotten emotional about it. He simply accepted it and used it as a way to justify his Internet habit. Until he allowed himself to feel how furious he was that his wife was not interested in exploring a richer sex life with him, and until he talked to her and let her know how it made him feel, he wouldn't be able to begin to work on the addiction he had come to see me about.

"Have you heard about those two girls?" he asked, his voice suddenly low and conspiratorial.

Not wanting to assume anything, I asked him what he was talking about.

"The two Web-cam girls. The one who died, the one who's still in the hospital."

"Yes," I said, thinking for a moment about being woken up when Noah got the call.

"This is very freaky, but I saw them on Saturday night."

"You saw it happen?"

He was quiet for a few seconds, then his fingers started to do their march on the leather armrest. "I was watching them, and then I heard my wife get up. I heard her go into her office. It was late. About midnight. I thought she was asleep. She'd told me she was going to sleep at ten-thirty. Some nights her antidepressant keeps her up—it had the night before, and she was tired."

"What did you do when you heard her?"

"I turned off the computer and went to bed."

"How did you feel?"

He thought about this—as if it had not occurred to him that he had any feelings about it. "I was angry."

"About what? What made you angry, Bob?"

"I wanted to keep watching those girls. I'd seen them before. The Saturday Night Specials, they called themselves. Only worked on Saturday nights."

"And you couldn't watch them because of your wife?"

"That's right."

"But doesn't your wife have a right to not have your sexual addiction thrown in her face?" This wasn't what I thought, but it was what I thought might get Bob one step closer to facing his own reactions.

"My wife has gotten everything she's wanted. One thing, one stupid thing—letting me jerk off in my own office on my own time—what is the big fucking deal?"

His voice was rife with feeling. Real anger flashed in his eyes. Good, we'd accomplished something. He was still controlled, but he was clearly furious. I was relieved to hear the shift. "Why is it so important that you have this one thing?"

"Because she has everything else. She has always had everything else. She didn't want children right away, she wanted a career, and she wanted to wait. We waited. She wanted to live on the Upper East Side, even though I wanted to stay in the Village. She wants…she wants…she wants me to keep my dick in my pants, unless she wants me to take it out." He was shouting and I didn't do anything to stop him.

We were moving toward a new stage where Bob might finally be able to face how hurt he was. We still had miles of feelings to traverse, but at least we were on the way. I was quiet, waiting, allowing Bob to sit with his emotions, letting the sound of his voice fill the room and then fade away, until there was only the sound of the little clock on the table by my chair, and the traffic outside.

"I can't stop thinking of those girls," he said, his voice now low and sad.

"Why is that?"

He didn't answer me.

Thirty-Three

Less than twenty-four hours after arriving in New York, Detective Jordain had flown back to New Orleans and appeared in court for the Hatterly trial, for what he hoped would be the last time. He spent a half hour on the stand and as soon as he stepped down, Jordain was again thinking about the two victims in New York. Once he was back in a taxi and on his way to the Louis Armstrong airport, he called Perez to get an update.

"ZaZa, whose real name was Cindy Conners, has been working for Global Communications for the past two years. Same company Debra Kamel worked for. Conners was an actress. Easy work in between auditions, I guess. She never landed much—mostly extra work—but she took a lot of classes over the years. Tania's an actress, too."

"That where they met?"

"We don't know yet, but one can assume."

Jordain watched the scenery whiz by. Leaving New Orleans was always bittersweet. Home had a pull all its own, even after he outgrew it.

"Did the forensic team find anything at the apartment?"

"Not yet. If anyone left behind one fiber, one hair, a single speck of dirt that had been stuck in the tread of a shoe, they're going to find it."

"Sometimes I think you believe the cop shows you watch on television. Even if someone left a fiber behind, what will it mean to us unless the same person left the same fiber behind at Debra's apartment and we find that one?"

"The TV shows are modeled after us, not the other way around. Don't get confused on me," Perez interrupted.

Jordain smiled and gulped lukewarm coffee from a foam cup. No matter, it was still his drug and would work its trick, regardless of its temperature.

"And, no. We don't have anything yet on Debra Kamel's apartment. I know that was your next question."

"No, actually, I was going to ask you how Tania is."

"It's still touch-and-go."

"Butler have any luck with the computers?"

"Still at it."

"We're *going* to find something on the computers."

"I hope so. But ZaZa's laptop is pretty much shot to hell."

"We don't have an option on this. We need to find something, and soon." Jordain wasn't surprised Perez didn't ask why. They both knew.

How many more girls were targeted?

How many could they save?

Damn. This case was getting under his skin. They all did. But there was something about this one that disgusted him. Maybe it was the spectacle of it. The horror of knowing that while these women gasped for their last breath, naked and vulnerable, they were on view before thousands and thousands of men who were sitting out in the wild blue yonder, all over the globe, watching them, jerking off to them, coming in their hands to them, without realizing that the girls were dying in front of their eyes.

"If they're going to die, they should at least be afforded some dignity."

Jordain hadn't realized he'd said it out loud until he heard Perez's sigh.

Thirty-Four

Bob stood up suddenly, said he had to go to the men's room, and walked out of my office. When he'd been gone for five minutes, I called Allison and asked her if he'd left. It had happened before—a patient bolting when a session got too rough to handle.

She hadn't seen him, and he did return after another few minutes. Silently, he took his place on the couch. His eyes were shut. There was little expression on his face.

"When was the first time you saw a naked woman?" It was a topic I'd wanted to broach for a long time.

"A real woman?"

"Whatever comes to mind."

"When I was twelve, I found magazines under my father's bed. Luscious, full-color pictures that made me drool. Those beautiful women, looking at me, lying there naked for me, showing me what I wanted to see—the way they'd make me feel. Christ. That slow burn, the build. I'd hide out in my room and sneak looks at them. I'd leave dinners to go upstairs. Five minutes with the right magazine in one hand and my dick in the other, the sounds of the busy house beyond my door. Is that what you asked me?"

"You're doing great."

"My father never seemed to notice when I took his magazines."

"Do you think he did?"

"I don't know, but I wish I knew if he was like me."

"Would it make you feel differently about him?"

"No. About myself."

"How?"

"But those were just photographs. Nothing like the first real woman I saw naked." It wasn't the first time Bob had skipped over a direct question about his feelings, and I didn't want to stop him to force the issue. "It was at an X-rated theater." His lips twisted into a smile that was also a grimace. His fingers flexed. "One Friday afternoon when our school let out early, two of my friends took me. They'd been there before and had been telling me about it for weeks. I can still remember how much I wanted to go, even now. This was really doing something bad. It was breaking big rules, and I knew if I got caught I'd be in a shitload of trouble.

"The theater was called the Playpen. It's still there. All boarded up, but still standing. It had been one of the city's really grand old movie palaces that had gone out of business. Turned into a smut palace." His voice had lingered over the last two words almost lovingly. Then he frowned.

I had seen this same kind of pleasure/guilt reaction from other patients. Like them, Bob found both release and a kind of exquisite hell in his addiction. It was a special kind of torture, his orgiastic needs overpowering his morality. The push/pull of his conflicting cravings.

"What a mess it was inside. Grimy and stinking. The rug was worn down to threads. Isn't it crazy that I can remember the rug? It was dark red." He shook his head as if his own memory surprised him. I didn't tell him that it wasn't unusual for someone to remember minute details of his first sexual encounter.

"The owners had broken up the old screening room and turned it into two smaller theaters—one where they showed the dirty movies, and the other was the live room. That's where we went. Each of us had our own small booth. I pulled the ratty curtain closed behind me. And then all I could see was the stage.

"She was sitting on a chair, dressed in a tight skirt and a tight sweater and high-heeled shoes. I was hard the minute I saw her. My buddies had told me that everyone pulled it out and jerked off during the show, but I couldn't believe it was really okay to do that. I'd only done it at home, quickly, while the world was going on around me. Now I had time. And this woman wasn't on a page of a magazine but staring straight into my eyes."

He licked his lips. His eyes remained shut. "Can I…do you want me to tell you what happened?"

"Yes, if you want to."

"She started to strip for us. First her blouse. Then her bra. She had silver pasties covering her nipples. God. I can still see her. Those pasties made her even sexier than if she'd been totally bare. And then she walked over to each booth, one by one, and pressed up against the glass with her breasts. When she got to me, I put my hand out. The smooth feel of that cold glass and the sight of those glorious breasts. Oh, God.

"I couldn't believe how fast it was over. But then she took off her skirt. Underneath, she was wearing a lace garter belt and stockings. I got hard again. Instantly. That had never happened before. Maybe I'd never given myself a chance before. I was always rushed, afraid someone would knock on my bedroom door. But this was different. She was naked except for those pasties and that garter belt, pressing her body up against the glass. I stood and pressed my cock against the glass, too, and it was almost as if I was fucking her." He sighed and breathed in deeply. Once. Twice.

"As I said, the theater's still there, at Forty-fourth and Eighth. A few years ago, someone bought it to turn it into some women's shelter. Make a statement. There was a legal battle over it and it—" He stopped suddenly. He'd been about to say something and then caught himself. What had he been about to tell me?

"Bob?"

"I read about it. That's what I was going to say. I read about it and saw a newscast about it and damn if I didn't get a fucking hard-on just hearing the name of the theater said aloud."

Thirty-Five

It had been a long day, and after my four o'clock patient left I got up and stretched. It was already dark outside and the street lamps cast a warm pink glow that seeped into the office.

The smell of chocolate made me turn around. It was intense. Bitter. Orange. Spicy. Sweet.

"I made these last night and thought you and Dulcie would like some," Blythe said from the doorway. She was dressed in a lavender sweater with a starched white collar and cuffs peeking out, slim black slacks and pointed cowboy boots. Her blond hair was pulled back in a ponytail and her face was scrubbed clean.

Some people have utterly transparent faces. You can look at them and know without any question how they are feeling. Blythe was like that. She really was pleased to be making this offering and it touched me.

"That's so sweet of you," I said, not meaning to pun. She smiled. I took the plate from her and peeled back the tinfoil.

"Do you want one?" I asked her as I tore off a corner of one of the thick, soft brownies.

"I only have a few minutes. I have a patient coming," she said, clearly nervous. Something was bothering her.

"First one today?"

"No, I have two on Mondays."

I chewed the chocolate treat. She watched, waiting to see my reaction.

"These are delicious. Thank you. Dulcie will love them. So how did your first session go?"

"Not great. I'm still feeling too much emotionally. I'm trying to separate myself from my patient, but it's not working. At one point, I had to bite my cheek to stop myself from crying."

"We'll keep working on it. We'll solve it."

"Can you really listen to your patients without feeling anything?"

"No. The point isn't to stop your feelings but to use them to inform the therapy and steer you in the right direction with the patient. That's healthy. What we have to work on is not reacting."

She nodded, but she still looked defeated. Being a good therapist mattered to her so much. "Sometimes I think I'll never get there and that I'm crazy to try."

I wanted to reach out and touch her hand and give her some kind of comfort. It was ironic that what she struggled with—connecting too deeply to patients—was what I was struggling with, with her. What was it about Blythe that tugged at me and made me want to shelter her?

What she had been willing to sacrifice to get to this point made me frightened for her. At first, I'd thought she had a self-esteem problem. Now that I understood she didn't, I cared about her even more. And I wasn't supposed to do that. Wasn't that what I was telling her her own problem was?

We are not supposed to care in a way that keeps us up at night, but some of us do, because we know that with effort there *can* be change. We've seen it. We've been part of it. Just a little bit of hope is all it takes, and you can't give up even if it destroys you to keep waiting to see it again.

Thirty-Six

"Ben wa balls painted with toxins," Perez said.

"Leather outfits with topical poison applied to the inside of the garments," Butler offered.

"Good one. How about whips soaked in poison that would enter the bloodstream when the strap broke the skin?"

Butler added it to her growing list of ways sex toys could be turned into deadly weapons. "You scare me," she said. "Dildos outfitted with explosive devices."

"I scare *you?*" Perez quipped.

Butler leaned back in her chair and looked out through the glass partition that pretended to be a wall. The station house was in high-activity mode, as if it was the middle of the day, but it was after eleven. She'd been working since eight that morning, after getting only five hours of sleep the night before, and was exhausted.

Until early Sunday, the investigation had been focused on Debra Kamel, whose death they'd assumed was an isolated incident. Now they were not only trying to solve two murders, but they were also strategizing on how to prevent countless others.

She looked up when Jordain walked into the office. He'd come back from New Orleans, been briefed, and then gone into a powwow with the lieutenant about what to tell the public.

"We're not going to release anything about the delivery systems of the poisons," he said. "No one—not the mayor or the police commissioner—wants us to start a panic, and I don't want us to tip our hand and lose any leads that might come our way."

"All three victims worked for the same porn site. Can't we at least get word to the rest of the women who work there?" Butler asked. "God only knows how many of them already have some deadly sex toys in their hands now."

Jordain nodded. "Sure, we can do that. As soon as you figure out how to do it without a list of who the hell all those women are."

He was frustrated. Although he'd gotten court orders to get a list of employees and all the customer records from the porn company, the man they were dealing with at the Global Communications office in Singapore wasn't accommodating them. They knew there was someone in the States running things, but they hadn't cracked the code and found out who he was or where he was.

"Any ETA on how long it's going to take to cross-reference the two computers?"

Perez nodded. "Another hour or two. Maybe more. Penny's computer files are complete, but ZaZa's are almost all corrupted."

"Let's assume nothing turns up. Do either of you have any doubt the same person orchestrated both killings?" Jordain asked.

Neither of them did.

"No details out of place?"

"There aren't any details to be out of place. We still have squat," Perez said.

"Any chance it was a copycat?"

Perez shook his head.

"We're sure no precise info about how Debra was poisoned has been leaked to the press? No one but us knows the poison was in the lubricant, right?" Jordain asked.

"Right. And we're assuming no one guessed about the delivery system and then put poison in the massage oil," Perez agreed.

"Okay. That means someone is targeting these women for a reason. Any ideas?" Jordain asked.

Butler drained what was left of her soda, yawned and shut her eyes for a second. When she opened them, she looked at the clock. It was almost 11:30 p.m. Jordain didn't even look tired, she thought. He was wide awake and ready to start brainstorming.

Detective Details they called him, only half joking, because he was obsessed with minutiae. But as often as not, that was what solved cases. Not the big, broad strokes but the infinitely small details that no one else noticed. Jordain was a perceptive man—he made it all look so easy, so possible. He was tireless and determined, and most of all, he was just. He had a heart. He balanced compassion with rationality and never wavered.

Perez was smart, too, but he wasn't that different from everyone else. She respected him, but she didn't look up to him. There hadn't been many men in her life she looked up to. Perez was a good guy, but still just another guy. Jordain was the one you stuck it out for. If he said you were doing a good job, that mattered.

She yawned once more.

"Maybe you should go home, Butler. How long have you been here?" Jordain said.

"It doesn't matter. There's a chance those women's computers might give up a name tonight, and if you can wait for it, I can, too."

Tuesday
Ten days remaining

Thirty-Seven

~~~~~∽⊙⊙⊙∽~~~~~

From the time Detective Jordain got the call from the hospital, it took him and Perez less than fifteen minutes to get there. Dr. Fred Klein met them on the seventh floor and briefed them. Tania was through the worst of it and was going to make a full recovery. They could talk to her for ten minutes.

Jordain sat by her bed while she slept. She was pale, but her breathing was even. Five minutes went by. Another five minutes. When she finally opened her eyes, he saw they were large and the color of the ocean during a storm. Her lips, though cracked and almost bloodless, opened to say something, but only a very faint whisper came out. He wasn't sure, but he thought she asked him who he was.

Even in this sorry state, Jordain could tell how tempting she must have been to the men who watched her online, and before his mind went further in that direction, he said hello and introduced himself.

"Do you know where you are?" he asked.

She nodded. "I know…" She coughed. "Woke up before." Her eyes searched the room and then blinked three times. He could read the panic. "My mother…?"

"She's downstairs with my partner, Detective Perez. She'll be right back. I told her I'd stay with you. You know, she's been here since Sunday morning when you came in. She hasn't left."

Tania nodded and licked her lips.

"Would you like some water?"

She nodded again and he poured some from the plastic pitcher on her nightstand—the same pitcher that was in every hospital room he'd ever been in. How many times had he done this? Gone through the ritual of soothing the patient and waiting until he or she was comfortable enough so that he could ask his questions and disrupt the fragile recuperation process with the last thing the patient needed: prodding that forced him or her to relive the trauma.

While Tania was drinking her water, Perez came in.

Jordain introduced them, and Tania gave Perez a hello that sounded slightly stronger than the one she'd given Jordain. All the time, her eyes searched. "My mother?"

"I convinced her to have a little breakfast. She's having some oatmeal. She'll be back in about fifteen minutes."

She nodded.

"We'd like to ask you some questions," Jordain started. "Not too many and not for too long. Is that all right?"

"I guess so. But first will you tell me how ZaZa is? I asked the nurse but she doesn't know who I mean."

Perez gave Jordain a quick look that said he didn't want to be the one to tell her.

Jordain nodded almost imperceptibly. Damn. Yes, he'd do it, but he had no idea how close the two women were. How was it going to hit her? He wished her mother had told her. Although, maybe even her mother didn't know. If he told her, he might lose her for an hour, a few hours, a day, but he couldn't lie to her.

The hesitation was enough for her.

"She didn't make it, did she?"

"I'm sorry, no."

"I already figured it out. We were both sick with the same stuff. If she was okay, even if she was as bad as I am, no one would have kept it from me. How stupid is this? Just like some dumb movie—" She stopped talking and closed her eyes. Tears rolled down her cheeks but she didn't break down. "She died of the same thing that made me so sick, right?"

"Yes," Jordain said.

"Do you know what it was?"

"Not yet. Not for sure. We're doing tests. We need you to tell us what happened. Okay?"

Tania nodded, but now she was crying too hard to talk.

Thirty-Eight

❧❧❧

I didn't get out of my office that day until it was time to leave for my session at the Park East School. It hadn't been snowing five minutes earlier, when I'd looked out of my window to check, but now it was coming down hard again and I didn't have time to go back for an umbrella without risking being late. But if I didn't find a taxi—which I doubted I would in weather this bad—and I had to walk, I'd get soaked.

Rushing inside, I grabbed one of the extra umbrellas Allison kept in a stand by her desk. She was on the phone and waved good-night to me, and then I saw Blythe coming down the steps, wrapping her scarf around her head.

"It's bad out there," I said as I opened the door and held it for her.

"What else is new?"

She was heading Uptown, too, she said, and so we walked to Park Avenue together, hoping we'd find a cab to share. The two of us huddled under the one small collapsible umbrella and blinked the snow out of our eyes as we forged ahead. The wind was blowing west and I had to swirl the umbrella to keep it from flying away. It wouldn't have mattered; it wasn't preventing the snow from stinging our cheeks and our lips.

The sidewalks were packed with that day's fresh snowfall, which covered previous layers of both snow and ice. Walking was hazardous, and halfway down the block Blythe hit a patch of ice and started to slide. Reaching out, I grabbed her arm, and she steadied herself.

"I can't believe how dangerous it is just walking to the corner." She laughed and thanked me for holding on to her.

We got lucky a few minutes later when a young woman with a toddler got out of a taxi in front of an apartment building on Sixty-seventh Street.

Once we were in the cab, I told Blythe I was going as far as Eighty-eighth Street and she said she'd drop me off then. She was going all the way up to 103rd Street.

"Mount Sinai hospital? Everything all right?" I'd felt an immediate lurch of fear in the center of my stomach upon hearing the address. There wasn't anything else up there.

"The girl who was poisoned on Saturday night—the Webcam girl—she's there. I don't think there's anything I can do for her, but I wanted to go in case she needs to talk to someone."

"Do you know her?"

"No. Not personally. But…I feel like I do."

The taxi was warm and I was wearing a heavy coat and good, thick gloves, but I shivered. Blythe, despite her degrees and her potential as a therapist and her desire to excel in my own field, was so close to the tragedy.

As the cab crept Uptown, I told Blythe where I was going and a little bit about the sessions I was doing at the school.

"I hope you can help them," she said earnestly.

"So do I."

"You don't sound as if you think you can."

I didn't know if Blythe was especially perceptive or if my

tone of voice had been too revealing. "These kids are encased in stone. Every week I chip away but make almost no progress. I can't find a fissure to use to crack them open."

"I never thought much about this before, but what's going to happen when I have to work with a patient who has this problem? Has my problem?"

"You'll be that much more sensitive and compassionate."

She laughed. "Compassion is hardly my issue."

"You're being too hard on yourself. You've only been seeing patients for a few months. You're going to learn how to deal with all these feelings you have. I promise. That's why we're working with each other."

She looked at me the way Dulcie used to and maybe would again when she was older—when she reached Blythe's age.

We all need someone whom we believe has the answers and whom we can trust to help us. But when that person disappears from our lives, we feel every shift in the wind as a threat—we become one of the lost girls. It had happened to me when my mother had died. Blythe was one, too; I knew the signs. At some point in her life, Blythe's anchor had disappeared. We needed to talk about it in a session, not in the back of a steamy cab.

The taxi stopped at a light at Eighty-seventh Street. I'd be getting out at the next block. I reached into my bag, opened my wallet, pulled out a ten dollar bill and handed it to Blythe. "Take this."

"No, I can pay."

"There's no reason for you to pick this up. It's a business expense. I'm on my way to a session." I forced the bill into her hand. The light changed. The driver pulled up to the middle of the next block. I put my hand on the door handle and then turned to Blythe.

"Thanks," she said.

"Really, it's not a big deal. I had to come Uptown, anyway."

"No, I didn't mean the cab. I meant what you said about me being okay. You always make me feel so much better. Like everything will work out."

She smiled. That wide-open smile. It pulled me in again.

I stood on the corner in the falling snow. Flakes landed on my hair and my cheeks. A fat one settled on my bottom lip. While I watched the taxi pull away, Blythe turned around and waved at me, and for a moment I felt it, too—that maybe everything that was wrong really could be fixed.

Thirty-Nine

⟡⟡⟡

"I was online but just goofing around. I wasn't surfing. I wasn't watching them…" Barry started and then stopped. He rubbed a spot on his left arm almost to the point of obsession.

We had a rule in the group, only one rule: if any of the kids watched porn or engaged in it, they'd come clean. They wouldn't get dissed or lectured; no one's parents would be told, but they had to be up front with me and with the rest of the group. And since the group was the only thing standing between them and expulsion or suspension, they were pretty good about it.

I waited, keeping my eyes on Barry's, keeping my body language neutral.

"But a bud IM'd me and told me that these two chicks were going at it and acting all weird and I clicked over to check it out. I didn't get what he'd meant by acting weird. I thought they were doing something kinky."

"How long did you watch it?" I asked.

He looked down at the floor. "Not long. I got sort of sick."

"Sick?"

"Like I was gonna throw up, you know?" He was embarrassed.

"Do you know why?"

"They were in pain. It was awful, you could tell."

I wanted to find a way to make him realize he was connecting to what he'd seen—understanding it was happening to two real women—instead of the detachment he'd felt with all the women he'd been watching online the past two years.

"How could you tell they were really sick?"

"They just weren't acting. I don't know. You could just tell."

"You kept watching it?" Jodi asked. "That's disgusting. How long?"

He shrugged.

"Did you do anything?" she asked.

"Like what? Jerk off?"

"No. Like call the fucking police or something."

He shook his head.

I waited for one of the other kids to get involved.

"You watched the whole thing?" Ellen asked. Unlike Jodi, she wasn't angry, she was incredulous.

"Yeah."

"You think that the one girl tried to kill the other one?" Ellen was playing with the button on her jacket, twisting it around and around.

"Come on," Amanda said. "That's so lame."

No one said anything. I waited. Watched her face. Felt the pain from across the room. Why was it so hard for her to talk about this?

"Why is it lame to wonder that?" I finally asked.

"They wouldn't hurt each other." Amanda's voice was low; I had to strain to hear her. "They were friends."

She seemed so sure. And so pained.

"Amanda, did you see those two girls on Saturday night?"

She shook her head.

"Have you seen other girls like them?"

She didn't answer.

Who had she seen? When had she seen them? How was I going to help her feel comfortable enough to share whatever she was struggling with?

A few seconds went by.

"When you watch women online, what do you think they're thinking? What do you think those two women were feeling before they got sick?" I asked.

"Nothing. They're being hot. They're ho's. That's all," Paul volunteered, and then shrugged.

I watched Amanda flinch.

"Do you ever really think about it, Paul?"

"About what? What they are feeling?"

I nodded.

"Shit, I don't know."

"Try now. Let's all try. First thing that comes to your mind—what do you think they are feeling?"

"They probably dig all that attention." Paul smirked. "They—"

"Maybe it was suicide," Amanda said in a very low voice. She was interrupting but didn't seem to be aware of it. She hadn't looked up when she said it but had kept her eyes on her shoes—suede boots with thick rubber soles. Most of the girls wore them. My daughter wore them. They were the accessory du jour in Manhattan schools.

Timothy quickly looked over at her, a concerned look in his eyes.

"What makes you think so?" I asked.

"Because you get to a point where the only way you can come out on the other side is to die."

The tone and timbre of her voice alerted me that her stress level was high. All the kids sensed something was happening and waited. I needed to keep her talking. "Amanda, do you ever feel like that? Like you need to come out on the other side?"

She shrugged.

I leaned forward. "What do you do when you feel like that?"

"I guess I do art stuff."

I nodded. "Me, too. When I feel like that, I sculpt. I know how it works. It helps, doesn't it?"

She was watching me—so much going unsaid, so much I couldn't read in her eyes, and so much I needed to say to reach her. "Yeah. Sort of."

"Amanda, what could have happened to the girls online that would have been so bad that they would have wanted to kill themselves?"

"Just because they were getting paid doesn't mean it was only about that. At first they probably liked knowing guys were watching. Like Barry said. They probably did like the attention." She wasn't looking at me anymore, or at anyone in the room. Her eyes were still on her boots.

"And then?" I asked, encouraging.

Everyone was still riveted, waiting. She had galvanized the group.

"It was what they did, right? They were pros. The ultimate Venus fantasy that every guy is stuck on, and they knew it. Two chicks. Going at it…putting on a show. But it wasn't…" Her voice shook as she went on. Her eyes were still cast downward, but her hands had curled into fists in her lap. "They probably didn't get off on it at first. Didn't even think about it. But then all that touching. All that touching each other, all soft and caring and naked like that…"

Hugh whistled. Barry joined in.

Amanda winced.

Timothy glared at both of them and hissed, "Shut the fuck up."

I was surprised. Real emotion. A protective streak.

I watched a tear fall from Amanda's eye and get lost in her jeans. Another. She did nothing to wipe them away.

Timothy got up. He walked across the room, knelt down in front of her, put his hands on the arms of her chair, and whispered something to her that I couldn't hear. I don't think anyone in the room could. She didn't respond but another tear fell, this one landing on Timothy's hand. He looked down and stared at it but didn't brush it off.

"Amanda?"

They'd all left the session and were walking toward their lockers to get their things. She turned, said something to Jodi and walked back toward me.

"I wanted to give you this," I said, and held out my business card.

She didn't take it.

"You left it on the seat three weeks ago when you joined the group. All the guys have my number and address. And the other girls took it."

"Yeah. So?"

"So who knows. It doesn't mean you have to call me, but if you don't take it, you won't have the choice."

She was staring at it. I was certain there was something she needed to talk about but that she was afraid of. Otherwise, taking the card would be meaningless. If she had it, she might be tempted, and something about opening up was scaring her.

"I promised everyone in the group. Nothing anyone ever says will ever leave the room. I'll never break a confidence. That's my job."

"Yeah."

"Why don't you believe me?"

"It's not that."

"Then what is it?"

She shrugged.

I took a chance.

"I really would like to see some of your artwork."

She nodded, seemed to be thinking about it. "Why?"

"I love art. I told you I sculpt a little. I think that making art is one way we explore our feelings. We can say things in a painting or sculpture that can be hard to put into words."

"Photographs, too."

I nodded. "Do you take photographs?"

"Yeah. And I make shorts."

It was quiet in the hallway; the voices and footsteps of the other kids had faded away. Her words lingered, not quite an echo, more like a piano note fading away.

"Short films?"

She stepped back, frightened.

"Amanda? What is it?"

She shook her head.

"I don't want you to tell me anything you aren't ready for. But I want you to take this. I know something is bothering you and that it's something that seems overwhelming and impossible."

"How?"

I smiled at her. I would have preferred to reach out and take her in my arms, but I couldn't do that. "It's what I'm trained to do, Amanda. I can help you straighten it out. Not make it go away. Not even make the pain go away. But help you put it in some kind of perspective, so you aren't controlled by it."

She shifted. A shield came down. She backed up. "Yeah, like you're helping the guys to get control over how much they go online? They still can't stay away. You're not helping them."

"We don't know that yet. It takes a long time to break an addiction."

"Amanda?" It was Ellen calling out; she was at the end of the hall. "You ready or what?"

"I have to go."

I was still holding the card. "Take it."

She stared at it for a few seconds.

"The secrets get bigger and bigger the longer you keep them." I extended it so that it was even closer to her. It almost glowed in the darkened hallway.

"Amanda?" It was Ellen again.

She turned with most of her body, broke eye contact with me, but somehow reached out with her left hand and took the card, as if it was an afterthought and didn't matter.

But it did. Very much.

Forty

My mother had a snow globe that sat on her battered dressing table in our dingy apartment downtown. Inside was a theater marquee with the words *The Lost Girls* on it, along with my mother's name spelled out in what looked like tiny yellow lights.

Now that globe sat on my dresser, among perfume bottles and picture frames. When she was growing up, Dulcie had loved it as much as I had, and would sit and play with it for a long time, enchanted by the way the snowflakes fell over the marquee.

I was having one made for her next birthday—with her marquee and her name and the title of the play she was appearing in. When my taxi pulled up to the theater, the marquee was indeed brushed with snow just like the scene inside the snow globe. Dulcie and I were still talking, albeit cautiously, but she'd accepted my decision about her not doing the audition.

For the first time in hours, I forgot about the kids from Park East and the strange sense I'd had that Amanda and Timothy knew something I needed to know—the sooner the better.

Inside, the doors to the theater were shut. Harold, the usher, saw me, smiled and let me slip quietly inside.

I stood in the back, behind the last row of seats, and looked at my daughter on stage. No matter how many times I watched the play, I was still surprised each time I saw Dulcie in the footlights. There was always a first rush of shock that she was there, on Broadway—not in her junior high school auditorium, not at a summer camp production, but a professional, performing for strangers every night.

At the same time that I was incredibly proud—the audience had burst into applause as Dulcie finished up her second-to-last song—I felt the rise of a low-lying anxiety fluttering up from under my ribs. She was so vulnerable. And as the play moved ahead to its finale, I saw the teenager on stage not as my daughter, not as my mother's granddaughter, but as a wholly independent creature—like the kids I'd been working with earlier. They each had secrets inside of them that their parents, their teachers and their families didn't know about, couldn't guess.

What secrets did Dulcie have from me? From Mitch?

I wouldn't know, even though I'd had secrets, too. Kept them close to me and away from my father, from my step-mother, and from Nina.

But that didn't make it any easier for me to accept when it came to my own daughter. At thirteen, her secrets might still be innocent and harmless, but with each piece of knowledge that she hid from me, afraid that I would not understand it or that I would interfere, she moved farther away from me. She was at the age when the chasms appeared. And I knew, because I had counseled patients about this—about how important it was to love your child for who she was, for who he was, to not be disappointed about whom your child didn't turn into. That the best a parent could do was to listen, be sensitive, not give up. But when it came to my daughter, following my own advice was far more difficult than I'd imagined.

The orchestra played the first notes of the finale. Dulcie found her position. She finished her line, took a breath, segued into her last song of the evening. Her voice, like liquid gold, poured into the cavity of the theater. The richness of it, the purity of it, melded with the orchestra and rode just on top of the music, merging but never getting lost. She carried the song for the first twelve stanzas and then was joined by the others.

When the song ended, the notes and the voices died out, and all that was left was the reverberation in the air. Finally that, too, was gone. Silence held for ten, fifteen seconds and cracked open as the applause swelled. I joined in, more excited than I thought I could be, more moved than I wanted to be, more caught up in Dulcie's moment—and feeling her excitement—than I was prepared to be.

Feeling her happiness should have pleased me. It would have had I not also realized that standing up there made my thirteen-year-old so much happier than anything else in her life had. I recognized the look in her eyes as she took her bow. I'd seen it before.

I knew better than to merge them like this. My mother. My daughter. They were two separate beings. Thirty years separated the last time I had seen my mother and tonight when I was seeing my daughter.

How could I begrudge Dulcie adulation because of my failing and my insecurity?

Mitch told me I was too protective of our daughter. So did Nina. But when I was in that state between sleep and wakefulness, when I talked to my mother in my head, she told me that I was right. That Dulcie was too young. That I needed to keep my daughter from the things no one had kept her from.

After the crowd thinned, I walked down the center aisle and onto the stage and then behind the curtain and into the wings. I knocked on my daughter's dressing room door and waited to hear her response.

No answer.

I knocked again.

Maybe she was in the bathroom. I opened the dressing room door and then instantly regretted doing that. She wasn't a baby anymore. I couldn't barge in on her.

"Dulcie? I'm sorry. I knocked, but—"

She wasn't there.

I walked over to the small bathroom. The door was shut. I knocked. No answer. I knocked again. Still no answer. This wasn't like her. Even when she was angry, she responded, her voice dripping with her effort at adult fury.

Finally, I tried the door. It wasn't locked. The bathroom was empty.

She must have gone into someone else's dressing room; I'd sit down and wait. Normally, she didn't linger when the play was over. None of the kids did. They were tired and hungry and had been with one another all day. But that didn't mean it never happened.

After a few minutes more of waiting, I went out into the hall to search for her. The car and driver the theater arranged for every night would be outside waiting and it was getting late and God knows how much more snow had fallen while I'd been inside and how bad the traffic on Broadway would be.

I asked everyone I ran into, but no one had seen her since the last curtain call.

Finally, I found Raul, the director, talking on his cell phone by the back door. At first he didn't get off the phone, but when I didn't politely go away, he cut the call short.

"Something wrong?"

"Have you seen Dulcie? I can't find her."

"Not since the last curtain call. Did you check in the car?"

He'd suggested the most logical place, and as I went back into the dressing room to grab my coat, I felt foolish. Of course. She didn't know I had been in the audience. I didn't always come inside. Dulcie had probably been in such a hurry to get home that she'd raced out of the dressing room and was waiting for me, wondering where I was.

Forty-One

The black town car was not where it always was.

I looked across the street.

No, it wasn't there, either.

The panic started deep in my chest.

I ran as fast as I could in the snow, twenty yards up the street, then backtracked in the other direction.

No car.

A rush of adrenaline set my heart racing and I stood there in the freezing cold, trying to figure out what I was supposed to do first. And then I thought of the phone. I called Dulcie's cell, and while I waited for her to answer, I tried to imagine her voice, curling at the edges with her smile, calling me Dr. Worry and clearing up the mystery of where she was with one simple sentence.

"Hi—"

"Dulcie where the hell—"

She was still talking. Damn it. It wasn't her, it was her message, saying she wasn't available.

"Dulcie? Where are you? Call me. I'm worried. Raul didn't see you leave. I didn't—" It was pointless to keep talking. What if something was wrong? What if—

I couldn't think. The wind was blowing and the snow was getting in my eyes. My coat was open and I was starting to shiver.

What the hell should I do?

Dulcie was old enough to take the car service home on her own but either Mitch or I usually met her. We didn't want her to be alone after a performance. It was a good time for us to talk, to find out how her day went, to reconnect. If one of us couldn't be there, she could take the car by herself. But I'd told her I'd be there that night.

I stared at the phone, glowing blue and green in the dark. *Call 911. Tell them—* No, I could do better than that. I punched in Noah's cell phone number. He answered quickly, listened to me, and then asked me for the name of the car service.

"Hold on, Morgan."

I could hear him dialing another phone in the background and then he was back. "Hold on, Morgan, we're calling the driver."

Now I felt stupid on top of worried. Why hadn't I thought to call the car service? Why hadn't I—

"Morgan, she's fine. The car service just dropped her off at home."

I couldn't say anything right away. The relief was overwhelming. Then I thanked him, told him I'd call him later, and dialed Dulcie's number at home.

This time when the machine answered, I was angry. She was avoiding my call, acting out because of the audition.

"Call me back. Now."

The bright neon signs and twinkling marquee lights were muted by the snow. Cars moved as if their drivers were unsure of what was happening beyond the windshield. A hush had come over the city. Winter storms mute Manhattan as nothing else can.

I pulled on my gloves, held the cell phone and walked west, figuring eventually I'd find a cab or get to a bus.

On the corner, a homeless man was huddled in the entranceway to a dark and boarded-up theater. All but one section of the theater's neon sign was covered with snow, but the wind had blown in such a way that a single pink leg wearing a red shoe was exposed. On another night, I'd stop and try to talk him into going to a shelter, but I needed to get home.

I'd gone five blocks without hearing from my daughter. Stepping into the entrance of a busy and well-lit Japanese restaurant, I shook the snow off my hair and dialed the doorman of our building.

"Good evening, Doc. I hope you're on your way home. It's nasty out there."

"I am. But listen, Gus, I've been calling Dulcie and she isn't answering. How long ago did she get home?"

"I haven't seen her, Doc."

"How long have you been there?"

"I've been on duty since six."

"But the driver said he had dropped her off at home."

Gus was talking but what he was saying didn't register. I ended the call and quickly punched in my ex-husband's phone number.

My daughter had gone home, Noah had said.

Dulcie had two homes.

Damn. How could I have been so stupid?

"Mitch, it's me. Is Dulcie there?"

"Yeah, didn't she tell you she was coming back here tonight?"

"No." I knew I was yelling into the phone—the patrons at the bar of the restaurant were staring at me.

"She left the theater without telling me. You can't imagine how worried I've been, calling everyone—including the police. What the fuck is going on? Is this about that damn television show?"

"I think you'd better come over," he said.

"First tell me, is she all right?"

"She's not sick or hurt. She's fine. But it might be better if—"

"I'll be there as soon as I can. There are no cabs. I'm walking," I said, and hung up.

A young man and woman were standing out in the street, just standing there, two faces looking up at the sky, letting the soft flakes fall on them, mystified and amazed by the storm.

I was mystified by the storm, too: the one going on within my family.

Forty-Two

"That's impossible," Alan Leightman said to his doorman through the intercom.

"Sorry, Judge. But I'm looking at their badges."

"Okay, Jimmy, send them up."

He stood in his hallway waiting for the elevator to stop on his floor. He was a New York City Supreme Court judge. The police treated him with respect. They certainly didn't show up at his home at eleven at night unannounced. But apparently that's exactly what they were doing.

Watching the numbers light up, charting the detectives' progress, he tried to imagine what had brought them here at this time of night.

Someone he was responsible for putting in jail must have been released. He would listen, nod, reassure the detectives that he was not only careful but was well guarded both in his luxury apartment on upper Fifth Avenue and in his downtown office. The city in the post-September 11th world did not take the safety of its officials lightly.

The elevator door opened and two men stepped off, their coats still flecked with snow. Alan nodded to them as they stood there stamping the last of the slush off their boots. He recognized both of them, welcomed them, and then ushered them inside.

He liked to watch people come into the apartment. Despite his high-profile job, it was his wife's salary that paid for them to live floating above the city. No one was unimpressed by the floor-to-ceiling windows that looked out over Central Park. At night, the view crept up on you, seduced you, pulled at you. The sparkling lights from thousands of apartments across the park, on the West Side, looked like stars.

Leightman led the detectives into his den and motioned to the seating area. Detectives Jordain and Perez sat down side by side on a couch. The judge took a chair facing them. A coffee table piled with papers and leather-bound books separated them.

"Would either of you like a drink? Coffee? A cigar?"

"I wouldn't mind some coffee," Perez said as he rubbed his hands together, warming them up.

Leightman nodded and looked at Jordain. "And you, Detective?"

"Sure, if it's not too much trouble."

"None at all. I just hope you're not here about something that's going to be too much trouble." He chuckled.

"It may be, Judge."

Forty-Three

⟪ ⟫

Waiting for Leightman to return with the coffee, Jordain looked around the room, taking in the two walls of fine walnut bookcases.

"How many books would you guess there are in here?" Perez asked, following his gaze.

"More than you could ever read in a lifetime, my friend."

Perez gave him a sideways glance.

"Okay, I'm underestimating you. About three thousand more than you could read."

"That leaves how many that you think I could read?"

"Maybe ten."

The sideways glance now included arched eyebrows. Perez was famous for looks that spoke volumes. Jordain laughed quietly. "That one I deserved."

The judge came back with a silver tray that Jordain recognized as the classic Georg Jensen acorn pattern that had enjoyed huge popularity more than fifty years earlier. The teaspoons, sugar spoon and coffee service belonged to the same pattern. He wasn't surprised. Not everyone could incorporate this kind of style into their lives, but in apartments like this, it was almost expected.

"It's a little late for a social call," Leightman said as he poured the coffee. "So I'm assuming this is urgent."

"Urgent and a little uncomfortable, I'm afraid," Jordain said as he took the fine bone china cup. Bringing it up to his lips, he tasted the steaming liquid, and over the gold rim, watched Leightman's reaction: There was curiosity and concern but no panic, no looking away, no discomfort.

"Judge Leightman, is your e-mail bob205 at standard dot com?" Jordain asked.

Leightman hesitated. He only used that e-mail for accessing porn sites; how did they know about it? Why were they asking? For a moment, he ran through possible reasons to hold back this early in the conversation. Could they find out what his e-mail address was if he didn't admit it? What would they think if he refused to discuss it?

"One of them, yes."

Jordain and Perez didn't look at each other, but a muscle in Jordain's jaw throbbed and Perez nodded almost imperceptibly.

"We have e-mail that was sent from you to a woman named Penny Whistle, and e-mail that was sent from you to another woman named ZaZa, no last name. We retrieved both pieces of e-mail off the women's hard drives." As Jordain spoke, he watched the judge take in this new information. First, Leightman's face expressed recognition. Next, relief, which was confounding. And finally confusion.

"You have e-mail sent by *me* to these two women?"

Before either detective answered, Leightman stood and walked away from the detectives, over to his desk, where a silver laptop sat open. He put his hand on the computer top and lowered it.

"Yes," Jordain responded, the one word drawn out and definitive.

The judge stood eight feet away from them, looking down

on them with a disdain that had not been in his eyes when he answered the door. "What do you want?"

"Do you know who these women are?" It was Perez's turn to take over the questioning.

"Can you explain precisely why you have come to my home, in the dead of night, to question me about this?" Leightman asked.

"Because these women are dead and because there is e-mail on their computers from you to them."

"Why is that relevant? There must be a lot of mail in those women's computers."

"The nature of the e-mail suggests that the person who sent it was involved with the women's deaths."

The judge opened and closed his mouth like a fish gasping for air, and then he regained his composure. "Someone is setting me up. Do you realize how many people know my e-mail address? This is clearly something you need to investigate, and I commend you for coming to me first, but I have nothing to do with this."

"Judge Leightman, it will save us a lot of time and you a lot of embarrassment if you talk to us now—"

"No," the judge interrupted Jordain. "I'd like you to leave. Immediately. I've never been so outraged in my life. How dare you come here and question me like this. You know how easy computer fraud is?" Leightman was whispering his shouts, so while they were not loud, they were resonant with fury.

"We're going to need to take your computer with us," Jordain said.

"Absolutely not. You won't invade my privacy for some wild-goose chase. Now, please, get out. Tomorrow morning you can call my office and my secretary will give you the name of my lawyer and his phone number and you can pursue this travesty through him."

"Judge, I'm sorry. I'm very sorry. But we have a search warrant. We need your computer." Jordain watched the judge's eyes narrow and his lips purse into one thin line. A vein throbbed in his neck.

Jordain felt sick to his stomach. He hated doing this to a guy who had a reputation of being a fair judge.

"I'd like to see the warrant."

Perez walked across the room and handed it to him.

For the next sixty seconds, Leightman read every single line as if he had never seen a court order before. "So. Larry Rosen signed this." Leightman laughed viciously. "He must have loved that. Well, you can arrest me and put me in jail and deal with the repercussions, but I am not letting you take my computer with you no matter what kind of paperwork you have."

Jordain and Perez had talked about the possibility of the judge pulling rank and flat out refusing.

If he was guilty, they'd figured he'd do something exactly like that. They had no choice but to insist. If they didn't take the computer, the judge could easily erase his files or destroy the hard drive overnight. They couldn't allow that to happen. Two young women had died. A third was still in the hospital. The only thing that they had in common was mail from a man whose e-mail address had been traced back to Alan Leightman. In both e-mails, he asked that the women use the gifts he'd sent. The gifts that had killed them.

Jordain nodded at Perez, who moved to the desk. Leightman lunged. They were well matched. Jordain ran over, pulled out his handcuffs and rushed the judge before he and Perez could hurt each other. The sound of the metal clicking shut stopped Leightman. He looked down, real horror on his face. "What the fuck are you—"

"I really don't want to do this. But I *will* arrest you if you interfere with us taking your computer." Jordain was thinking about the bodies, about the description of what the poisons had done to the women's insides. He knew how tortured their last hours had been. How ill Tania still was.

Sweat broke out on the judge's forehead. "Okay. Take the fucking thing, but be forewarned, Detective, I'll have your ass for this. By tomorrow morning, the two of you won't know what hit you. Now—this minute—you take these off me."

While Perez unplugged the laptop and put it in a case he'd brought with him, Jordain fished in his pocket for the key to the cuffs.

At just that moment, they all heard the noise of the front door opening and closing, and before anyone could move, Kira Rushkoff was standing in the room looking at the scene.

The expression on her face was strangely calm.

Forty-Four

—◦⤚⥤⧉⥢⤙◦—

"Dulcie, your mother is right," Mitch admonished. "You owe her an explanation. Actually, you owe me one, too. You never told me that Mom didn't know you were coming here."

My daughter gave her father a withering look—one you'd barely expect a much older teenager to manage. A glance that not only accused him of treachery but also conveyed her disappointment in him for not taking her side.

She was sitting on the oversize white couch in her father's living room. Her arms were crossed over her chest and her chin was lifted high into the air. Mitch was sitting next to her, and I, the outsider, the enemy, was on the opposite couch.

In the last ten minutes, she had yet to speak directly to me.

The ignoring tactic was my mother's trick and yet my daughter had learned it on her own. I'd hated it so much when my mother had done it, I would never have repeated it.

So how did it come to be part of my daughter's repertoire? No matter what I knew about science and nature and genes and what we inherit, I was still shocked by how much my daughter was like her grandmother, despite having been born eighteen years after she'd died. Even the way she held her head, thrust out her sharp chin, flipped her hair, widened her eyes, contradicted her smug words with sweet facial expressions—all were just like my mother.

Sometimes it comforted me that my mother lived on in my daughter. Other times, like that night, it made me furious. The rage I'd felt when I'd walked in, which had been stoked by the twenty-minute panic of not knowing where Dulcie had gone from the theater, had not dissolved. I wanted to scream at her and shake her and tell her what it felt like to have your heart fall out of your chest from worry.

"Daddy, I want to move back here. For good."

"Even if you stay here, you can't do the TV series. Your father is one hundred percent with me on this. Aren't you, Mitch?"

"Absolutely."

"I know that," she said, talking to her father as if he was the only one in the room with her. "I'm not staying here because of that. You understand me. If you won't let me do the series it's not because of your problems, it's because of me. So that's it. Decided."

"Talk to both of us, Dulcie. Not just to me." Mitch's voice was raised. "And before we discuss anything else, I want you to apologize to your mother for scaring her half out of her mind, and I want you to do it now."

She glared at him. He stared her down.

"I'm sorry." She said it low and under her breath and without looking at me.

"You don't want to know what is going to happen if you don't turn around and face your mother and apologize to her loudly enough that she can hear it. Now."

Finally, reluctantly, she turned toward me but looked somewhere to the right of my face. Mitch couldn't tell this from where he sat, and I debated whether or not to bring it up.

In a voice that was devoid of any emotion at all—as if auditioning for a part she did not want to get—she said, "So, I'm sorry, but I'm staying here. With the parent who understands me. Not with the one who wants to rule my life because of stuff that's not about me. At all."

I stood up. I knew Dulcie, I knew myself, and I knew Mitch. This was not going to get solved tonight. "Mitch, is there somewhere we can talk?"

Yes, I wanted to speak to him, but I also wanted my daughter to know that, try as hard as she might, she was not going to get us on opposite sides of her battle.

He followed me out of the living room and then led me to his bedroom. If it was an odd choice of rooms, I didn't think of that then.

Mitch sat on the upholstered window seat and I sat on the edge of the bed, facing him. The duvet cover was cool to the touch and my fingers sunk into the fluff. I was suddenly overcome with a desire to lie down on the bed and pull the coverlet up over me and sleep. To have all of us rest under one roof again. It was the last thing I expected to feel, and it took me by surprise.

"I don't think you should try to force her to go home with you," Mitch said.

There were four pillows on the bed; if I lay down, they would cushion me.

I faced my ex-husband. Mitch, at forty-two, had thick, dark brown hair and a boyish smile that included dimples. He hadn't changed as much as I thought I had over the past few tough years. Suddenly I was picturing him, in the hospital, holding Dulcie in his large hands only minutes after I'd given birth to her. There were tears on his cheeks and he kept shaking his head and saying, *Look at her...just look at her....*

"I thought we'd straightened it out the last time."

"So did I."

"Well, we didn't do a good job. This is even more serious now that she's playing us a second time. We need to work this out once and for all. She can't keep running away from me every time she doesn't get what she wants."

"I know that, but not tonight. You're exhausted. She's exhausted."

"I was so frightened. Last time she was here, she just refused to leave with me. But when I couldn't find her…it never occurred to me…I thought…" I was surprised to feel the tears. I didn't cry often, but I wasn't often afraid for my daughter's life.

He got up, came over to the bed, sat beside me, pulled me to him and stroked my hair. For a few minutes, he soothed me the way he had when we'd been together. There were problems in our marriage, but they had never interfered with our caring about each other and being friends. I didn't cry for long—a fast release of pain and fear and then I straightened up and wiped my eyes.

"Morgan, are you seeing a lot of Noah Jordain?"

The question took me aback. "Why?"

"I think it might have something to do with Dulcie's attitude."

I thought about it.

"I don't want to believe that. But the first time she pulled this wasn't long after I started seeing him."

"And now that the relationship has been going on for a while, I think she's getting more worried that we'll never get back together again."

"You think she's doing this so that we spend more time together? You think she wants me to get upset and wants you to comfort me?"

"You're the therapist, not me."

"You're not doing bad for a layman." It was an old joke between us. No one is a good therapist in his or her own family, and Mitch had more often than not been the one who had realized what was going on with us.

He looked at me with an expression that I hadn't seen for a very long time.

Whenever Mitch had wanted to make love, his features became less animated and his eyelids became heavy. I used to tease him that he practiced the expression, but of course he didn't. I'd seen the "sex look" on some of my patients' faces when they discussed their relationships. I'd never imagined I'd see it on Mitch's face again. And then he reached up and with his right hand began to massage the muscles in my neck, where he knew I stored all of my tension. He was good at it. He'd been doing it for years. I let my head fall forward. I let him touch me and try to work out my tightened cords. And then his lips were on the skin he had just warmed, and I could smell his familiar amber-scented cologne.

For a few seconds, I sat there under the spell of old memories and an easier time—before Dulcie became a teenager, before Mitch told me he wanted more from a relationship than he got from me, before the fabric of our family had been ripped apart.

And then I picked up my head and pulled back.

"What is going on?"

"You're different," he said, and then he grimaced. "That was the worst sentence. I can't believe I said it. Listen, I don't know how to say this. And I know it's a bad time to even bring it up, but lately I've been thinking that maybe we shouldn't have split up so fast—"

"Mitch, don't do this." I stood. "It wasn't fast. It was a year. And it was what you wanted. And you can't change your mind now after—"

He reached out and took my hand. "Can't we even talk about it?"

"You are falling for it. Our daughter is sitting in there manipulating us. You're the one who noticed it."

"I know that. But I also think there's something to the idea that we should be together again. At least try."

"No. Not now. We have a big problem here. Our daughter is not talking to me. She ran away from home tonight."

"She didn't really run—"

"She did, Mitch. We need to discuss Dulcie. About how much she wants to test for this TV series, and how we are going to explain to her, in a way that she understands, why it is not right for her. And in the middle of that you are thinking about us? We had months and months to think about us!"

I was trying to keep my voice down but it was hard.

"I know, but what if it's all unnecessary. What if we did get back together? You're different now than you were. I don't think we'd have the same problems. And we'd solve what's bothering Dulcie. She could stop acting out. Believe me, I'm more surprised than you are. I didn't expect to feel this way about you again, but I do."

In the middle of this crisis, in the middle of a nightmare night, why was Mitch pushing this? I knew better than to listen to my ex-husband, but I really hated the idea that I was going to walk out of that apartment and leave Dulcie there. I had missed her so badly the last time. She was only thirteen. I wasn't ready to let her go. Was there really a chance that it could work between Mitch and me, and the three of us could once more be a family?

I'd give up anything for that.

Anything?

Noah?

Noah, whom I couldn't even think about without feeling

confusion and exhilaration. Who moved me and got inside my head in a way no one, *including Mitch*, ever had. Would I give up Noah to have Dulcie smiling and home with me for the next five years? Even if Mitch would never understand the darkness in me the way Noah did?

Would anything ever matter again if together we were able to make Dulcie's life lighter?

Forty-Five

$\sim$⟨⟩$\sim$

Amanda was alone at home. Her father was away on a business trip to somewhere or other—he was always gone—and her mother was at her book club meeting. She'd stayed late at the office and gone straight there, calling Amanda at seven o'clock to make sure she was home and had found the dinner the housekeeper had left for her.

She'd told her mother she wasn't hungry. That she had a sore throat. That maybe she was coming down with something. She wasn't sure why she'd lied, except that she really didn't feel that good. But not because of a sore throat—it was worse than that. It was everything she had read on news sites about Penny Whistle, ZaZa and Tania and what the guys had been talking about at school before Dr. Snow showed up.

And it was Dr. Snow, talking to her as if she knew everything. As if she really could look right inside her and see how it was all twisted up and scary.

Her fingers on the keyboard, she stared at her desktop, hesitating before clicking the Internet icon. She thought she'd be over this by now, but every fucking time she signed on, she got a cramp in her stomach. Sometimes it lasted a few seconds. Sometimes it was so bad she had to lie down. She never knew why it was worse some days than others. She wanted to tell Dr. Snow about it tonight. She almost had. Almost asked her how long it would hurt. How long it would take before she stopped missing Simone? How long it would take before she'd stop thinking of her when she did the things they used to do?

Simone had lived online.

Amanda used to sign on and instantly an IM would appear. Wht r u dng?

They'd instant-message back and forth while they did their homework, talked on the phone to other kids and watched TV. They were never not in touch with each other.

So when she went online now and the IM box didn't pop up right away, she noticed it. And when someone else contacted her, she felt sort of disappointed when she saw the user name and it wasn't Simonesez.

Amanda's hands perspired and shook a little as she typed in the URL. She didn't have to even think—it was right there. Literally at her fingertips.

She was holding her breath, not knowing what to expect. She hadn't gone there since Simone had died. It had been months and she still missed her best friend as much as she had the very first week she had died. But she had to make sure. If she was going to tell Dr. Snow, she had to make sure first that she was right.

Silently, the Web site appeared. Amanda stared at the checkerboard of women's photos. How was she going to find the other two girls? The ones that they had found before. She didn't remember their names. She and Simone had just clicked on anyone who had New York in her profile, and then watched, sometimes laughing and sometimes getting disgusted and sometimes admitting to each other that it was a little sexy to watch this stuff. And then they'd sit and talk about Timothy and Hugh and the other guys they knew who watched this stuff all the time and why the guys liked these girls so much more than them. They finally went shopping at Victoria's Secret so they could get dressed up to look like the Webcam girls. They posed each other in front of the Web cam Amanda had bought for just this purpose with money she'd saved up and watched themselves on the screen to see if they looked as good as the other girls.

They never did.

It hadn't seemed like a big deal when they'd started. It seemed pretty normal for them to want to know what the guys were watching. They were curious. There was nothing wrong with that, was there?

In her mind, Amanda was defending what they had done to someone who wasn't there. She was explaining it as if she were on trial.

No, she wasn't.

She was trying to imagine what it would be like to explain to Dr. Snow. But first, she had to be sure.

Amanda started clicking on all the New York names. They all looked familiar. She and Simone must have gone to dozens of these sites after that first night they'd stumbled on the guys surfing the Net at a party at Hugh's house. She and Simone weren't even invited. But Les, her brother, who was friends with Timothy and Hugh, had dragged them along. He was supposed to be babysitting them, not taking them out. Timothy had been nice to her. He'd been the only one who even noticed her and Simone in a normal way. He'd stayed nice to them. He'd even gone to Simone's funeral with her. Sat next to her. Not like it meant anything. But it was nice, anyway.

That long-ago night, when she and Simone had walked into

the darkened bedroom, they'd seen three boys glued to the computer, the screen's light reflecting on their faces, and instantly sensed they shouldn't be there, but they were too curious to leave. The boys never heard them—they were way too involved watching two women making out in a bubble-filled bathtub.

"What ho's," Hugh had said in a voice that gave Amanda goose bumps. "I'd like to be that bar of soap."

"Wrap those legs around me like that. Fucking A," Barry said.

Only Timothy hadn't spoken. It was a small thing but it had meant something to her.

So what? Then, at sixteen, Amanda had already seen stuff. She wasn't too freaked out about it. When you're a teenager and you have a brother eighteen months older than you, there's not that much you don't know about. Her parents had lectured her about going online and giving out her real name, and she'd heard them fighting with Les over what he was looking at on the Net. She'd even wound up on smutty sites by accident, but she'd never watched any porn before. She'd never seen anything that was as down and dirty as what the boys were watching that night.

She and Simone sneaked out before the guys caught them, but a few months later, when Simone was at Amanda's for a sleepover, they'd asked Les if he'd show them what sites he went to. He said no about a hundred times and then Simone had offered to give him a blowjob in exchange for some of the URLs. He said yes.

Amanda was dumbfounded and sat there without moving the whole time that Simone and Les were out of the room.

"Why did you do it?" she asked her friend later.

"I like him. I thought maybe it would make him like me," Simone said. Her voice was flat. "The worst part was he kept watching the Web the whole time I was doing it."

After that, she and Simone became obsessed with figuring out what was so special about the online girls, and what was wrong with themselves.

No. She wouldn't start thinking about it. It would just make her cry. And that wasn't the point. She needed to figure it out. She needed to understand what was happening. It was too creepy. There was no way that what she and Simone had done had anything to do with the girls who were getting killed.

But what if it had?

Forty-Six

The message light was blinking when I walked in the door that night. I dropped my coat on the couch, but before I had a chance to hit the play button, the phone rang.

"Hello?"

"Dulcie's gone to bed," Mitch said. "I thought we could talk."

"Did she say anything?" I unwound my scarf from around my neck and walked into the kitchen. There was a bottle of wine in the fridge; I poured myself a glass.

"No. She asked me if I'd pick up some things for her from your place. I told her that I wouldn't. That she needed to ask you herself."

"I'm not going to force the issue with her," I replied. "I need some time to figure it out, to try to come up with a way to reach her."

"While you're thinking about that, I want you to think about us, too."

"Okay."

"That's all? Okay?"

"Yes. That's all. I'm tired. I'm angry with Dulcie. I can't think about us, too. Not tonight."

The apartment was so stuffy. With the phone up to my ear, I took my wine back into the den and walked over to the window, put the glass down on the floor, reached up, opened the window, felt the quick rush of cold and took a gulp of sharp air.

"What's that noise?"

"I just opened the window."

"It's freezing outside, Morgan."

"I know, but it's hot in here. I left the heat on too high. Mitch, I'm tired. Let me go, we can talk tomorrow."

I sat on the couch, thinking about the words I'd used when I'd said goodbye to him. Nothing was an accident. I'd said *let me go* but I'd really meant *I want to go.*

I didn't want to think about Mitch.

I wanted to work out what to do about Dulcie.

What could I say to her to make her understand that everything I do, I do for her?

The red light was still blinking. I hadn't listened to my messages. Over at the desk, I looked down at the machine. The flashing LED light showed fifteen calls. It *had* to be a patient in crisis. I hit the play button.

"Morgan? Are you there?" It was Noah, his voice low and soft and just a little concerned. "I'm at work. Can you give me a call when you get home?"

I felt the tug of wanting to pick up the phone and call him right away, but the next message had already started and was so loud it startled me.

"Dr. Snow. It's Bob. Call me as soon as you get this message."

The mechanical voice on the answering machine told me that he'd made that call at 11:40 p.m.

The next twelve messages, only minutes apart, were all from him, and in each he sounded more disturbed and agitated than the one before.

And then the last message. "Christ, where are you? You

have to help me figure out how to deal with this. I have to see you. I have to tell you what a mess this is. I have to tell you who I really am."

Forty-Seven

❧─◦◦◦─❧

At one-thirty in the morning, Yasmine pulled down the blinds and shut out the building across the courtyard. At night, it was so easy to look into someone else's apartment. Even though all the lights were out, someone could wake up. Someone could look in when she wasn't paying attention.

That task accomplished, she walked over to the table where everything she needed was waiting for her. Her pulse quickened. The anticipation felt good. And not much else did. She savored it.

The pain was so bad. Had been bad all day and kept getting worse. But soon she'd chase it away with the silver savior.

She got undressed down to her bra and thong and inspected the scars on her thighs. She wanted to pick at the scabs, but that wouldn't hurt enough. She needed a big jolt. Today had been that bad a day.

Yasmine switched on the Web cam.

Sitting on the floor, she unwrapped a new razor blade, smiling at herself in its reflection. She was aware that while she was alone in her apartment, she was being watched, and that mattered to her because being watched meant getting paid, and getting paid for something she was going to do, anyway, was just great.

Damn easy.

Easy? Are you nuts?

Nothing is ever easy.

It's easy enough, though.

Compared to everything else, it was easy enough.

The voices were always in her head, talking about how wrong she was, how bad she was, how messed up. Sometimes an old voice came back and let loose with a familiar litany: Get up, clean up this mess, feed your little brother, stop at the store and buy food for dinner, and don't forget beer for your father. And beer for your father. And beer for your father. The man in the grocery store knew her and her father and even though she wasn't old enough he let her take a six pack home. All that matters is the beer so he can fucking drown himself in the beer and then give you orders. *Lie down. Open your mouth, bitch.*

He'd hit her when she refused. The back of his hand against her cheek. His belt on her back. Over and over.

Sometimes she thought it would be easier to do what he wanted than it was to take the beatings. Other times she thought the beatings were easier because they took away the real pain. The deeper pain. The screaming for mommy pain that got swallowed up in the craziness of the beer-driven nightmare.

She didn't even remember anymore when she got the idea to cut herself. Maybe it was something she read about online. Probably was. It was so long ago. Now the shiny little razor blade was winking at her in the light and she lifted it up.

The sharpness would sting and the sting would take away all the voices and all the worries and all the real fucking pain.

Tonight was special.

He was watching tonight.

He'd even sent her a present.

And she had promised him that she would use them when she was done.

Had anyone ever cared that much about her before? To go out of his way to buy her bandages to use after the cutting?

He was so sensitive. He told her he understood why she cut herself. And how lovely she looked and how sexy she was and how much it hurt him and at the same time excited him to know that when she cut herself she felt euphoria. He told her to rent a post office box and e-mail him the address. And she had. And then she'd waited. And then the present had come.

Do you know that your nipples always harden when you make the first cut on your thighs? Do you know that? Do you know that your little pussy gets all slicked up and is literally dripping by the time you are finished cutting?

What does it feel like?

Do you come when you cut herself?

Does it feel the same every time?

I want to know that. And to be the one to comfort you when it is over. So use these Band-Aids for me. They are medicated with a special rare dark aloe, so that your skin will heal without marks. You are too beautiful to have scars. Don't be afraid of the color of the salve on the cotton. I promise it will heal your beautiful skin, it will make it whole.

The cutting was like a drug that night. The blade made such a thin line and the blood came to the surface so quickly. She sat in front of the Web cam and smiled into its unblinking black eye while blood dripped from her leg onto the floor, and she floated away from everything she knew.

"This is for you," she said out loud as she picked up the blade and made another tiny horizontal cut on her upper thigh. And then another. And then another.

Finally, when she was all done, when she was cocooned in the new pain and removed from the old, she saw the bandages he'd sent by the side of her computer and remembered that she'd promised to use them.

Slowly, she reached for one.

Wednesday
Nine days remaining

Forty-Eight

Jordain closed the file filled with résumés from forensic psychologists. There wasn't one candidate in there who he thought was senior enough for the job. He knew someone who'd be perfect, though. Perfect, except for a million personal reasons. Besides, why would Morgan ever want to leave the institute to work for the NYPD?

It was just that there was no one he'd rather have advising him on the twists and turns the human mind could make.

"Detective?"

Officer Butler was standing in the doorway to his office with a sheaf of papers in her hand. Jordain had given her Leightman's computer last night and told her to keep the geeks working on it 24/7. He hadn't expected them to have anything this soon.

"Do you want some coffee?" he asked as he got up to refill his mug. She shook her head. He knew she never said yes, but still he asked.

"Leightman is very definitely a Global client. Global and a few dozen other sites. He's got a serious habit. Always uses the bob205 handle and—"

"Are there e-mails to the women on his hard drive?" he interrupted.

"Nothing. But there's always the possibility—and the geeks are looking into it now—that he sent the e-mails we're looking for and then deleted them. That should take a few more hours."

"Someone could be setting him up. Like he said."

"Either way, we'll find out."

"You need to find out soon. He is a judge, Butler."

"You don't have to remind me…" She hesitated.

"What is it?"

"We did find something you should know about."

"I don't like the sound of your voice."

She shook her head. "You're going to like what I have to tell you even less."

"Okay. Enough of the buildup. What is it?"

"Judge Leightman is seeing Dr. Snow. There's e-mail from him to her setting up appointments. E-mail back from her confirming."

"Shit." He thought for a few seconds. One possible way out. "Old e-mail?"

"Current. As recently as last week. Going back months."

"Thanks. Let me know what else you find, or what you don't find, as soon as you can," he said, dismissing her.

Jordain leaned back in his chair and stared up at the ugly acoustical tiles on the ceiling. He hated those white squares with their ugly wormhole patterns.

Oh, Morgan, he thought, *how am I going to sit across a table from you and not ask you about this?* His fist came down hard on his desk and he felt the impact shoot up through his wrist.

Forty-Nine

When I arrived at the institute at 7:30 a.m., I had to use my key to let myself in. It was dark in the foyer. Allison didn't come in until eight and those who scheduled earlier sessions had to fend for themselves.

Dark, cavernous spaces never spooked me, but that morning I was already nervous, and I didn't like being there alone or hearing my footsteps echo on the marble.

Flipping every light switch I passed, I unlocked the annex door and then went upstairs to my office. The shadows receded. The furnishings took on their everyday appearances.

It was cold, too, the way an empty building is before everyone arrives and fills it.

After sleeping less than four hours, I should have been exhausted. But between an espresso, which I'd drunk too quickly while I got dressed, and being unnerved by the empty building, I was wired. Everything that was bothering me was bouncing around in my brain.

I sat down at my desk, checked my watch and picked up the phone.

He answered in the middle of the first ring.

"Bob, I'm in my office."

"I'm in the garage."

"I left the annex door open. Just lock it behind you and come straight up."

He talked nonstop for the first ten minutes, and I sat quietly, trying to keep from reacting with surprise to anything he said. That he was Judge Alan Leightman was the first shock. And as soon as I'd absorbed that, I realized that meant he was married to Kira Rushkoff.

Kira Rushkoff, Alan's wife, was a prominent lawyer specializing in First Amendment issues. I'd seen her on television, standing on the steps of the courthouse in Lower Manhattan, imposing and imperious, looking down at the camera and speaking with passion about the case she'd just won. A strong wind had been blowing her chestnut hair into her face, but she ignored the annoyance. The civil case—between Kira's pornography-king client and Stella Dobson—had garnered a lot of media attention. I didn't notice if she was pretty, or how old she was, or if she was tall or short. I had been too engrossed in her fervent speech about how important her client's victory had been for the Constitution.

And my client—who was desperately addicted to Internet pornography—was that woman's husband? I'd been looking at this case, at this patient, with only half a pair of glasses. I needed to reevaluate everything he had ever told me, in light of this new and obviously relevant information.

"Then Detective Perez said—"

"What?"

"I said that Detective Perez had a search warrant."

"There were two detectives?"

"Yes, Perez and Jordain. I've met them before. In my goddamn courtroom. The fucking indignity! This is a disaster. Oh, and the best part is that Kira walked in on the charming scene. She saw me in cuffs."

"They handcuffed you?" I was having a hard time keeping with him and processing what I'd just heard. My patient was saying my lover's name.

Was I going to have to step down as his therapist because of Noah? No, we weren't at that point yet.

"Only because I tried to keep them from taking my laptop. Once I gave in, they took the cuffs off and left. Kira locked herself in the bedroom." His voice cracked.

I focused on his face, on the expression in his eyes, on his demeanor. "Alan, are you all right?"

"I haven't done anything illegal. You know that."

"Yes."

He hadn't slept at all and there were deep circles under his eyes. The worry lines in his forehead seemed to have doubled since the last time I'd seen him.

"So how could they think I'm involved with these disgusting crimes?"

"What did they tell you?"

"That two of the victims received e-mail from me."

"Do they have e-mail addresses for the women right on the sites?"

"Yes."

I watched him carefully as he spoke. There was no suggestion he was lying. He didn't look away from me, but held my gaze. He didn't bite his lips or lick them or put his hands over his mouth when he talked.

"Did you send them any e-mail at all, Bob—Alan?" It was going to take me time to stop thinking of him as Bob-without-a-last-name.

"Of course not. I signed on to their sites, but e-mail? Can you imagine me doing that?" He gave a derisive laugh.

"If you didn't send either of the two women e-mail, what are the police talking about?"

"Someone is setting me up. It's obvious. Someone is preparing to blackmail me. My lawyer spoke to one of the detectives late last night and all I know is that the girls both have e-mail from the e-mail address I use to access the porn sites I visit. Mine is the only e-mail the two of them have in common. And apparently the content of the e-mail is damning."

"What does it say?"

He shook his head. "They won't tell Adam, my lawyer. And obviously, since I didn't write it, I don't know."

"If the e-mail isn't on your computer, your lawyer will be able to work this out. You need to focus on that."

He shook his head furiously. "I'm not concerned that I'm going to be charged. I know I didn't send the e-mail. But I have accounts at those porn sites. I visited those girls. I watched them. That will come out. It's going to ruin everything. Once people know that I'm an addict, that I'm seeing you—"

"That's not going to happen."

"The police have my computer, Dr. Snow. And there *is* e-mail to you on my computer—"

"What goes on in this office is privileged information."

Sweat beaded on his upper lip. He looked like a man with vertigo who had found himself on top of the Empire State Building.

"I need you to tell me about the law of doctor-patient confidentiality the way you understand it. What will happen if they ask you if you treat me?"

"I can't and won't tell them you are my patient. The only circumstance that would allow me to talk to the police about you is if you told me that you intended to hurt someone and I believed you."

The wind had picked up and was blowing tiny pellets of

icy snow against the windowpanes. I turned to look. The garden on the small balcony was cut back and wrapped in burlap for the winter. Four or five inches of snow covered all of it, rendering the planters and pots into amorphous blue-white shapes, abstract and strangely foreign. The weatherman had predicted the possibility of a blizzard moving in from the north sometime late this morning, but it looked like it was already here.

"If they get a court order—"

"Alan, think, you know this. They can't order me to tell them anything. Each and every word between us is protected unless you were suddenly to tell me that you are planning to commit murder or abuse a child and I was certain that you were telling me the truth. And there's nothing you've said to me in the past six months that would even come close to suggesting that you're a danger to anyone—except possibly yourself."

Alan buried his face in his hands and sat still and silent for the next sixty seconds.

It was true.

From what I knew about him, I couldn't imagine that he could be involved in the murders. He'd been in therapy long enough for me to understand his psychology. Yes, he was disturbed, but Alan didn't have the characteristics of a psychopath. He was addicted to Internet pornography and he had intimacy problems. He also suffered self-doubt and self-loathing. He was torn between needs and knowledge, passion and logic. But no matter how deep and devastating any of those issues were for him, his rage was not directed at the women themselves. He was not capable of making the absurd leap that if he could get rid of the women, he would get rid of his obsession. If I found out that he had killed himself, I would not have been surprised. But to be responsible for those poor girls dying?

No. That was not possible.

"Alan, do you understand that I believe you?"

Of everything I could have said, of anything I could have asked, I knew that it was important for Alan to feel this was a safe place. His wife had invaded his fantasy life, the police had invaded his home and taken away his computer. He'd had to expose not only his secrets to me but also finally, his identity.

Finally he spoke, but into his hands, and his voice sounded as if he were deep under water.

"Yes."

"No one can come in here and get your files."

He nodded.

"No one."

He relaxed just enough for it to be noticeable.

"You can talk to me today the same way you talked to me last week, when I thought you were Bob. Nothing is different except your name. Has anything changed for you? Now that I know your name? Are any of your feelings any different?"

"No. What I do is still repulsive, and I still can't stop myself. No, I can say that more precisely. I still don't want to stop myself. The only thing that I care about anymore is the feeling that comes over me when I sit down at the computer, when I bring the image of one of my girls up on the screen, when she's looking right at me, and moving for me. Kira is gone then. My office is gone, too. The work I have waiting for me, the trials I have on my docket. Not in my consciousness. Shit. The decisions that I've made that may not be right, the ones that are definitely wrong, I don't think about any of that. Not while I am sitting there in the dark, all by myself."

"Alan, what decisions are you talking about?"

"Decisions?"

I repeated his sentence.

"We have all made decisions that, in retrospect, were not

the right ones. We are human. We're influenced by all sorts of things about people. Hasn't that ever happened to you, Doctor? Haven't you ever misjudged a patient?"

Of course I had, but this wasn't about me. And I wasn't going to allow him to turn the question around.

"What do these decisions you're talking about have to do with what's going on?"

"I am not about to let some overzealous detective turn me into a laughingstock. Do you understand what would happen to me if it came out that I have this problem?"

He hadn't answered my question. "I understand, Alan, but what I'm asking is—"

"You don't know why I'm here this morning, do you?" he interrupted me.

"You're in therapy with me. You wanted a session so that—"

He interrupted again. "No. Not today. I came this morning because I need to know that no matter what the police ask you about me, you plan on keeping silent."

There was something about the way he was staring at me and the intensity in his voice and his eyes boring into mine that made me afraid. If I hesitated, I was sure he would threaten me. What was going on?

There was a knock on the door.

The judge jerked back and stared at the door.

"Who is it?" I asked.

"Terry Meziac."

Alan relaxed.

"Come in," I said.

The door opened and the young man Alan sent to my office once a month to check for listening devices, who was the judge's driver, and possibly, I thought, his bodyguard, entered the room. He didn't say anything, but looked with questioning eyes at Alan, who checked his watch and then glanced up at me. "I have to go, Dr. Snow. But we have an agreement, don't we?"

"We always have. Nothing's changed."

Fifty

The fourth victim lived on 110th Street and Park Avenue, in a studio apartment in an old tenement building.

"What took us so long to find her this time?" Jordain asked Perez as they climbed the first flight of stairs, trying not to pay too much attention to the stench or the filth.

"Cutting isn't the most popular scene and it was late. Fewer men were watching. Fewer men, fewer calls."

It took from two in the morning, when the first call was taken by a 911 operator in Miami, until 10:30 a.m., when the fifteenth call came through in Georgia, for New York to be alerted and start a trace on the woman's IP address.

"Every damn police department in the country knows about this. Even one call should have gotten the ball rolling. How does a 911 operator not get what she's hearing when someone describes a woman on the Internet who looks like she's dying? We might have saved her."

"It wasn't as clear that she was sick this time, Noah. She'd finished cutting herself and put on a Band-Aid. Then she sat back down again in front of the camera. At first, she didn't do much but play with the razor blade, teasing the guys who were still watching. This went on for ten, fifteen minutes according to the reports. The few guys who hung around weren't sure that anything else was going to happen. But there was something sort of mesmerizing about her, one of the men said. That's when she started to get sick."

Inside the third-floor apartment, Jordain looked out of the window that faced into another building. A woman in an old flowered housedress stared at them from her apartment.

"Can I lower these blinds?" he called out to the forensic team working by the body.

"Sure, boss."

The woman looked annoyed when she saw Jordain pulling the cord.

He joined Perez by the body.

Yasmine was an extremely thin, young, very pale woman whose long black hair spread out around her like a raven's wings. Except for her legs, her skin was smooth and luminous.

But her thighs were disfigured with welts, scars and cuts—some so fresh there was still a trail of dried blood, others so old they were only faint lines. Hieroglyphs of pain, telling a story that Jordain couldn't translate into a language he understood.

"I don't get this. Not why she'd do it—I understand why people are cutters—but who the hell would find that a turn-on?" Perez asked.

Jordain sighed. This was one of the toughest parts of the job. Seeing the brutality of perversity and trying, but always failing, to bring some sense to it. When he attempted to imagine the mind of the person who had perpetrated a crime like this, he saw a morass of writhing worms, twisting, feeding on themselves, sick and sickening.

"We've got something," one of the forensic cops said, and within seconds Perez and Jordain had crowded around the garbage pail where Officer Keller was working.

In his rubber-gloved hand he held an ordinary Band-Aid box. Taped to it was a note on a small card, the kind that comes with a bouquet of flowers.

"I want to help you heal" was printed on it. It looked as if it had been computer generated.

"If we're lucky, there's something on this."

"If the perp is stupid, there's something on it." Perez shook his head. It was rare that the clue that broke a case was in the most logical place.

In the car going back downtown, Jordain's cell rang, and he spent the next five minutes caught in traffic, listening to the lieutenant warn him that he'd better break this case soon, and it better be with Leightman as the killer. The powers that be were not happy about the judge's search and seizure. If it was warranted, they'd deal. If not, there was going to be hell to pay.

Back at the station house, Jordain stopped at Butler's desk.

"This is for you." He put Yasmine's computer in the middle of all the paperwork. "You know what you are looking for, right?" he asked.

"Same thing I looked for on the other two computers."

"God help us if you find it. God help us if you don't."

As Jordain walked back to his office, he took a small vial of extra-strength aspirin out of his pocket and popped three. He got headaches when he didn't sleep enough. Too bad. He'd live. That was the shame of it. On days like today, he almost didn't care.

Judge Leightman.

That was what everyone was pissed about.

Even though he'd followed all rules and regs and gotten a legit warrant, the powers that be were taking him to task for treating Leightman like an ordinary citizen instead of one of the most powerful judges in the city of New York.

Even though the Web-cam women had e-mails that came from Leightman's address entreating them to use the very items that had killed them, what Jordain had done was still unacceptable according to the top brass.

Perez was standing by the cork wall in their office, pinning up lists and photos of items found at the scene.

"We have to find out if someone has it out for the judge. Someone who would know he has a little porn problem. It's hard to imagine the guy who sat there in his study with us last night did this, much less let this fourth poisoning happen after he knew he was under suspicion."

"He could be a lot more psychotic than anyone realizes. And it could be that he couldn't call it off."

"Possibly."

"We just better make sure nothing about this leaks before we know one way or the other. You and I, partner, are going to be paraded through the city streets, tarred and feathered, if this gets out and we're wrong."

It came as no surprise to the two detectives when Butler stuck her head in their office a half hour later and told them there was e-mail from Alan Leightman on Yasmine's computer.

"Same kind of note that you found on ZaZa's and Penny's?" Perez asked.

She nodded.

"Same e-mail address for him?"

She nodded again.

"But the geeks still haven't found any deleted e-mail to any of them anywhere on Leightman's hard drive?" Jordain asked.

"Nope. Lots of proof he's visited their sites. But, no. No deleted e-mail."

"Damn it!" Jordain pounded his desk with his fist. He looked down at the yellow pad full of his notes. "You know what I don't understand? What does it mean that so far all the women who have been targeted are living in New York? It's not a coincidence. There are hundreds of girls at Global. And why Global? Do you think this is a vendetta against the people who own the company?"

Perez shook his head. "Well, you're asking good questions. If we could just get ahold of the people who run the company. You know, now that this has happened, we really need to rethink alerting the women at Global."

"How can we do that without the company's help?"

"We can have someone go to the site and send each girl e-mail directly. One at a time. I don't see how we have any choice."

"Neither do I. Let me get clearance for that. Even if we start a panic—it's that or tell the press."

"Listen, there's something else. It makes it more complicated…." Butler said.

Jordain uttered a small moan. "Just what I love. More complications."

"There is e-mail sent from Leightman's computer to someone in his office that's time-stamped within ninety seconds of the e-mail that ZaZa received from him."

She handed Jordain two printouts.

"What does this mean?"

"Just that he was online at that time. At home."

"Why can't we find his fingerprints on the tube of lubricant? Would that be too much to ask for? And while we're at it, how about a motive. We still don't have a new forensic psychologist. I'm still waiting to borrow Dr. Schoenfeld for a few days."

"I'm sorry, boss," Butler said.

"Hell, what of all this is your fault?" Jordain looked at her for what seemed like the first time. Her eyes were hollow and haunted. She had some kind of personal history that had led her to work in SVU, but she'd never shared the whole story and he'd never pushed.

"I want you to go home early today. Eat something good. Get some sleep."

"I will."

"But?"

She smiled at him, and for a minute her face softened. "You're really good at reading people, but do you ever think that not everyone wants to know you can tell what they're thinking?"

Perez laughed. The phone rang and he answered it. While he proceeded to carry on a conversation, Jordain and Butler continued talking.

"Point taken," Jordain said. "But you were thinking about something and it was bothering you, so what was it?"

"What I just can't stop thinking about is why these women? Is there an order to these poisonings? Why make them do this to themselves? Someone needs to watch, obviously, but why?"

Jordain smiled and pushed the yellow pad across the desk so that Butler could see it. She read down the list of questions he'd scrawled. In similar words, each question she had just asked was among the questions he'd written down.

"Now all you have to do, Officer Butler, is figure out the answers and you can have my job. I'd be proud to work for you."

She stood up. "Yeah, I bet. My guess is that you have never been proud to work for anyone. You like running the show too much."

"That's not true," he said, but he wasn't thinking about work. He was thinking about Morgan just then. He wasn't running the show there. She was setting the pace of the relationship and it was too slow. And just when he'd get ready to speed it up, a case would break, like this one. Now it was going to get confusing again. And they didn't do well when that happened. There was no way around it, though. Jordain was going to ask her if he could see her that night.

He needed to tell her about Alan Leightman.

If nothing else, she could be in danger.

Fifty-One

──⟨⟨⟨⟩⟩⟩──

My cooking class started at seven and I just made it. The building on Houston Street was lit up and glowing in the snow, which was still falling and had been falling, it now seemed, forever.

Inside the Culinary Institute, I hung up my coat and rushed into the classroom.

Until Dulcie had gotten the role of Mary Lennox, I never would have signed up for this, but since she was at the theater until ten-fifteen five nights a week, I had the time—and God knows I needed the help.

"Tonight we are going to work with some basic sauces," Sarah Neery, the chef and teacher, said once we were all assembled.

As soon as she started talking about a basic roux, my mind started to wander. The truth was I was as much a disaster in the class as I was at home. After three weeks, I was slowly realizing that I really wasn't interested in cooking. It was only eating that interested me.

I whisked the melting butter as I poured in the flour. Whisked more. It was turning golden. That was good. Then the golden turned caramel. And then the caramel color darkened even more. I whisked faster. The mess had turned almost black. Great, I was burning it.

"Morgan, you're not supposed to let the roux go that dark. Why don't you try again? This time stop when it turns a nice, warm light brown."

Light brown? Dark brown? How fast did it turn? Why was I doing this?

Noah was waiting for me in his car in front of the school when the class was over.

"I burned the butter," I told him once I got inside the car. "And not once. I burned the butter twice. No, not the butter— I burned the roux."

He reached over and brushed snow off my cheeks and then kissed me softly on the lips. "You're freezing." He put his arms around me and kissed me again. For a few seconds, I let go of everything and lived inside his arms.

"Not anymore," I said when we finally broke apart.

"So if you burned the roux you must be hungry. I haven't eaten yet but I have some shrimp Creole in the refrigerator."

"Could we go out? Somewhere nearby?"

He gave me a sidelong glance but didn't ask me to explain why I didn't want to go to his apartment. I wasn't sure what I would have said. I only knew I needed to be in a neutral place. I was afraid that Alan Leightman's name was going to come up. Afraid of how I was going to avoid talking about him if it did. At least in a restaurant, I could get up, go to the ladies' room—there were distractions I could use.

Five minutes later we were ensconced in a booth in a small, dark restaurant called Lucky Strike. Noah knew it was one of my favorites—a French bistro that served fries almost as good as what you could get in Paris.

We both ordered dirty martinis, which arrived quickly, and Noah held his glass up to mine in a silent toast.

"I need to talk to you," he said after we'd each taken our first sip. "About Alan Leightman."

I didn't say anything and hoped that my face wasn't showing any reaction. "What?"

"You're good at this, Morgan, but you don't have to pretend. I know he's your patient. It's not a question. I have to tell you about Leightman. You don't have to say anything. Just listen. The man may be a killer. We don't have enough on him yet to arrest him, but we're working on it, and in the meantime, I'm worried about you."

I fingered the stem of the glass. "I appreciate that, but I'm fine. I'm not in danger."

"I've heard that before."

I made a face at him. I'd been sure of my ability to judge people in the past and had not always been right. "I knew you were going to say that," I said.

"I'm becoming predictable?"

"Only about this one thing."

"Well, I am worried about you. Do you understand how powerful he is? If you know something that could help us convict Alan Leightman—"

"I can't have this conversation with you. I can't even sit here."

"Yes. You can. You can sit here and listen. You can help me save your life."

"That's overly dramatic."

"No, Morgan. No. It's not. And if you won't take this seriously, I'm going to talk to Nina about it."

I laughed. "Going over my head? Like I'm a bad little girl? She's the last person who would take your side."

"No, not like you are a bad little girl, but like you are a stubborn woman who isn't being as cautious as she should be."

The tension swirled around our heads. In the time we'd

known each other—in the past seven months—we had come to this place before, and we had not navigated it well.

"I know. Professional ethics. I know. Our principles represent a line neither of us can cross. We admire each other for respecting the line until it gets in the way. Every damn time." He was angry. At me. At us.

I heard a small sigh escape my lips. "I had hoped we wouldn't get here again."

"So did I."

The waiter arrived and we ordered without even having to look at the menu. French fries and mussels in white wine for both of us.

After the waiter left, I took a deep breath. "Dulcie still hasn't come home…."

His eyes registered immediate worry and his reaction made me feel a wave of emotion that I wasn't prepared for. "She's decided I'm the devil incarnate. Mitch thinks this is about more than the audition, that it's her way of punishing me for the divorce—"

"But you didn't instigate the divorce—"

"I know, but it's easier for her to blame me…." I took another swallow of the salty vodka. "Mitch thinks we should try again. He's convinced that—"

"Try again?" he interrupted. "As in, the two of you try as a couple again?"

I nodded.

He was waiting for me to say something. To tell him how silly an idea it was. I could tell; I knew him that well.

I started to, because I knew it was. Because I knew how I felt about him. But what if Mitch was right? What if we did owe Dulcie one more try?

Noah fished an olive out of his drink with his fingers and ate it. "So since I'm always Mr. Nice Guy, I should understand this and step back and offer you my best wishes." His voice was tinged with iciness.

"Noah—"

I'd thought nothing could scare me as much as Dulcie's disappearance the other night, and probably nothing could. But the expression on Noah's face was ripping at my heart, leaving ragged edges that I knew were going to hurt me for days. For weeks. Maybe forever. I couldn't do this.

"Noah—"

"No. Don't interrupt me. Let me say this, and when I'm done you can talk. We'll take turns. We'll pretend we are utterly civilized and sophisticated even though what I feel like doing now is getting up out of my seat, taking you by the shoulders, and shaking you until your brains rattle back into place. So can you—you who always has something to say and who loves to control everything—be quiet long enough to let me talk?"

He didn't understand. I needed to explain. To stop him before—

Before I could answer, the waiter arrived with our food. The iridescent black shells glistening in their fragrant broth should have been tantalizing, but suddenly I wasn't the slightest bit hungry. Noah, on the other hand, didn't seem to be affected, and popped a steaming mussel in his mouth.

"I don't want to go backward, Noah."

"With me? With Mitch? What do you want, Morgan?"

I didn't want to hurt anyone. I didn't want to break any promises. I didn't want my daughter to become a stranger. I missed Dulcie so much my eyes hurt when I got home at night and I couldn't see her, my arms ached at not being able to hug her before she went to bed.

I played with the mussels, tried to eat a few, and then gave up.

When he was halfway done with his food, he pushed his plate away, took a long, slow drink, sat back in his seat and said: "I can't believe we're here again. But we are. Listen, I'm not a hard-ass, Morgan. I understand that this fight with Dulcie is torturing you and that you'll do anything to make it right again. I'm not even going to suggest that if you do get back with your ex-husband that it won't help your relationship with Dulcie get better. Because I don't know that. It might. It just might."

He stopped to drink what was left of his martini and then waved the waiter over and ordered another for each of us, even though I hadn't finished mine.

I started to say something but he put up his hand. "I don't have a lot more to say, so if you can, I'd appreciate it if you could continue not interrupting me till I'm done."

I didn't want to. I hated seeing him in any kind of pain. But this was so complicated. There were too many questions on the table, along with all the forks and spoons and knives.

"You should see your face. This is hurting you like hell. Well, it's hurting me like hell, too. But you know what? It's too complicated. So let me make it easy." He smiled sarcastically. "Go do whatever it is you think you have to do. But understand, I don't believe for one goddamn second that you are really doing this because it will solve everything between you and Dulcie. She's thirteen, she has to rebel. She has to argue. She has to want things you can't give her. It's a rite of passage for both of you. Hell, you know that. You are a goddamn shrink. That's why you know you wouldn't be going back to Mitch for any of the right reasons, but because it's the path of least resistance. It's goddamn easier."

This was a mess. Like the stupid roux. It had gone from golden to burnt and I hadn't even known where along the way I'd screwed it up. Reaching down, I grabbed my bag off the floor, prepared to leave. I couldn't quite see where I was going because of the stupid tears. I wanted to hold Noah and tell him how I felt about him. Instead I said, "You can't know what my reasons are. The presumption behind everything you just said is astounding." Out of the corner of my eye, I saw that the couple next to us were listening. It was too late to care.

"You'd be right if I was wrong. But I'm not wrong." Noah shook his head. "I'm not the one who you want to hear this from, but I'm the one who is sitting here and I'm the one who is crazy about you and I'm the poor fucker who is going to lose out here. What you're doing is wrong. It's not that it's wrong for me, or Dulcie, or Mitch. It's wrong for you, Morgan."

Fifty-Two

The apartment was not only empty but it was cold. Too cold. It wasn't until I went into the den that I found out why. When I'd left in the morning, in a hurry to meet Alan Leightman early, I'd forgotten that the window was cracked open from the night before, and now there was a small pile of snow on the carpet.

For some reason this, of everything that had happened, overwhelmed me. I shut the window, then kicked at the mess with my bare foot, not caring that it was freezing or that it was wet or that I was only making a bigger mess. Snow did not belong inside. It was an intrusion in my home.

Down on my knees, I rubbed at it, freezing my fingers until it melted and the rug wicked it up.

After that I took a bath, went into the kitchen and made some tea. I picked up the phone and dialed Mitch's number so I could talk to Dulcie, but I hung up before it connected. Instead I punched in Nina's number. She wasn't home either and I didn't bother leaving a message.

It was quiet in the house and I kept hearing Noah's words in my head. I didn't want to think about what he'd said. He didn't know me that well. He had no idea what he was talking about. I had been married to Mitch for fourteen years. It had been good with him. With us. It would be again. Dulcie would have her family back. It was a happy ending.

No. It wasn't a happy ending. It was a happy beginning. That was even better. A new start.

Then why did I feel as if I were in mourning?

Thursday
Eight days remaining

Fifty-Three

❧∿◦◦∿❧

Dearest,

One more candle has been lit to commemorate one more death. One more step closer to full retribution and one act closer to fulfilling my promise to you. There are only eight days left and then I'll be done with the fun and the blood and the guts and the gore and nothing will matter because you are still gone.

I am so tired. Tired from being careful and from keeping track. I have so much to do, to monitor, to control. There are a million details, just like the millions of men out there addicted to Internet porn. Addicted to watching women, women who are not women. I pity the men who come up against them and, more than the men, I pity the boys who have had their first sex on screen. Watched virtual women undulate and whisper to them and them alone long before they'd ever approach a real young woman. All during their developing years, the Web lifts its shirt and flashes these spoiled boys the prettiest breasts and tightest vaginas and never ever asks them to give anything back. Not a word, not a thought, not compassion and not caring, no, none of those, just a credit card number that their parents give them, or they steal.

No one, not therapists, not lawyers, not teachers, not parents, has the experience or the knowledge to deal with our troubled children because they are a mutation—the first generation who have been suckled by twenty-four-hour, easily accessible and practically free instant gratification. Twenty-four-hour poison.

The more I watch what you watched, the more sacred this quest, the more critical these rituals and important this cleansing. We need to burn every one of them at the stake until there are none left to tempt, lure, entice, bait and seduce. To set the devil's examples that young women follow into hell.

It was frightening to watch that girl cutting herself and watch the razor blade slice open her skin and see the blood rise so quickly to the surface and to think you once watched her cutting, too. This time she made fourteen cuts until her skin was ribboned with thin, sad lines of blood.

When she was done cutting the computer did not go black and she didn't realize what was happening. She never went for the phone and no one came to her aid.

She was dark and alien—the kind of witch woman who lured you and swayed you and turned you into something dark and alien, too, and that's one thing I can never forgive her for. It's not just that because of them you're gone, but because of them you thought you lost me, because of them I lost you.

Soon, I will have gotten to them all, in exactly the way they got to you. I promise.

This I do for you.

Fifty-Four

$\sim$—●○○○●—$\sim$

Alan Leightman sat in the kitchen across the breakfast table from his wife and watched her stir her coffee. Over and over the spoon circled the cup, long after the sugar had dissolved, and all the while tears dripped down her cheeks. He wanted to get up and wipe them away, and with them her pain.

Until the past few months she had not cried often. He could count the times: when her father died and when she'd had her miscarriages, and even then only for a few minutes. She had always been so stoic. She moved past sadness. She had a bigger agenda than her own personal disappointments. She had a Constitution to save. And she'd been saving it, year after year. He was so proud of her. He had been. So proud of her.

But ever since she'd lost the big privacy case and gone on antidepressants, her emotions had been out of whack. Weeping one minute, furiously angry the next. This morning had been no exception. She'd started out angry. Now she was crying. Scared, he'd say, if the word wasn't so incongruous when used in conjunction with his wife.

How disturbed was she? How badly was the medication affecting her? He couldn't take his eyes off her stirring the coffee. Over and over. Only someone deeply disturbed became obsessive like that. She needed help. More help than he could give her. How was he going to help her? He had to help her. Because whatever had happened to her was his fault.

"What are you going to do today?" she asked. The spoon did another revolution, the silver stem glinting in the overhead light.

"I need to finalize which criminal lawyer to hire. Adam can't handle this if it goes to the next stage. I also need to hire a software genius who can figure out how my credit card was charged with visits to those girls' Web sites on days when I didn't go there and—"

"Hard to do," she interrupted. Another revolution.

"What?"

"That will be hard to do."

"It's not like you to suggest that it's a lost cause before we even get started."

"Did I say it was a lost cause?" Another circle with the spoon.

"I heard it in your voice."

"It amazes me that you think I'd still be on your side."

Finally, she laid down the spoon, and he almost cheered. She took a sip of her coffee, then grimaced. "It's cold." Getting up, she walked to the sink and poured it down the drain.

She put the kettle on to boil again, and then, standing there, staring down into the flames that were licking up around the black enamel, she said, "No matter which lawyer you hire, the best they can do is figure out a way to get you off, but you do understand it's too late for you to come out of this totally clean."

"You're smiling through your tears, Kira. Does the idea of my humiliation make you that happy?"

"Happy? That your reputation is going to be tarnished? That I'll be a joke? That our marriage will be exposed as a sham? No, Alan. I'm not happy. Of all the things you could have done to humiliate me, you had to do this? You had to go online? You had to deal with those women? Those women? Alan?" She was screaming. "If you had stopped and thought about it for two minutes, you would have realized it would be the worst thing you could have done to me." She shook her head and then reached out and touched the pot with her forefinger, pressing her flesh against the kettle as if she were testing to see how cold it was, not how hot.

How could anyone just hold her finger against burning metal like that?

She grimaced, but she didn't move her finger.

"What the hell are you doing?" Alan yelled as he leapt out of his chair and pulled her hand away.

She struggled with him. "Leave me alone," she growled.

He backed off.

Kira smiled. Turned back to the stove. Reached out and touched the kettle with her middle finger.

Alan pulled her hand away again and wrestled her away from the stove. She fought him, beating him with small fists that he hardly felt. She was acting crazy. He expected anger and recriminations. Even tears. But she was being irrational.

"Let go of me. You don't have the right to touch me. Not anymore. Not since you stopped loving me. Not since them. Not since you don't love me."

Even her voice, instead of being in the mid-range, was now low and edged with madness.

He let go.

She straightened up, ignoring her fingers, even though, he thought, they must have been throbbing with pain.

He wanted to tell her that he did love her. Had never stopped loving her. No matter what he did online—that was something else. But he knew it wouldn't make any difference.

"Can't I do anything, Kira? Won't you let me help you?"

"Help? Your help?" She giggled. It was unexpected and totally out of context. A six-year-old's glee escaping in the midst of a forty-five-year-old's rant. "I'll survive, but I don't think you will. I don't think they'll find out that someone else logged into your account at those sites. I think they'll find out you were connected from your own computer. Will that convince them that you were responsible for those women dying? Who knows? The press is on a rampage, Alan. They are all over these murders. They can't let go of all the salacious details. It's becoming a media sensation. Just imagine how they will jump all over you once your dirty little secret is out and your name is linked to the Web-cam murders. Your career will be over."

"I didn't have anything to do with those girls dying. You know that, don't you?" He heard his own voice, pleading, begging the one person who had always been on his side to tell him that she still was. "Kira, you can't think I'm capable of anything like this."

But to his astonishment and horror—because if she didn't believe him, would anyone else?—she didn't give him what he was asking for. She just stared at him, and for those few minutes he did not know if he would be able to ever breathe normally again.

"Kira, do you really think I could have killed those girls?"

"Of course not."

He started to breathe.

"If I wasn't your wife, I might even be able to convince them you're not involved. But I am your wife. Isn't that the ultimate irony? Even if I could prove it, no one would believe me."

And then Kira walked out of the room, leaving him sitting there at the table, listening to the kettle shrieking its song.

Fifty-Five

❧~✦~☙

Blythe had brought two cappuccinos and two large black-and-whites to her appointment, so we sat across from each other at my desk, drinking the coffee and munching on the sweet cookies. I knew she was ambivalent about talking to me that day. The food and coffee was a distraction.

"You didn't want this to be a session today, did you?" I asked.

"Why would you think that?" Blythe gave me the slightly mysterious smile that was unique to her: As her lips moved up in the corners, her eyes closed for just a moment. The viewer's attention was, again, pulled from Blythe's eyes to her mouth.

"Is it true?"

"Maybe, but how did you…" She eyed the cookies and the drinks and thought it through. Then she smiled. She got it. "That was impressive."

"No, it's good training. You have it. You'll get there."

"I guess I'm going through a crisis of faith that I can do this job."

"Okay. Do you know why?"

She shook her head. "I don't suppose you'd just tell me why?"

"No, I can't. Even if I was sure I knew, which I'm not, it

won't help unless you get there yourself. You know that, Blythe. But I'll help you get there. What's happened in the past few weeks that's set you back?"

"The Web-cam girls, the ones who have been getting killed."

I nodded. "What else?"

"There's something else?"

"How do you feel about what's happening to the girls?"

"There but for the grace of God…"

"Right, but you stopped doing Web cast work months before all this started. Why is this affecting you so personally now?"

She thought about it. She looked up at me. I wasn't going to help her make the last leap. She had to do that herself. And then she did.

"The interview with Stella Dobson."

I didn't have to tell her she was right.

"She was someone I looked up to, Dr. Snow. She went on a hunger strike for three weeks to protest that judge in Alabama who was trying to prevent a teenager from having an abortion unless she got her parent's permission. When everyone else stopped talking about women's rights, she talked louder. And now even though she'll never know my real name, and even though I'll disguise myself, it will still be me, meeting her." She stopped talking and looked away from me. "How do you know when you're doing the right thing?" Blythe asked.

"With a patient?"

"No. Personally. When I'm working with a patient I have a good sense of whether her behavior is destructive or not, but I can't turn my intuition on myself." She leaned forward and clasped her hands under her chin, focusing her attention back on me. It was slightly affected but charming, and made me feel as if my answer mattered to her very much. It also drew attention away from her eyes and to her mouth.

"It's hard to do. Our own neuroses and needs get in the way."

"What kind of process can I put myself through to test my decisions and make sure I'm doing the right thing? How can I be my own therapist?"

I shook my head. If there was an easy exercise, I wouldn't mind knowing it myself. "You can't be. That's why most therapists are in therapy."

"I don't want to be in therapy forever."

"You won't be. Most of us need to be in therapy at the beginning of our careers, but then, like any other patient who has gone through the process, we terminate, knowing there's always the option of coming back when issues resurface."

She seemed to be taking mental notes, nodding her head slightly, studying me with her inscrutable green eyes.

"I told Stella Dobson I'd do the interview, and I want to do it because I'm curious. I'm flattered. Isn't that nuts? I'm flattered she wants to interview me about the big secret of my life. I'm excited that someone wants to know about it. But I'm embarrassed about it at the same time. I'm afraid of what she's going to say if I'm really honest with her. I mean, what is a feminist going to think about the fact that I loved showing off?"

"What do you think she's going to say?"

"That it was wrong of me to crave the attention. That it's part of what's wrong with our society. That I exacerbated the problem. Set a bad example."

"Do you think you did?"

"I don't know. I just loved the idea of the attention. I loved the idea of invisible hands stroking me. Of the eyes staring at my body. Taking me in."

"Did you feel powerful?"

She nodded. "You can't imagine how powerful you feel when you know you can move men without even being in the same room as them."

"Go on."

She hesitated, then took a breath. "It's crazy when you first realize that just watching you can give them a hard-on and make them come. It made me feel so sexy—"

Another hesitation. "It's okay. Tell me."

"Sometimes…there were some times when the session was over and I'd shut off the Web cam and masturbate for real because I was so turned on. And the…the orgasms I had then were more intense and better than any I ever had with anyone." She was whispering. Her flawless skin was flushed with pink. Her eyes sparkled. "And then I'd get paid for it, the check would come in the mail, and I'd feel so disgusted."

"Why?"

"It turned it into something else."

"Into what?"

"Into something disgusting."

"Is that how you feel about the interview?"

"I'm worried I will. But I could use the money. Since I've given up webbing, I'm strapped. I've even asked Nina if she can give me some more patients from the clinic. In the meantime, Stella Dobson is giving me five hundred dollars for this."

"I'll talk to Nina. If you'd be willing to work another day at clinic, I might be able to make that happen."

"Yes, that would be great."

"Will that help you decide about the interview?"

"I'll probably still do it. I'm excited to meet her, to talk to her, to help her with her book. Although I know it's another form of showing off. That's one thing I need to work out. That and wondering how I'm going to feel when she pays me." She sighed deeply and tossed her hair again. "I've been dreaming about being on camera again. I wake up and when I realize it was just a dream I'm so depressed. I miss how it used to make me feel."

Her eyes filled with tears but her face didn't crumble. She contained herself and then started to laugh. "Can you believe this? I must be the only woman in the world who gets weepy at not having to play dirty in front of a Web cam anymore. I hope I don't do this in front of Stella Dobson next Friday."

"Is that when the interview is?"

"Yes. Can you imagine?" She was excited again. "I'm going to meet her! A real hero."

Friday
Seven days remaining

Fifty-Six

It had taken Amanda's parents forever to leave. First her father was late getting home from the office. Then they'd had a fight about some bill for a new couch that he said cost as much as some people's monthly rent, and her mother said there was nothing for him to worry about because she was using her money to pay for the redecorating.

Amanda tuned them out. They always argued about money. She didn't understand how they could stand to go over the same thing all the time. Her mother shopped too much. Her father got annoyed. Why didn't one of them change? Why did her father even care? Her mother was a really successful designer. He was a high-powered businessman. What did the cost of a couch really matter to either of them? So what if the apartment never looked the same for more than two years. At least her room never changed. She'd got her father on her side and he'd convinced her mother to let her keep it the way she wanted. Her sanctuary, her father had called it.

But there were no sanctuaries. That was an adult fantasy about what being seventeen was like. How could he have forgotten what it was like? He was only forty-four. When did you forget?

She wouldn't. She'd hold on to it. She'd remember how it was all a gray landscape. A dreary, endless day that was complicated with feelings that didn't go away and work she had to do for her classes that hardly ever interested her.

Except for her art classes. She wished she could just take art classes and nothing else. Art and photography and film. She loved the way you could sit down in a theater and relax your shoulders and your neck and your hips and let the chair hold you and let the darkness be the door between what was real and what was more interesting than real.

She made movies with a digital camera and edited them on her computer. Short ones. They were her private diaries. Images that meant something only to her. Simone had acted in a lot of them. There was only one movie she'd shown anyone else. And that had been the worst mistake she'd ever made, no matter what Dr. Snow had said about secrets. It should have stayed a secret forever.

Amanda wrapped her long black scarf around her neck as they walked to the corner. It was so cold out. She had a hole in the thumb of her glove and felt the freezing air stinging that one spot of skin. It was snowing, of course, but only lightly.

"What if you're wrong?" Timothy asked as they crossed Park Avenue.

"I'm not."

"But we'll get in so much trouble. And we're already in trouble. At least, Hugh and Barry and I are."

"This is more important." Amanda's words came out in a puff of white air. She watched them disappear.

They walked another block in silence and came to a huge snowdrift on the corner.

"Can you fucking believe this snow?" He climbed up over the messy pile that was crusted with ice. She followed in his path, using the footprints he had made.

"It's snowed every day for more than two weeks." Amanda's scarf had come undone and she wrapped it around her neck again as they trudged on. It was a cashmere scarf her mother had given to her last year. She never took it off anymore. Not because she was always cold—well, she was pretty much always cold—but because with her neck swathed she felt protected. Sometimes she'd pull it up and hide her mouth and chin in its soft folds. If she could have hidden her whole face, she would have. As it was, she wore long bangs that partially covered her forehead and eyebrows, and she'd recently started wearing lightly tinted glasses she'd found in her mother's drawer. They had stupid gold *C*'s on the edges but she'd gotten black paint and covered over them. Her mother hadn't noticed. As if. She hardly noticed anything Amanda did.

They continued west on Seventy-seventh Street until they got to Fifth Avenue, and then they walked two blocks north and entered Central Park.

It was only 8:00 p.m. and there were still people heading home from work, or taking their dogs out for a run. There were also some couples, arm in arm, who just seemed to be strolling.

"Weird, huh. Why are these people out?" Timothy asked. "It's so cold."

She looked around. There was a full moon and the snow was still falling. Everything was dusted white and sparkling. It looked like a dream. Someone else's dream.

The deeper they walked into the park the fewer people there were. After a few minutes it was all quiet, and she could hear their boots crunching on the path. They went west and north. Neither of them hesitated about what direction to take. This was their playground; they'd grown up in the park.

They'd been walked here in baby carriages, played in the sandboxes as toddlers, spent afternoons visiting the zoo. Their schools had brought them here for ice skating in winter and softball in spring. Once they were old enough, they'd come on their own to escape from their parents, sitting on the hills or the edges of ponds and fountains, disappearing with their friends into smoky hazes.

"I've never been here this late," Amanda said.

Timothy shrugged. "There're lights everywhere."

"People still get murdered in the park, though. It's always in the news when it happens."

Timothy nodded. "But they're alone. We're not."

A few more steps brought them to the crest of the hill. The pond where kids and hobbyists sailed toy boats was frozen over. The fresh coating of crystalline white on all the trees and benches shimmered. The sky looked like velvet, Amanda thought, suddenly remembering a dress that she'd had when she was eight or nine years old.

"Amanda, c'mon. Let's get the damn thing and get outta here."

"So, you're nervous." She smiled. It felt strange to smile on this mission.

"No, just cold."

"I'm nervous, though. One of them is still alive."

Even with the thick gloves they both wore, she felt it when he took her hand. She'd given three guys blowjobs, but this was the first time a boy had ever done that.

An oversize bronze Hans Christian Andersen held a book in his lap as he read one of his own fairy tales. Tonight his head was dusted white and the pages of the book were hidden under inches of snow.

As kids, she and her friends had sat at his feet while their teacher read them story after story, each with a happy ending.

She and Timothy approached the statue.

Hans sat on a bronze platform atop a large pedestal made of tightly fitted limestone blocks. Or, at least, they seemed tightly fitted, but there was a crack in between the third and the fourth blocks on the right side. Timothy had found it when he was a kid and his second grade class was here racing toy boats. He grew tired of hanging over the edge of the pond watching the stupid toys whizzing across the water, and he'd wandered off on his own.

"Timothy?"

Amanda was staring at him, her eyes wide, her cheeks red from the cold. Most of the time, when he looked at her, he forgot about the movie. She looked like any other girl to him. Most of the time.

He pulled his army knife out of his pocket, extracted the nail file, and inserted it into the crevice. He felt a connection and moved the file forward. The edge of a transparent CD case became visible. He reached for it and pulled it out.

Timothy held it flat in his hand and Amanda stared down at it, noticing how the moon was reflected in its surface, full and round and silvery. At that moment, it didn't look lethal at all.

Monday
Four days remaining

Fifty-Seven

~~~~~~~~~~

Alan Leightman was sitting on the couch holding a large cup of coffee. I was still having trouble not calling him Bob. He kept wrapping his fingers, first of the right hand, then the left, around the cup as if he were warming himself. But by now, surely the coffee had grown cold. It was the idea of warmth he was in search of.

"She kept stirring the damn spoon around and around."

"That bothered you?"

"Everything bothered me. My wife—the brilliant woman I've lived with for all these years—has turned into a drugged-out zombie who hates my guts."

"What happened in the kitchen?" I asked, getting him to refocus.

"She said her coffee was cold and turned the heat on under the kettle. Once the water was boiling and the kettle was whistling, she did the strangest thing…she reached out and touched it."

"What do you mean touched it—to see if it was hot?"

"Yes, but she had to know it was hot, it was whistling. She was burning her fingers on purpose. Twice. Why would she do that? And then she said she knew something that could help me with the police." He rubbed his face. "But whatever it was, she said it wouldn't matter, and she's right—no one would believe her, she's my wife. Everyone would assume she'd lie for me." He shook his head. "She's punishing me for what I've done to her. I deserve it, too."

"Deserve it?"

He nodded. There was anguish in his eyes.

"Alan, if you want I can talk to—"

"No." He was on his feet. "You can't talk to the police. Do you understand? You can't talk to anyone."

"I wasn't suggesting I go to the police. Sit down. I was going to say that if you want me to talk to you and Kira together, in therapy, I would."

He collapsed back on the couch. "I didn't write to those women. I certainly didn't kill those women."

"I have no doubt of that. None at all."

And I didn't.

"Dr. Snow, why was she burning her fingers?"

"Maybe she wanted to punish herself. Or sometimes inflicting pain distracts a person from a deeper pain."

He nodded, twisted his hands in his lap. Crossed one leg over the other. Then uncrossed it. His eyes were darting around the room as if he was going to find answers hiding in the corners and behind the books.

"She blames herself for my addiction, doesn't she?"

"It's certainly possible."

He nodded, nodded again. He was thinking. A moment went by.

"She takes responsibility for everything. Damn. She takes responsibility for the First Amendment."

I was watching him put himself through some kind of difficult process. The pain intensified in his eyes and then he closed them. When he opened them a few seconds later, he seemed as if he'd resolved something, was almost elated.

"Alan? What is it?"

"Do you think her moods and erratic behavior could have something to do with her meds?" he asked.

"Technically, yes. It is not unheard of for medication to have the opposite of its intended effect. Patients being treated for depression can become more depressed. Or more paranoid. Would she allow you to call her doctor and—"

"Can they become violent? Seriously violent? Delusional?" He interrupted me.

"Yes."

He looked down at his hands. His wedding ring glinted. He covered it with his right hand.

"She takes those pills because of me."

"No. No, she doesn't."

He wasn't hearing me. I could see that.

"Alan, are you all right?" I asked.

He was looking through me, oblivious of where he was or what was going on around him. I waited. One minute passed. And then another. He started to speak and then stopped. Shook his head as if he was having a silent conversation with himself.

"I've made a decision."

I waited.

He didn't say anything. Then he cleared his throat. I nodded, encouraging.

"When I leave here I'm turning myself in to the police."

"For what?"

"I lied to you. To you and to Kira and to the police. I killed those girls, those Web cam girls, and I think… I think it will be better for everyone if I admit it now and prevent an investigation."

I might not have known his name until a few days before, but I knew this man's psyche. "Alan, you didn't kill anyone."

His face was devoid of any emotion except resolve. "Yes, I did. I'm confessing. And I am asking you not to discuss me with the police. Not to tell them whether you think I am or am not capable of murder when they ask."

"They won't ask me. We've talked about this. I can't discuss your therapy with anyone unless you want me to."

"Even if you believe that I am a threat to society, you can't go to the police?"

"I'm confused. Are you confessing to me so that I will go to the police and help you do this?"

"No. God, no. You can't talk to them. Do you understand? I'm turning myself in. You don't have to protect anyone. The only one who knows I was in therapy with you was Kira. No one else. I don't want you to tell anyone else. All right?"

"Alan, why are you doing this?"

"Dr. Snow, the best thing you can do is to stop asking questions and stop looking for answers. Do you understand?"

He was staring intently at me and, for a second, I felt a jolt of fear.

"Yes."

His eyes were unflinching, unrelenting. "You won't discuss anything I've told you with anyone?" His jaw muscles tightened and a cord stood out on his neck.

"No. No, I won't. But I think we should talk about this before you make a mistake you can't undo."

"I have to go now. Will you call my wife's doctor? Will you ask him to go to our apartment? To give her whatever she needs? Will you go see her? If you can't find him, will you go? I don't want her to be alone when the story breaks on the news." He was speaking clearly, but he'd begun to disassociate.

"Alan, listen to me. You are paying me for forty-five minutes, let's use them. Let me help you. I know you didn't kill anyone. I don't even think you are capable of killing yourself. Your ego is too strong. No matter what you're doing online, sexually, you care about your career. About your wife. You don't want to do this to Kira, do you?"

His eyes blinked three times in succession.

"I am not doing this *to* Kira."

"No. You're not, are you? You're doing this to protect her."

He looked surprised that I'd guessed.

"Alan, is that what you're doing?"

He smiled just a little and then it disappeared. "What do you mean protect her? I don't understand, Dr. Snow. What do I have to protect her from?"

"Alan, please. Tell me what is going on."

"I wish I could have completed my therapy with you, Morgan. I think you would have gotten me to a better place."

It was the first time he'd ever called me by my first name. He stood.

I wanted to lock him in my office and make him talk to me, explain why he was taking this drastic step. "If you need me, I'll come. Wherever you are. Do you understand? In prison, you'll be allowed to see your therapist. They'll let me see you."

He nodded, reached out and shook my hand. His skin was dry and cold but the handshake was strong.

Judge Alan Leightman could not have killed anyone. I was right about that. But I was wrong about him being able to commit suicide. Because he was doing that, in front of my eyes. And there was nothing I could do to stop him.

He turned, walked to the door, opened it and left my office. I watched him march down the sweeping staircase. It was the first time he'd left the Butterfield Institute through the front door.

Fifty-Eight

$\sim\!\!\infty\!\!\sim\!\!\infty\!\!\sim$

Noah Jordain and Mark Perez were in the interrogation room, questioning a Hispanic boy who was far too young to have been picked up on rape charges, though that's why he was there.

"So, who were you there with, Juan?" Perez asked.

Neither detective thought this kid was the one they wanted, but so far they couldn't get Juan to crack.

"Nobody. I told you that already, man."

"Hey!" Perez shouted. "No attitude. It doesn't matter if you told us twenty times. You tell us again. You understand?"

Butler opened the door and stuck her head in. Jordain looked over. "I need you both for a few minutes," she said.

Jordain got down on his knees in front of the kid. Where Perez had been tough, he was almost gentle. "Listen, Juan, you're only twelve. If you tell us what really happened last night and the name of the friend you're protecting, you won't get into trouble. But if you don't, you're going to grow up in jail." His voice got cold as ice now. "And when it comes to girls? Hell, you won't see one for years. Think about that for a while. By yourself."

The two detectives walked out of the room. Butler was waiting for them.

"What have you got?"

"Better to show you than tell you," she said, and led them down the hall.

"Tease," quipped Perez.

Butler didn't take the bait. She didn't turn around. She just kept walking.

"Have you got something on the Web-cam case?" Jordain asked.

"Maybe."

He was frustrated that they still were nowhere. Sure they suspected Leightman, but they still didn't have enough evidence to arrest him. They all knew they couldn't hang a case on the e-mail. It was too easy. It had to be a setup. If the judge was going to ask the girls via e-mail to use poisoned lubricants, massage oils and Band-Aids, would he use an e-mail address so easily traceable? Okay. So who was setting him up? Why wasn't he screaming bloody murder and pointing fingers? Was it blackmail? Skeletons in his closet? How were they going to find out?

Butler watched their faces when she opened the door.

"I'm willing to tell you what you want to know, who killed those three women," Leightman said once everyone was seated. "But I need your word of honor that you won't ask me to explain anything or discuss any details with you now."

"We don't bargain for information," Jordain said.

"Bullshit, Detective. You bargain all the time. I'll tell you what I have to tell you. And then I'll just shut up. Like it or not. My lawyer will handle the rest."

Jordain hated games. "You're here. We didn't call you. Talk or don't talk."

"I'm turning myself in voluntarily. I'm responsible for all three deaths. That's all I have to say until my lawyer gets here."

Fifty-Nine

Nina came by my office to say good-night, took one look at me and asked what was wrong. I told her about Alan Leightman and the confession he had probably already made to the police. We sat and talked for a few minutes, and then she suggested we leave the office and have drinks.

Usually we went to Bemelman's Bar at the Carlyle. It was a twelve-block walk that we normally enjoyed, but the narrow pathways carved out of packed snow were uninviting, so Nina and I pulled up our coat collars and walked to the small French bistro four doors down.

It was about fifteen degrees out but felt even colder because of the brutal wind that whipped around us. We were all getting tired of the weather. Everyone was talking about it constantly. Every night now, news shows did special segments on coping with it. More of my patients were depressed than usual. There was an epidemic of SAD—Seasonal Affective Disorder.

The waiter came and took our order—a vodka and tonic with lime for her, a dirty martini on the rocks for me—after which we continued talking about Alan. I explained how ludicrous it was and why I was so certain he wasn't the killer that he claimed to be.

"He's going to need help, but it can't be you. You know that. You can't treat him anymore," Nina said.

"Why?"

"You need to ask?"

"You mean because of Noah?"

"Of course."

The waiter brought our drinks. Nina was watching me. I knew what she was thinking. "I'm not seeing Noah anymore."

The waiter returned with a terra-cotta pot of black and green olives, glistening with oil, and I took one.

"Since when?"

I told her what had happened with Dulcie, how I'd reacted, what Mitch had said, and ended with the fight I'd had with Noah. I went through it all, trying to be as objective as I could and not be defensive, but it was difficult since Nina's facial expressions were speaking volumes: There wasn't much she liked about what she heard.

"You're so good at denial, Morgan. But you can't expect me to believe that you think this whole plan will solve anything, can you?"

She sat back and refolded the cuffs on her camel-colored cashmere sweater.

"Why not? I loved Mitch. I never wanted the marriage to end."

"Nope, you didn't. But it did end. And you met someone else." She reached out and took my hand. "What's really going on?"

I shrugged.

"Do you even know what you're afraid of?"

"I'm not afraid." My voice was only slightly above a whisper.

"Yes, you are."

"You're going to make me do this the hard way."

"I don't ever *make* you do anything."

I laughed. "No. But you never let up if you think I'm taking the easy way out of something." I drank some more of the martini, noticing for the first time that it was cold and good.

"Morgan, do you know why you are considering going back to Mitch?"

"Because he was my husband and I was happy with him, and our daughter would be better off if we were together."

She shook her head.

"What then?" I asked.

"You're smarter than that."

"I want to give Mitch a chance. I want my daughter home."

"Of course you want Dulcie home. But you are also damn afraid of getting involved—no, let's call this as it really is—so damn afraid of *getting intimate* with Noah and having him disappoint you that you would rather run away from him than face up to it and work on it."

I took another sip of my drink. And then another. I tried to keep quiet until the moment had passed and I felt able to carry on a civilized conversation without shouting.

"Why the hell can't you just get mad at me?" Nina was leaning over the table, whispering.

"Why can't you let me do what I have to do to get my daughter back? This is about Dulcie."

"Okay, let's talk about Dulcie. This is what's supposed to happen to her at this age. Rebelling is healthy for her. You know that."

"I know it intellectually."

"Good. At least we can start there. And you know being a teenager is rough. By the very nature of what she is going through developmentally, she is supposed to fight you for what she wants. It's the last stage in her self-individuation, and it's not only important but critical that she go through it. Without a mother to fight…you know how not rebelling hurt you. You need to allow her to fight you now. Nothing that you do or don't do with Mitch will prevent that process. And you don't want to. It's not healthy to."

I looked at my watch. Nina frowned. "Sure, tell me it's late and that you have to go. Good response to confrontation." Nina glared at me. "Don't bother. I'll get the check."

She waved the waiter over, and while she waited for him she pulled out her wallet and opened it to get a credit card. I saw the picture of Dulcie and me that she kept there.

My father had known me longer than Nina, but no one knew me better than she did, and she was right. I hadn't rebelled. I'd been too timid as a teenager, followed the rules, emulated the adults. I emulated Nina by going to both her undergrad and grad alma maters. I'd married relatively early—someone my father knew and liked. All that time, I'd never stopped to examine why it was all so effortless for me and so difficult for all my friends.

The result of my not rebelling was that I didn't always connect to my self—to my innermost thoughts or to my physical self. I had worked on that in therapy when I got out of college and during grad school, but I'd never quite resolved it. My feelings were there but buried deep down and I didn't always have the energy to dig for them.

Only with Dulcie had love come to the surface with ease. I held my baby in my arms and did not have to search for emotional connections. And yet, even with Dulcie, the problem manifested itself in its own way. Maybe because she was one of the very few people I did connect to, my feelings for her were magnified. The way I felt pain that she experienced. The way I woke even before I heard her stirring. It was not psychic so much as it was inevitable, with all of my attention focused on her.

Together Nina and I walked out the door and into the street. The wind blew our coats around our legs and pushed at us. Tiny pinpricks of snow hit my face. It had started up again. Not lush, fat flakes that landed gently and made the world into a soft winter scene. This was an icy attack of pellets of snow mixed with freezing water. We walked the half block to Madison Avenue, and by the time we reached the corner, my cheeks were already stinging. I took Nina's arm to help her across the street, knowing that there were patches of ice hidden under this fresh layer of snow, the argument forgotten for the moment.

We turned north and went another half block and then I spotted a taxi discharging a woman. At the same time, across the street under the light of the street lamp, a man was watching us. I couldn't be sure, but it looked like Terry Meziac. Alan's bodyguard.

What was he doing here?

I shivered, and it wasn't from the cold. Noah had warned me that what I knew about Leightman could put me in danger, and I'd shrugged it off.

The snow was falling. It was dark. The taxi was going to pull away.

Maybe it wasn't Meziac.

I forced myself to look away from the man, to focus on catching the cab. I called out *"Taxi!"* and quickened my step, and that's when I slid.

Letting go of Nina's arm—somehow knowing better than to drag her down with me—I fell forward, fast, put out my right hand, felt the cold ice on my palm, felt my legs fold, felt the cold all around me. Hard, stinging cold.

Sixty

Five hours later, Nina and I left Lenox Hill Hospital. I'd dislocated and broken a bone in my right wrist. The doctors had reset it and put my arm, just below the elbow to the knuckles, in a cast.

"Morgan? C'mon, sweetie. Let's go."

"Where are we?" I was groggy from the painkillers. Where was I? I looked around. In a taxi. In front of Nina's brownstone on East Fifty-sixth Street, across from the East River.

"You're spending the night with me," she said, and she helped me traverse the sidewalk and get into the building safely.

Inside, she put me in the bedroom where I'd spent so many nights as a kid, and brought in a cup of hot milky tea laced with honey—a concoction that she never drank herself but foisted on anyone who was hurt or sick. I loved it.

More than that, the milk and the honey with the slight bite of the tea was what comfort and caring tasted like to me. I made the same drink for my daughter when she didn't feel well, and she always drank it slowly, the same way I did, making it last, the way I was doing now.

Tuesday
Three days remaining

Sixty-One

❦

There wasn't a moment when I was asleep and then awake. There was only the slow emergence from a complicated dream of a giant checkerboard, Noah standing in the middle of it, holding out both a red and a black checker to me, asking me if I was ready to play.

I had a hangover from the painkillers, a headache, and my wrist was throbbing.

Sitting up, I looked down at the pajamas I was wearing. I didn't remember getting undressed. Nina must have helped me. I stood up, felt woozy and slowly made my way to the bathroom.

Navigating with one hand proved more complicated than I had imagined. It was difficult to pull the pajama bottoms down and then up with only my left hand.

It was going to be a long six weeks.

I found Nina sitting in the kitchen at a small table by the window that looked out into a winter garden.

"You must be in a lot of pain," she said when she saw me. "Come, sit down. I'll get you some juice and some pills."

"It's not that bad," I said, maneuvering the chair.

"You're not going to play martyr, are you?" She put a crystal glass of orange juice down on the table, along with a plate that had two white pills on it. Without thinking, I reached with my right hand for the juice, felt the stab of pain, grimaced, put my hurt arm back in my lap and took a deep breath.

"Where's your sling?"

"I forgot."

"I'll be right back. In the meantime, take the pills."

When Nina returned, she was holding a lovely silk Hermès scarf. It was black with large copper poppies on it. She draped it over my chest and tied it around my neck.

"I have a sling from the hospital."

"It's hideous."

"Nina, you're crazy." I couldn't imagine using something so expensive to hold my arm in place.

"You're worth it." She smiled.

After I'd finished the juice, Nina looked down at the plate, where the two pills still sat, untouched.

"Am I going to have to sneak these into your food?"

"I don't need them."

"Of course you do."

I shook my head.

"You are the most stubborn creature. Aren't you in pain?"

"I'll get over it."

"Morgan, you are not going to get addicted to pain pills if you take them for two or three days."

"If you have two extra-strength over-the-counter pain-killers, I'll take those."

We'd been over it before. About me. About what kind of medication I'd give Dulcie. I was afraid that we might have inherited my mother's tendency toward substance abuse. She'd been on uppers and downers and muscle relaxants and pain pills, all washed down with vodka, during my short life with her.

Nina left for the institute at eight and it didn't take much urging on her part for me to agree to let her cancel my appointments and stay in bed. I slept most of the morning, woke up about noon, ate some of the soup and sandwich she'd made for me before she left, and then spent the afternoon watching old movies on television, avoiding the relentless news coverage of the confession from Judge Alan Leightman.

There was a lot I had to work out, but the pain, as gripping as it was, had given me a short reprieve.

Sixty-Two

With Alan Leightman in jail, Jordain and Perez spent the morning catching up on paperwork. At lunchtime, Perez kept a long-overdue dentist appointment while Jordain stayed at his desk, and that's where he was when Ken Fisher, one of the computer geeks, stopped by to tell him he finally had some new information.

"All the e-mail the women received from bob205 originated from a computer at NYU," Fisher said.

"Makes sense. Leightman teaches at NYU. So now we know why there was nothing on his home computer."

"Listen, Noah, I don't want to tell you how to do your job, but there are some things that don't match up now."

"Tell me."

"Okay, but you are not going to like it. Remember we said that at the same time the letter was sent to Debra Kamel, there was e-mail sent from Leightman's computer that definitely went out through his own DSL line?"

"Humor me and explain what that means."

"It means that if Alan Leightman was at NYU sending that mail, then he couldn't also have been at home sending mail. I'm sorry, boss."

"Don't be. Not yet. Maybe his wife was using his computer at home and sending mail from her husband's e-mail account. Isn't that possible?"

"Sure."

"So then it's also possible that he was home and someone else—say, his wife—was at NYU using his e-mail account."

Fisher nodded.

"Can you find out which computer at NYU the e-mail came from?"

"Sure, we can do that. Let me get back to you." He turned and almost walked into Perez.

"Butler just grabbed me in the hall. It's all over the news— Kira Rushkoff was just taken to Bellevue. Sounds like a nervous breakdown."

Sixty-Three

Officers Davis and Lynds escorted Alan Leightman Uptown to Bellevue Hospital and took him upstairs to his wife's room. They were about to take him in when he asked if he could go in alone.

Not much could happen in a hospital room, Davis figured. There was only one entrance. A nurse was there. Leightman was wearing handcuffs. They could watch Leightman through the glass in the door. Afterward, he or Lynds could ask the nurse what the judge had said.

"Sure, but we'll be right here."

Inside, Alan stood and stared at Kira, who was lying in the hospital bed, hooked up to an IV. She looked ravaged, as if she'd been deathly ill. As if most of the life force had left her. Was she sleeping? Awake? He couldn't tell. Her eyes were open, but she hadn't looked at him or said a word. There'd been no response when he'd said her name. He felt his knees go weak and held on to the foot of the bed. He waited until he felt a little stronger, and then asked the nurse if she would step outside for just a moment so he could speak to his wife alone.

She didn't mind, shrugged and got up, stretching her legs

and walking slowly. He watched her leave. When the door was closed behind her, he watched one of the cops walk up to the door, station himself in front of the glass window, and look in. Alan didn't care about being watched. It was being listened to that mattered to him.

Sitting beside Kira, Alan took her left hand, the one that wasn't hooked up to the IV, dipped his head down and kissed her palm. How was it possible that this woman, his wife, had committed such twisted crimes?

"Kira?" he whispered.

Nothing.

It was possible because he had driven her to it with his addictions. With his lack of empathy for what she had suffered when he turned away from her and turned on the computer every night.

Reaching out, he smoothed down his wife's hair as he whispered her name again, but there was still no response.

Who do you blame when a child commits a crime? Only the child? Or the parent also? No, he wasn't her parent, but he was just as responsible. How many cases had he heard in his career? How many pleas? He knew how to weight both sides of every issue.

Even, and especially, this one.

His whole life was a matter of justice. And if there was going to be any justice here, it was going to have to be his to mete out. Here, now, he was sitting on the bench at their trial and while there was no question hers was the more heinous crime, his was the instigating crime. There was no way he'd ever right the wrongs he'd done to her or the wrongs she'd done to those poor women, but he could pay the penalty that he deserved.

He felt tears prick his eyes but blinked them away. What good would any of that do now?

"Kira, sweetheart, can you hear me?"

Nothing.

"Kira, please." His voice was on the verge of breaking.

Finally, she turned her head and looked at him through a drug-induced haze.

"You're in the hospital but you are going to be all right. Can you hear me?"

She had to be able to hear him. She had to be able to understand what he needed to tell her.

"Kira, you can hear me, right?"

She nodded.

"You don't have to worry. I'll never tell anyone. I love you too much. I'm sorry. I'm so sorry. Nothing you did will ever be discovered. I did do it, really, didn't I? It *was* my fault. You only reacted. You shouldn't be punished for reacting."

Her eyes opened wider, in alarm. There were deep hollows under her cheekbones. Without the deep red lipstick that had been her trademark, her lips looked thin and dry.

"You can't..." she said in a feeble voice.

He bent down, awkwardly because of the handcuffs, and kissed her forehead.

"You have to get better. And when you go home, you have to remember to destroy anything you have on paper, anything on your computer, anything at all that's left. You have to make sure there's nothing to tie you to all this. They won't come looking for you. They won't have any reason to. But you have to take care of every shred of evidence. Do you understand?"

Kira opened her mouth to say something but only a sob came out.

Sixty-Four

❧❧❧

At four-thirty, instead of going to her favorite art class, Amanda left school early and got on the Fifth Avenue bus. No one cared if she skipped art. Hell, no one really cared what she skipped anymore. She was a senior and she'd already applied to colleges. This last semester was a joke.

She was nervous during the ride and almost got off twice. What if Dr. Snow broke her promise and went to her parents? What if she went to the principal? What if this fucked up her chances at getting into the school she wanted? Would the guidance counselor write to Brown and Cornell and tell them?

Anything was possible.

There was no way to know.

First she'd get Dr. Snow to promise not to tell anyone. But could she take her word for it? She didn't know. Timothy had told her that some of the guys had told Dr. Snow some pretty heavy shit over the past few months and she hadn't blabbed to anyone.

She should have called. She shouldn't just show up. But she didn't want the doctor to ask her anything over the phone.

The bus finally stopped at Sixty-fifth Street and Amanda

walked quickly from Fifth to Madison, then continued down the block until she found the wrought-iron doors and the small bronze plaque identifying the building as the Butterfield Institute.

She tried the door but it didn't open.

Then she found the buzzer and pressed it.

What was she going to say if anyone asked who she was? Should she give them her real name? Her whole name? Or just her first name? Would Dr. Snow know who she was if she only used her first name?

She was starting to panic. Then she heard a click and a woman's voice asking for her name.

"Amanda. I'm here to see Dr. Snow."

"Come in."

Inside, Amanda looked around at the high ceiling, the crystal chandelier sending soft light down on the peach walls and bronze leather chairs. Surprised, she kept searching for something that would identify the place as a sex therapy institute.

She was in the right place, wasn't she?

"Can I help you?"

She walked over to the receptionist, holding on to her backpack so tightly the strap was biting into the flesh of her palm.

"I wanted to see Dr. Snow."

"I don't see you down for an appointment?"

She shook her head. "I didn't have one."

"Dr. Snow isn't here today. She had an accident."

Amanda hadn't really heard anything after "isn't here today." It had taken so much to decide to come. She didn't know if she could do it again. Tears started to fill her eyes. Fuck, she was not going to cry in front of this preppie chick.

"She'll be back tomorrow. Do you want to make an appointment?"

Maybe she should just give her the damn CD and ask her

to give it to Dr. Snow. But what if she looked at it? What if she figured it out?

"When?"

"She has an hour free on Thursday at five-thirty. Would that work for you?"

Amanda nodded her head quickly. Yes.

But could she really wait? Should she say something? She was afraid—afraid to give herself a chance to say no, to chicken out, to screw up. She'd done enough of that already. Delivering this CD to Dr. Snow was something she had to do. Dr. Snow would know what to do. She had to. Enough people had died already. Nothing would happen between now and then. Nothing would.

Amanda shuddered.

"You okay?" the blonde asked.

"Not really," Amanda said, but before the girl could ask her anything else, she ran out.

Sixty-Five

I left Nina's late that afternoon and took a cab home. Everything was slightly difficult to manage. And everything exhausted me. I dropped my bag on the floor and my coat on the back of a chair, then sat down on the couch.

The room was still and quiet and smelled slightly of the heated air coming up through the pipes. I went to light one of the many scented candles that I keep handy—not as an affectation or an aid to romance, but because they were necessary to get rid of the odor—but couldn't manage the matches with only one hand.

When Mitch rang the doorbell forty minutes later, I was still sitting in the den, trying to ignore the throbbing in my wrist. It was strange to open the door with my left hand.

He kissed me, gently and softly, on the lips. I smelled the cold that he brought with him and shivered a little, surprised that the freezing temperatures would follow him upstairs and linger so long.

"Does it still hurt?" he asked, looking at the cast in the sling.

"Yeah, but I'm okay."

"I bet you're being stoic beyond logic and not taking anything stronger than aspirin."

Instead of the comment sounding endearing, it was as if he'd flung an insult at me.

"I'm okay."

He shrugged as if he'd heard this before. And he had. I took a big breath. Of course it would be like this at first. We had to work back into knowing each other. We had to find a new way to be together.

"Do you want a drink?" I asked.

"I'll get it. You sit."

I let Mitch make us both drinks—Scotch neat for him, a club soda for me. I was concerned about mixing alcohol with the residue of painkillers in my system. He brought them over to the couch, handed me mine and took a swallow of his.

"How is Dulcie?" I asked.

"Resolute."

"So am I."

"I know." He smiled ruefully.

"You won't try to get in the middle and convince me to give in, right? I won't."

Mitch was handsome in a way that should have been more attractive to me. But sitting in the den that used to be *our den,* watching him, it wasn't. When he'd kissed me, I hadn't felt anything. Of course not; I was in pain. I'd broken my wrist twenty-four hours earlier. What was I supposed to feel? But there had been no startled acceleration of my blood, no heat in my cheeks. I'd smelled his cologne and had stepped back, finding it slightly unpleasant, the way a memory can be.

"No, I won't."

"Mitch, she doesn't have the tools yet to deflect the dangers out there."

"You're lecturing me, Morgan. I already told you I wasn't going to try to change your mind."

"Right. Sorry. I really am sorry. I just hate not having her here. I hate being the one to say no, being the bad guy again."

"It's going to be fine." He smiled. "Do you want to go out and get something to eat?"

I didn't. *I wanted to see Noah. I wanted to talk to him and tell him how I was feeling and sit in the kitchen with him and have him make us something to eat.* Damn. I needed to stop thinking about Noah. I had told Nina I could do this and that I needed to do this and it was what I wanted.

"Sure, let's go."

"Where?"

"It doesn't matter, wherever you want."

"Morgan, just pick someplace." He sounded irritated. This was all too familiar. A pressure was holding me down, a tightness wound around my chest. I recognized the signs. I'd forgotten how we had been together.

My marriage to Mitch hadn't ended because he wanted it to. I hadn't been happy, either, even if I chose not to think about it, even if I chose to hide behind my daughter and my work.

"Mitch," I said, "my hand hurts and I'm tired from all the painkillers. I think I need to stay here. I need to go to sleep."

I got up and walked him to the front door, where he leaned over and kissed the top of my head. "Call me tomorrow. And please, Morgan, stop being so stubborn. Take something to help with the pain."

But once he had left, once the door had shut behind him and I was alone again in my home, my wrist wasn't that bad and I wasn't so tired anymore.

Sixty-Six

⟨◦⟩⟨◦⟩

I struggled out of my clothes. Everything took so much time and effort with only one hand. Finally in my robe, I went into the kitchen and tried to get a glass of water from the dispenser, but I couldn't push down the lever and hold the glass with the same hand. I gave up and used tap water.

Holding the glass in my left hand—which still felt odd—I walked down the hall toward my bedroom, but stopped first at Dulcie's door.

I missed her. Not the willful teenager who looked at me with determined cold blue eyes and pinched her lips together, but the little girl who curled herself up in my arms, put her head on my shoulder and fell asleep in my lap.

There was something comforting about the small bed. I put the water down on the nightstand, lay back, turned on her television and channel-surfed until I found the news. I wanted to see if anything new had happened with Alan since I'd been hurt.

First up was an international story, about a bombing in the Middle East. Then a national story about a missing corporate jet over the Rockies. Then what I expected: a photograph of Alan Leightman filled the screen. It shouldn't have surprised me at all, since I was prepared for it, but as I sat in my daughter's bedroom, my wrist aching, listening to a reporter I didn't know read the news that would ruin my client, I felt the sting of tears. A man's whole reputation, after a life dedicated to the law, to doing the just thing, was being destroyed. Nothing, no matter what happened after this, would ever restore his stature, or probably his spirit.

I picked up the phone. I wasn't going to call Noah to tell him that I missed him, or that I'd fallen, or that I was having second thoughts about Mitch, but to tell him that they had it all wrong: Alan couldn't have killed anyone. I knew he couldn't have. And that meant someone else was still out there. Someone dangerous. Someone they had to keep looking for.

I'd already dialed; I heard the first ring.

But what if I did tell Noah all that and he asked me how I knew—what could I say? I still didn't have Alan's permission to speak to the police about him.

I heard the second ring.

No, Alan had been insistent that I not tell anyone. Almost to the point of being threatening. And then, for the first time since the accident, I remembered the man in the shadows under the street lamp in the snow. The man who looked like Alan's bodyguard, Terry Meziac.

"Hello?"

So instead of telling Noah what I called to tell him, I told him how I'd fallen and broken my wrist.

"Are you crying?" he asked.

I nodded, realized he couldn't see me, and was about to say something when he said, "You shouldn't have to cry by yourself. I'm on my way out. Would you like me to bring you something? Did you eat?"

I cried harder.

Sixty-Seven

~~~~~~∽◦⟋⟍◦∼~~~~~~

Most men would have brought chicken noodle soup from one of the ubiquitous coffee shops on New York's Upper East Side. Not Noah. He showed up with a quart of chicken gumbo with big chunks of tender white meat and tiny round slices of okra in a spicy tomato base that brought different tears to my eyes.

While we sat at the kitchen table and ate bowls of the thick Creole stew, I answered all his questions and told him everything but the one thing I wanted to talk to him about the most—how I'd seen Terry Meziac on the street, how I thought he was following me. About the threat Alan Leightman had almost made in my office. About how hard it was to reconcile the Alan who I had been treating for so long with the one who panicked at the thought of me telling anyone that he was in therapy with me, even if it helped him with the police.

Noah had warned me once that if Alan wasn't guilty, then I was in danger. He'd meant that whoever was guilty might want to keep me quiet.

It had never occurred to him that Alan might have other reasons for wanting me kept quiet.

"Are you in much pain?" he asked.

"No."

"I don't believe you."

"Really, no. It was worse before. I took some painkillers."

"The prescription kind?"

"No. But they helped."

"Okay. But if you need something stronger, do you have it?"
I nodded.

We were both quiet for a few seconds.

"I need to tell you something about Alan Leightman. I can't talk about it. I can't tell you why I know. Or anything. Is that all right?"

"It will have to be all right."

"There is no way that Alan Leightman killed those girls."

"I know you believe that, but he confessed. We have evidence proving he watched them online."

"That's not evidence that he killed them, is it?"

He looked at me with a sympathetic smile. "No therapist wants to believe that she could have misread her patient. You can't blame yourself."

"Damn you. Damn you for patronizing me. First of all, I never said he was my patient."

"I am not patronizing you. I'm telling you something you know is right. You don't want him to be guilty. You don't want to have missed the signs. I know how you feel. I understand."

I stared down at the empty bowl. I'd never be able to make food that good.

How could I tell Noah that Alan didn't have any of the personality traits of a person capable of carrying out those four macabre murders without revealing that he was my patient—and without breaking my promise that I would protect Alan's privacy.

Was that the real reason I didn't want to tell Noah? Or had Alan scared me? Had seeing Terry Meziac, or someone who I thought was Terry, scared me?

No, Alan wasn't capable of harming me, even to keep whatever secret he was keeping. I'd worked with him long enough to know that. He'd been excited by risking his reputation and visiting those women online. And at the same time, he was shamed by it. But he had no interest in any of the women he watched. No need to reach out and try to get to know them, help them or hurt them. He didn't see them as his tormentors. He'd been viewing Internet porn long enough to know that even if he got rid of three or four or five Web-cam girls, there would always be more just a few key strokes away. Yes, he needed the Web-cam girls the same way a coke addict needs a fix, but there was nothing violent about his obsession.

Noah got up, took our bowls and relit the flame under the pot. "My mother never believed that I had gotten drunk and smashed up our car when I was nineteen, either," he said.

"This isn't going to work."

"What isn't?"

"Telling me some sweet family story about how your mother didn't believe you were capable of acting out. It won't convince me that I'm wrong."

He didn't argue and he didn't try to finish the story that he'd started to tell. Using a fancy ladle I'd never used before, he refilled our bowls and put them back on the table. The fragrant, piquant smell wafted up in the steam.

"Eat," he said. "Nothing you are saying will convince me."

"Nothing?" I asked after swallowing a spoonful.

"Probably something, darlin'—but it's also probably something that you won't tell me."

I thought about that. Even if there was something I could tell him, I didn't have any facts, either. I only had my educated guess after listening to a man talk about his demons for weeks and weeks.

Yes, Alan was destructive, but only toward himself. He had devoted his whole life to justice. To protecting the innocent.

Who was he protecting now?

I spooned more of the gumbo into my mouth. If I kept eating, I wouldn't be tempted to speak.

"If there is something, you really should tell me."

More gumbo.

"Morgan?"

Okay, maybe I could do this. Maybe I could steer him toward what I'd realized without saying anything that was privileged. "Why those four girls, Noah? Why poison? Why would he go to all that trouble to kill them in front of the whole world? And if he did, why admit it? What did confession buy him? There are a million questions. Do you have answers for them all?"

"Not yet, but we'll get them. I know how you feel, but I don't really care why he confessed. Besides, even if he hadn't, there's enough circumstantial evidence on his computer that most juries would convict him."

"That may be. But he didn't do it."

Before I knew it, I was looking into the bottom of the soup bowl again.

"Do you want more?" Noah asked.

I shook my head. "Three bowls? No." I laughed.

"So how *did* you break your hand?"

"Wrist. I slipped on a patch of ice helping Nina over a snowdrift."

"There have been more broken bones in New York City in the past three weeks than in the past two years combined. You sure it doesn't hurt?"

"Sure. Yesterday it was throbbing, now it's just a dull ache. You get used to pain."

"You can, but why would you want to?"

"Sometimes you have no choice."

I was following the subtext and was sure he was, too. He got up and began clearing the table. It felt luxurious to have him do this.

"You want some tea?" he asked. "I'd suggest coffee but it's late, and I think you need to sleep."

"Thanks. Tea is fine."

He filled the kettle, got out the mugs and the chamomile tea bags, and cut a lemon.

"Honey?"

For a second, I thought he was using the word to address me, then realized what he meant. "Sure." There must have been something in my tone because his hand froze in midair and he held my glance for a few seconds. "You're having a rough time, aren't you?" he asked.

I nodded. "You, too?"

Now he nodded.

We were like dashboard figurines, silently bobbing our heads.

I stood up. Walked to him. Pushed him away from the stove. "Let me. Let me make you tea."

He watched me clumsily take out two tea bags and put one in each mug, then use one hand to spoon in the honey. The kettle started to sing.

It was awkward but I managed it, poured the hot water, stirred it together and squeezed in the lemon. Then I picked up the mug and offered it to him.

"I'm sorry about the other night," I said. "I didn't mean to hurt you. Not you. It wasn't even about you. I know I have a lot of work to do with Dulcie, but I'm going to do it on my own. Mitch isn't part of the solution."

He smiled. "At least you're thinking straight about one thing. Come on, bring your tea. I think you need to get into bed, with the covers pulled way up to your chin, and the television turned on to an old movie." He held out his hand.

Sixty-Eight

I stood by the bed and Noah undressed me—slowly, without any suggestion of sexuality, but with extreme tenderness. He pulled my sweater over my head and then smoothed down my hair where it had gotten ruffled. His hand soothed me like a lullaby. "Where's your nightgown?"

I pointed to the bathroom. "Back of the door." I stepped out of my shoes.

He came back with it and laid it on the edge of the bed. He undid the button and the zipper on my slacks. I started to tug at them with my one good hand, but Noah pushed my hand away and pulled them down. He held my left arm up by the elbow and I stepped out of my pants. I knew I should object and tell him that I could do all this alone, that I didn't need anyone to help me. I meant to say it. But while I was thinking about it, he knelt down and pulled the sock off my right foot, and then my left. It wasn't so bad having him help me.

Standing behind me, he unhooked my bra and helped me pull it over the cast on my right arm. I slipped it off my left. He did not touch my skin with his fingers, but I felt his breath on the back of my neck and felt the rough fabric of his jeans where his left leg touched mine, seemingly inadvertently.

He stayed behind me and lowered the nightgown over my head, holding it while I maneuvered my right arm through the sleeve, and then pulling it down for me.

"Now," he said, folding the comforter back, "get in."

Noah pulled the covers up, then found the remote, turned on the TV and surfed through the channels until he found what he was looking for.

"Perfect," he said, even before I knew what it was.

He was right, though.

Roman Holiday, with Audrey Hepburn and Gregory Peck.

It was exactly the right movie for a night when everything is complicated and there don't seem to be any solutions.

"Before I fall asleep, can you hand me the phone? I need to call Dulcie. I need to start getting this straightened out."

"What are you going to say?"

"I'm going to explain how I feel about—"

"Can I make a suggestion?"

"You can try."

"Tell her you miss her and you are picking her up on Sunday after her performance and that she's coming home with you."

"That might not be the best way to deal with—"

"Morgan, you have spent so much time trying to handle Dulcie and analyze just the right way to deal with her. Some rules won't hurt her. And one of them is that you are the mama and she does what you say. Call."

I started to argue, but there was something so simple about what Noah was saying. He wasn't overthinking it. Wasn't worried about ramifications and psychological issues. Just the truth: I am your mother and there are some things you have to do.

I called.

Noah got up and stood by the window, watching out for

me, I thought, as I kept my eyes on his back and shoulders until my daughter got on the phone.

Dulcie asked me how I felt. I said I was fine. I didn't want to tell her about my accident over the phone. I'd ask Mitch to tell her. Or I'd wait until I saw her. We talked for a few minutes about how her performances had been going. She didn't bring up the television audition. She was a little distant, but agreed to come home without any argument.

"I'm exhausted," I said to Noah when I hung up the phone.

"I bet you are." He walked over to the bedside table, turned off the light, took the remote, set the timer so that the TV would shut off when the movie ended, and then pulled the covers to my chin. "Time to go to sleep now, darlin'."

"Are you going home?"

"No, I'm going to stay in the living room. The couch there is more comfortable than a lot of beds I've slept in. I'll be fine."

"No, that's crazy. Why don't you—"

"Shh. I don't want to roll over and smash into your wrist. Don't worry about me. Just go to sleep. No alarm, no ugly buzzer set to wake you up. I'll do it, just tell me what time, and I'll do it."

I closed my eyes and listened to the movie soundtrack. My wrist still hurt, just enough that I was aware of it, and it was awkward to find the right position for the cast, but I fell asleep more easily than I had in a long time.

Wednesday
Two days remaining

Sixty-Nine

I woke up to the sound of music playing—bluesy jazz that somehow fit a cold winter morning. First I thought it was a CD, but then realized it was Noah, playing on the small upright piano that had been my grandmother's and then my mother's and was now mine, stuck in a corner of the den—not a worthy instrument, but a sentimental one.

He played for ten minutes and I stayed under the warm comforter, thinking about him, about how he'd slept on the couch, thinking mostly about the fact that he'd stayed.

"Good morning," he said when he came in a few minutes later with a mug of steaming coffee that smelled stronger than what I made. Even though coffee was my finest hour in the kitchen, compared to Noah's mine was only passable.

While I drank the coffee, Noah ran my bath, and when it was full and steaming, he helped me into the bathroom.

"I can take my nightgown off."

"Okay, just holler if you need any help."

I pulled the nightgown over my head, eased it over my right arm and then carefully got in the tub, resting my right arm on the ledge, hoping it would stay dry. I'd just sunk down under the hot water when I heard the knock.

"Yeah?"

"Can I come in?"

"Sure."

"If you sit up, I'll wash your hair. I know how tough it is to do this stuff with only one hand."

Grateful, I sat up, leaned forward and shut my eyes.

Noah massaged my scalp with shampoo. It was an utter indulgence to lie there in the fragrant water and have this strong man minister to me. I'd never be able to go to work after this, I thought. After he rinsed my hair, he took the washcloth, squirted my fragrant lime and verbena body gel on it, and then he washed me. It was gentle, helpful, and not erotic at all. And then he was done.

"I'll leave your towel here," he said, putting it on the hook near the bath. "Or do you need help getting out?"

I wasn't sure. "Maybe. I feel a little off balance."

He picked up the towel, threw it over his shoulder, then held out his hand. As soon as I was out of the water, he wrapped me up in the big terry-cloth sheet.

Standing behind me, he patted me dry. I'd never felt so indulged in my life. Then, taking a fresh towel off the rack, he used it on my hair, gently squeezing out the excess water.

It was warm and humid and smelled so good in the bathroom, and Noah's hands were so large and sure of what they were doing. I couldn't remember anyone ever having done these things for me before. My mother certainly had dried me off after bathing me when I was a very young child, but that memory wasn't accessible. Besides, she was my mother, and as avuncular as Noah was being, he was still a man. A man who had once been my lover. He was standing in my bathroom without his shirt on, and under my bath towel I was naked.

Over at the sink, Noah turned on the dryer and worked the hot air through my hair, using his fingers instead of a comb.

"That's dry enough. We have to get you dressed now and make you breakfast," he said, leading me out of my own bathroom as if I were the guest and didn't know where to go next.

We stood in my walk-in closet and Noah unwrapped the towel. Now, finally, his eyes moved over my flesh. I felt the look as if it was a touch, but he didn't acknowledge either his appraisal or my reaction. Instead, he let me stand there naked as he went hunting through the drawers, finding first a black bra and then a pair of black lace underpants.

Then he started to dress me.

Noah pulled the bra up over my right and then my left arm, lifted the straps into place, snugged the cups around my breasts, and then pulled the two ends around my back and hooked it. I let out a long breath. My flesh goose bumped. My nipples hardened. I wondered what he was thinking. If he had any idea how he was making me feel.

He bent over, lifted my right foot, and put it through the leg opening of the panties, then did the same with my left foot. Using both hands, he pulled them up over my calves, my knees, my thighs, my hips, and then smoothed them into place.

I shifted, rotating my hips involuntarily.

Noah was looking through my clothes again. I willed him to turn around and touch me more. Nothing happened until he grabbed a dark gray cashmere sweater off the shelf, turned back to me and manipulated the sleeve over my cast and then up the rest of my arm, adjusting it with his hands, smoothing it with his fingers so that I wasn't sure what created the sensation—his fingers or the soft wool. Then the other arm. Done, he buttoned the sweater from the bottom up and tugged at it so that it lay smoothly around my waist and over my hips.

Once more, Noah went looking through my clothes, now

finding a pair of gray flannel slacks. I put my hand on his shoulder and he pulled them slowly up to my waist. He zipped up the fly and snapped it closed.

Except for his shirt, we were both dressed then, standing in my closet, face-to-face. My hair was still damp. His hands were still on my waist, and then there was no space between us anymore. We were wrapped up in each other, Noah's lips smashed against mine. My good hand was on the back on his neck, pulling him even closer to me.

His hands moved to all the places they had just been, no longer innocent and helpful; now they probed. Over my sweater, cupping my breasts, running up and down my spine, slipping between my thighs, tickling me though the flannel.

There is a kind of want that takes over your consciousness, that blocks out time and logic. Your body responds to it involuntarily. You stop thinking. You don't care about anything but the touching and the feeling. Wings flutter inside your rib cage. You are lifted up.

My hips ground into him, his arms went around my back, his hands grabbed me and pulled me closer, until there was no closer that I could get.

Slowly, in the same order he put my clothes on me, he now took them off. He unbuttoned my pants, unzipped the fly, pulled them down around my ankles and helped me step out of them. Then he got down on his knees, I thought to help me take off my underwear, but he buried his head between my legs, blowing hot breath through the lace, making me squirm and thrust forward.

I gasped. I couldn't get a deep-enough breath. I couldn't get what I wanted fast enough. I wanted it to take forever.

Noah unbuttoned my sweater and pulled it off of me, going very carefully when it was time to manipulate it over the cast.

While he unhooked my bra, I went to work on his jeans with my left hand, fumbling with his fly but managing.

Finally, all of our clothes out of the way, his glorious bare skin was pressed against mine.

"You need to understand…" Noah said in between kissing me on the neck and behind my ear "…that it's not wrong to want to feel something other than pain."

Did I answer? Nod? Say yes, you are right?

I don't think so.

It was all in the movements. All in the sensations. There was nothing I needed to put into words. There were other ways to tell him that he was right—with my lips, with my fingers, the way I opened my legs to him.

We were on the floor and Noah was hard against my stomach and his fingers teased me, making me finally ask him for what I wanted, still not with words but with my legs wrapping around his waist as I pulled him to me and thrust up against him until he slipped inside of me.

I bit into the soft skin of his earlobe and my tongue licked inside his ear. He kissed my lips. Then pulled back.

"This, what we're doing now, it belongs to you."

And it did. Noah making love to me, with all of his body, with all of my body responding, with the smell of him, rosemary and mint flooding my senses, with the softness of his hair on my chest and the heat of his breath on my neck. There was just the two of us in that small space. In a normal room, where there would have been space, the ghosts of my patients and their issues and problems would have come along for the ride. But this journey was closed and tight, and there was no room for anyone but us. The two of us. Our bodies intertwined, my cries mixing with his one deep sigh that reached out and stroked me as softly as the fingers that were fluttering across my back.

And then, there, with only the two of us in a space that could barely contain us, I forgot that it was morning and that it was cold and that there were people who would be waiting for me, or that I was scared to let someone inside. Noah was already inside. It was out of my hands. And then there were no more thoughts.

Seventy

-------~◉◉◉~-------

Dearest,

I am almost done. I thought I would feel some elation at my accomplishment; after all, everything has gone according to plan and I'm still not the one they blame. I should feel something, shouldn't I? A sense of completion, at least? Or some satisfaction at having outsmarted the police?

But there's nothing except a big gaping hole inside of me, and at the very pit of it is some feral forever-hungry animal—jaws wide open—ready to snap at every morsel thrown down. It sinks its sharp, pointed teeth into each chunk of flesh I feed it, and yet its appetite only grows.

Why won't it stop? What else do I have to do to prove that I loved you?

Love is all I had for you. Yes, it was, and yes, it is. Don't even whisper anything else. I would tear my guts out and eat them in front of you to prove how much I love you.

There's nothing left I want to know, nothing left I need to do except make it up to you, make you understand that. There are only two days until your birthday. Eighteen years ago, I could never have guessed at the power of love and now I can only be amazed by its force.

When I lie in bed at night and think about you, what obsesses me still is the shame that you felt. What did I do to you that you never understood what you had, who you were, how much the world was open to you? How did I look right at you and not see that? It must have hurt you so much to have gotten through all the rest of it intact and then to have had me strip you so bare?

These women, who are not what we ever meant for women to be, rely on their bodies, their twisting, writhing, undulating bodies, and do their dances for the eyes that watch, and they never think about who is suffering because of their exhibitionism.

No one takes responsibility and no one can be held accountable because nothing is illegal and nothing is immoral, or if it is, it doesn't matter.

You were a sacrifice to an idea and you were a dream that ended too soon. You should have been exempt and immune. You, of everyone, should not have been a victim of this, not with who I was, not with what I believed and fought for.

But you were and so I claim victims in your name because it's not enough that they die. It's almost enough that others watch while they die. Now all but one have been crossed off, and she will be the most satisfying because once I can cross her off, too, then I can burn the list and turn it into red-hot fire, then ash, and then from ash to dust, and it will all be done.

This I do for you.

Thursday
One day remaining

Seventy-One

It was still dark the next morning when I left the apartment. According to the weather report, it would be yet another day without sun. Overnight, the snow had again dusted the rooftops, the trees, the fire hydrants and the parked cars with one more layer. The details of the landscape were long buried. The street signs were mounded with snow.

Alan Leightman's lies were hiding the real killer of those girls the same way. No one could see past the snow. No one could see past his confession.

Kira's doctor was waiting for me in the lobby of the hospital. We shook hands—awkwardly for me, since it was my left—exchanged a few minutes of conversation about her condition, and then proceeded upstairs.

Alan had given me permission to talk to Kira. The morning he told me he was going to confess, he'd asked me to call Dr. Harris, and if I couldn't get him, to go and be with Kira and help her process the news.

That's all I was doing. Just a few days later. If I was crossing a line, it was a very thin one. I had to talk to her. Someone had to figure out what was going on.

For someone so tall and broad-shouldered, Kira Rushkoff was diminished by the chair she sat in. I wasn't sure I'd ever seen anyone become so small. I had still been expecting to see the handsome woman who never appeared rattled or wrinkled. She was all of those things now. Her hair was dirty and tangled. Her hospital gown was crumpled and stained. Her fingernails were broken and the polish was chipped off. Her eyes couldn't focus and darted around the room.

No matter who she was, I would have known that this woman had only a tenuous hold on reality. One thin, silken thread separated her from being one of the lost girls.

"How are you feeling?"

She shrugged.

"Thank you for agreeing to talk to me."

"Don't thank me yet. I'm not sure I want to talk to you. I think I do, and then I don't. I'm mad at Alan. But I'm in love with my husband."

"I understand that and—"

"What did you want to see me for?" She picked up a green plastic straw, bending it forward and back.

For a second or two, I watched the movement. "I wanted to ask you if you could tell me why Alan confessed to crimes he didn't commit."

"How do you know he didn't commit them?" She squeezed the opening of the straw closed, her fingers tight on the end of it.

"Because I've been working with him long enough to know he is not capable of doing what he's confessed to. The only possibility, the only thing that makes any sense to me, is that he knows, or thinks he knows, who did kill those women and would rather take the fall for it than put the perpetrator through that."

"Noble of him, isn't it?" Her sarcasm only lasted for a moment and then she started crying.

I shot a look at Dr. Harris. He nodded, giving me permission to keep going, and remained where he was.

Her swing from forlorn misery to bitterness to tears didn't surprise me. I knew from Alan how betrayed she'd felt by his addiction. Of all the vices he could have engaged in, he'd chosen the one that she felt was the biggest slap in the face.

"I know how angry you are. And you're right to be angry. Alan degraded you. He broke every promise to you that he ever made."

I was watching her carefully. Her posture became more rigid. She bit her bottom lip, holding herself back from speaking. A few seconds went by. Then she let out a breath and started to speak in the same sarcastic tone. "He deserves to be sitting in that jail. The great and lofty judge, behind bars." Despite the tone, her tears still flowed, a total contradiction.

"I don't know how you stood it for as long as you did. It must have been the worst thing you ever went through in your life. Having your husband turn to the Internet, turn to those young girls, abandoning you—"

"It was terrible."

"I know. Horrendous."

She was staring at me, intently, not bothering to wipe away the tears dripping down her cheeks, or even noticing that her nose was running. "He didn't realize that I loved him all along. I should have told him. I should have touched him. I should have gotten help, sooner."

"He's done some very bad things. Terrible things," I added.

"But he shouldn't be in jail," she whispered. "I want him to suffer and pay for what he did, but he shouldn't be in jail."

"But he thinks he should be. Do you know why?"

She nodded.

"Why?"

She didn't answer.

"Kira, did he confess because he thinks you killed those women and he's protecting you?"

She looked down at the cup in her hands and moved the straw backward and forward again. I watched her movements, waiting to hear her response.

After five minutes, I realized she wasn't going to say anything else, and so I left.

In the elevator, I was struggling to put on my one glove when my cell phone rang. There was no one else in the elevator so I answered it. Allison was calling to tell me my next appointment had canceled, in case I wanted to come in later.

Downstairs the doors opened and I walked through the lobby. I got to the door and realized that I didn't have my glove. Had I dropped it in the elevator? Just outside? I turned to retrace my steps.

Terry Meziac was twenty feet away from me, watching me. I froze. Was he following me? Why? Or was it just a coincidence? Alan's wife was in this hospital. Alan was in jail. Maybe Terry was watching out over Kira for the judge, not watching me at all.

I saw the glove on the ground in front of the elevator. Bent down. When I straightened up he was gone. I spun around, did a quick search of the lobby, but I didn't see him.

Of course he was there protecting Kira Rushkoff. He was a bodyguard.

A bodyguard with a record, Noah had told me.

I hurried outside in time to catch a taxi.

After I gave the driver the address, I turned in the seat, and as we sped off I watched out the rear window, but there was nothing to see.

Seventy-Two

"I know what I thought I was going to get out of her, but I didn't get it."

"You actually *thought* she was going to confess and you were going to get a reprieve for your client," Nina said. "You're sure that he didn't have anything to do with the murders and that he's covering up for someone, and it makes perfect sense that the someone is his wife."

We were sitting in Nina's office. It was too cold to go out, so she'd ordered up lunch—tuna sandwiches on rye bread for both of us. She'd finished hers but I'd only taken a few bites of mine.

"I don't understand love any better than I did forty years ago when I first started studying human psychology. We're such pathetic victims of our emotions."

I didn't want to philosophize. We had to figure out a way for me to ethically talk to the police about Kira.

"How is your wrist?" Nina asked.

I looked down at the white cast. Like the snow, it was going to get gray eventually, long before it was time to remove it.

"It's all right."

"Do you still feel any pain?"

"A little ache. It doesn't matter."

"It does matter. To me. You're in pain and there's nothing I can do about it."

"Oh, there's a point to this. A little parable. Go ahead, O wise one."

"If I could take your pain away, Morgan, I would. You feel that way about Dulcie. I've seen you with her when she's hurt herself. But you're not supposed to feel that way about your patients."

"I can't stand by and watch Alan take responsibility for something he didn't do, that he thinks his wife did—something I'm not even sure his wife was capable of doing. Someone *did* kill those girls, and that person is still out there."

"What is Alan's problem, Morgan?"

"I'm not a neophyte like Blythe, I've been a therapist for years. I don't appreciate the idea that you are handing me."

"Play along. What's his problem?"

"He has intimacy issues. His wife is a real woman. Dealing with her means dealing with his emotions. He doesn't want to do that. So he shies away from sex with her. In the meantime, she can't deal with his distance, so she distances herself further. She was powerful, she made a lot of money, got a lot of press, and she pushed it. She became more powerful, made more money and got more press. She gave herself an excuse. He won't love me the way I want to be loved because I'm not needy enough. I'm too successful. It works. They split off. She works. He has the Net. It allows him gratification without emotional risk. He can find pleasure and excitement without a connection and still not feel as if he is really cheating on his wife. How am I doing?" I asked sarcastically.

Nina's phone rang and I didn't need to look at the clock on the wall to know that her next patient was there.

"I'm trying to help you," she said.

"I know."

But on the walk back to my office I wasn't sure how she could help me. It wasn't until I sat down at my desk that I finally figured out why Nina had asked me those precise questions.

How did she know enough about Alan to know that I had identified with him and felt that, if I could save him, if I could help him, it would mean that I could save myself, too? Not from Internet porn, but from a cold, emotional landscape that I kept running back to whenever I got too close to the sun.

Seventy-Three

The cell where he was being kept was in the Tombs in Lower Manhattan. I'd been there to see patients before, but no one had ever looked more out of place than Alan Leightman did.

"I don't understand why you're here. You're a New York City Supreme Court judge," I said, once we were sitting across from each other in the visitors' room.

"I'm a killer, Morgan. That's why I'm here." He couldn't even make eye contact with me when he said it. "I deserve this." Now he looked at me. That part was true. He didn't think he was entitled to any comfort or leniency. He was a successful man who believed he was a bad boy and should be punished.

"It was kind of you to come down here. You know, you shouldn't feel you failed with me."

"I'm not so sure. My job was to help you see yourself more clearly. To balance the real person you've become with the tortured kid you were. To give you the tools to fight your way out of your addiction. I didn't do any of that. If I had, you wouldn't be taking the blame for this."

He looked away from me again. "That's not what I'm doing."

"You can't convince me of that. I met with Kira."

"That was kind of you. How is she?" He had leaned forward, engaged again. Concerned. More connected to me now.

"I don't know, Alan. There's no way for me to measure—I didn't know her before. But I don't think she's doing very well."

"I want you to be her therapist. I want you to take over."

"I can't do that. Technically, you are still my patient. I can't treat both you and your wife. Besides, she already has a good doctor."

"You're sure he's good enough?"

"Alan, no one is good enough to help Kira with what's bothering her. She knows that you didn't kill anyone and she's racked with guilt that you are doing this to protect her."

His whole body went rigid. "What are you talking about? Protect her?" He was suddenly nervous, twisting around in his seat, looking behind him, then to the side, then to the other side, checking to see if anyone was listening.

"She wanted to punish you. She wanted you to worry that your addiction had driven her crazy. But what if that's all she wanted? What if you're wrong and she didn't kill those women, either? Did you think this through?"

He started to speak, and then stopped. No matter how much pain Alan had been in when he came to my office, no matter how angry he had been or how ashamed he'd felt, I'd never seen him like this. His strong bone structure seemed to have softened. His eyes, which had expressed wisdom even when they had glazed over with embarrassment, were now filled with hopelessness.

"Alan, why won't you talk about this with me?"

He searched for the words, speaking with halts between the phrases. "If Kira…if she…whatever she had to do…everything is my fault. I won't explain it any more than that. Don't ask me to. Don't ask her to. This is just how it has to be, Morgan."

"Your wife is sick over what you've done."

He nodded. "What wife wouldn't be sick to find out her husband had murdered three young women?"

"That's not what I mean."

"I don't want to talk about what you mean."

Somewhere someone cackled and let out a string of expletives. Neither of us tried to talk over it.

"I have put men here," he said.

Our eyes locked.

"Alan, you don't belong here."

"How do you know? Don't you see? I'm where I need to be. There is evidence on my computer that I visited those women. Evidence on those women's computers that I contacted them. That I asked them to use those tainted products. If I didn't do this, Dr. Snow, who else but my wife could have used my e-mail account? Who else knew that I visited those sites? That I had, indeed, watched those women over and over."

"But what if you are wrong? What if she's just trying to make you think she did it. What if—"

"Dr. Snow, listen to me." His voice was low and urgent. "There is proof on my computer that I visited those sites on days and times when I did not go there. Clearly Kira went there. She followed my trail. She watched those women. I told you that weeks ago. There is proof on those women's computers that I sent them e-mail asking them to use the items that were poisoned. What don't you understand about what I'm telling you?"

I ignored the sarcastic snipe. The pressure he was under excused him.

"Alan, do you understand that the police won't keep working this case as long as you are here? If your wife didn't do this, and if you didn't do this, then there's someone out there who did kill those women. I know what I'm asking of you, but what if I'm right? What if you go to jail and I'm right and whoever has done this does it again? Then you really will have someone's blood on your hands. You'll be a judge responsible for a murder. How will you live with that?"

He shook his head. "And what if you are wrong? What would happen if Kira went on trial? Can you imagine what that would do to her? To her reputation? Her stature? Her sanity? It's been hard on her. She's given up so much to be Kira Rushkoff, Esquire." His voice was pleading again. "She doesn't have anything left to give up.

"What happened to your wrist?" he asked, suddenly noticing my arm.

I shrugged. "I slipped."

"Is it broken?"

I nodded.

"It will heal. In six, seven weeks." There was a weight to his words. And he was looking off into the distance as if he could see the day when my cast would come off and he knew where he would be by then, what would have happened to him.

"You can't talk to the police about any of this. You understand that, don't you? No matter how sure you are of what you think, I will not allow it. You do not want to test me on this, do you understand?"

"Are you threatening me, Alan? Are you trying to scare me?"

"If that's what it takes, yes. You will not discuss this with anyone. Is that understood?"

"Do you have Terry Meziac following me?"

Like his wife had done earlier that day, Alan stopped answering.

The frustration I felt made me want to scream and cry at the same time. "I want you to know I had no intention of talking to anyone without your consent. You didn't have to scare me, too. But you have."

And then for the first time since I'd gotten there, I saw Alan's mouth lift. His smile was the saddest I'd ever seen.

"Call him off, Alan. I won't bother you anymore. You're on your own."

Seventy-Four

~~~

The whole way back to the office, I forced myself not to turn around to see if anyone was following me. When I got out in front of the office, I didn't look over my shoulder to search for Terry Meziac. I knew that even if he was following me, he wasn't there to hurt me, but to scare me. And no one could do that to me anymore.

I was getting a cold and my throat was sore. I wanted to go home and crawl into bed. Instead, I popped a throat lozenge, made some tea and saw my next patient. And then the next. I was waiting for Blythe when Allison called. "I forgot to tell you, the day you were out—yesterday—Blythe canceled, and I gave a new patient her spot. She's on her way up."

Moments later, Amanda stood at the door to my office, snow dripping off her boots and melting in her hair. There were bright spots in the middle of her cheeks. She couldn't seem to cross the threshold.

"You can come in," I said, encouraging her. "It's okay. I'm really glad to see you."

Tentatively, she took a small step forward. Her skinny body

was wrapped up in a big black down coat, and she had her suede boots on her feet. She left melting snow in her wake.

Once inside, she froze again, holding her knapsack close to her chest and looking at me as if asking me to get up and usher her farther in.

"Take off your coat—it's warm in here."

She took one cautious step after another, as if she were walking on a bed of nails. Finally, she made it inside and over to the couch, where she shrugged out of her coat and sat on it. She went through that whole maneuver without letting go of the knapsack.

"Me being here, it's a secret, right? Like at school?"

"Yes. Completely."

Despite my response, Amanda didn't relax.

"Do I have to pay you?"

"We can work that out later, okay?"

She nodded.

"This is harder than you thought it was going to be, isn't it?"

She nodded again.

"What did you think it was going to be like?"

"I was hoping that somehow you'd know what I wanted to tell you, and I wouldn't have to say anything."

I laughed. "I think all my patients wish that I could read their minds and they wouldn't have to talk. But I can't, so you're going to have to tell me. I can promise you, though, that I won't be shocked or surprised, and I won't judge you."

"I know that from what goes on at school."

I nodded and waited. Amanda still hadn't looked around at all. Her fingers had not loosened from the knapsack strap. A few seconds went by. And then a few more. She started to play with the tab on the zipper, teasing it up an inch and then rezipping it.

As much as I wanted to coax her, I didn't want to scare her off. Not when she had come this far.

Finally: "This is really complicated, Dr. Snow. It has to do with things that no one knows about." She frowned. "Well, some people know but…"

"Do your parents know?"

She shook her head adamantly.

"Okay. They won't find out. Not unless you want to tell them yourself."

She wasn't listening to me anymore but staring intently at a glass box that hung on the wall behind my desk. Inside was an iridescent blue butterfly, a gift from Nina.

"That's weird," she whispered.

"What is?"

"That you have a butterfly like that."

"Why?"

"Do you like them?"

I nodded. She looked around my office now and noticed the butterfly print on the wall and the glass butterfly paperweight on my desk. Her expression became tortured. Without saying anything, she stood, reached down for her coat, muttered a few unintelligible words and ran out of my office.

Seventy-Five

~~~~~~~~~~~~~~~~

In retrospect, there are always reasons for what we do, if we stop and examine them. Following Amanda that afternoon was not something I stopped to think about. Now I know that I went after her because I knew she was deeply troubled, and I was afraid for her. Also because of her age. She was just a few years older than my daughter, and I wanted to protect her the same way I wanted to protect Dulcie.

It was some sort of karmic exchange. If I took care of Amanda, then someone would take care of Dulcie if she were ever in this kind of distress. But it was also the horror on her face when she saw the trapped butterfly on my office wall that made me get up and follow her. What made her respond like that? What kind of trouble was she in that she had made her way all the way to my office to talk about something and then left?

By the time I reached the street, she'd reached the corner, walking west toward Fifth Avenue. I hurried to catch up to her, forgetting for the time being about my wrist and the doctor's admonition to be more careful on the treacherous city sidewalks.

"Amanda!"

She turned, saw me and was about to run, but the light changed and she was trapped.

I was at her side in four steps and put my left hand on her shoulder, not actually holding her back, but suggesting it.

"Can I walk with you?" I asked.

"I guess."

When the light turned green, we crossed Madison Avenue and continued west, walking in silence, passing the Rita Ford music box store, which was one of my daughter's favorite places in the city. Amanda's teeth were chattering, either from nerves or the cold. Her coat wasn't buttoned up, she wasn't wearing gloves and her head was bare.

Halfway down the block, we reached a set of wide doors. "Come in here for a while. You can warm up. We can just sit. You don't have to talk about anything. I'll just keep you company."

Amanda followed me through the doors, into an unimposing lobby.

"Have you ever been here?" I asked.

"It's where I went to Sunday school," she said.

We turned left and went through another door and into the main sanctuary of Temple Emanuel.

"I went here, too," I said. *And my daughter goes here now,* I thought but didn't say. As much as I wanted Amanda to feel comfortable with me, I didn't want her to think of me as a parent, but rather someone she didn't have to keep her secret from.

The sanctuary is almost the whole width of a city block and has a lovely stained-glass rose window above the entrance that washes the interior with soft red and blue light. I slid into one of the pews not far from the altar and looked up at the familiar golden doors that protected the Torah. Amanda took the seat beside me.

The quiet and emptiness of the temple was soothing, and I hoped it would calm Amanda.

We had only been there two or three minutes when the first sonorous tones of the organ wafted out and surrounded us. Someone was practicing, but flawlessly and as Beethoven's music filled the space, Amanda became less tense.

"It's really peaceful here, isn't it?"

She nodded as she started to play with the zipper on the knapsack she was once again hugging to her chest.

"Is there something in there you wanted to give me?" I spoke softly, hoping my words would meld with the music and not alarm her. She didn't respond. As if talking to a three-year-old who needed to be cajoled, I said, "Why don't you let me have it, Amanda."

She looked at me. I attempted what I hoped was an encouraging smile. Finally, Amanda unzipped the knapsack and pulled out a clear plastic square. Now the satchel was abandoned, useless, no longer important to her. The thing clutched in her hands held all the value.

"Do you know who Simone is?" she asked.

"No."

"None of the guys told you about her?" She seemed incredulous.

"No. Is she a friend of yours?"

"We were best friends."

"Did something happen to her?"

Amanda sighed and then sucked her lips in so that they disappeared. "They said that it was an overdose." The weight of the words defeated her and she slumped down farther in her seat.

"What kind of overdose?"

"Pills and vodka. But the thing is she never…we never did drugs."

"When did she die?"

"Last June. It wasn't an overdose. Well, it was, but it wasn't an accident the way it was reported." As hesitant as she had been to speak before, now she was in a rush to get it all out. I was having trouble understanding all the words over the music.

"What do you mean it wasn't an accident?"

"She'd been depressed and miserable for like a whole year, and she finally told me that she was going to do it. She even told me what the note was going to say. All the day before, I tried to talk her out of it, but I couldn't. I didn't know what else to do, so I threatened to go to her mother. I told her I'd help her find someone to talk to. I told her I'd get the name of a therapist that a girl in our class was seeing. She said okay. She promised me that she wouldn't do it. I called Robin that night. I got the therapist's number. The therapist even gave me an appointment for the next day and said he'd give me a break on the price. He was only going to charge me fifty dollars and I had way more than that in my savings account. I called Simone back—it was still only seven at night. She sounded much calmer. She promised me that she really was okay. That she'd go with me." Amanda had started to cry.

I felt more maternal than was good for me if I was going to be her therapist, but I didn't want to keep asking her questions and remain at a distance. I wanted to gather her up in my arms and promise her that I'd help her, and do whatever I could to make her pain go away.

"What was bothering her, Amanda?"

She looked down at the thing she still held in her hands. "This. What we did. It got around. Her mother found out. She was so embarrassed."

"With the other kids?"

"No. With her mom. She just wanted her mom to, y'know, to try to listen or understand what had happened or something…" She was running her finger up and down the spine of the plastic case.

"Do you want me to play it?"

She nodded but didn't hold it out to me yet. "Before… first…I have to explain." She took a deep breath, as if she were getting ready to dive underwater, and then launched into her secret, speaking now at an even faster pace so that her words blurred the way scenery does when you pass it by on a train going more than one hundred miles an hour.

"We just wanted the guys to see that we could do what the other girls did. I knew how to use the digital camera. I'd made movies before. It didn't seem like it would be too complicated. We decided that we needed to watch what they were watching and copy it. You know, we'd just do what those girls did and then we'd send it to them. They'd see that we could do the same stuff and they'd want to be with us. Simone liked Timothy. She wanted him to, y'know, be with her. I wanted… well, that doesn't matter. So we had to watch first to know what to do, y'know? It was a little gross when we first tried to copy the Web-cam girls, but the more we did it, the easier it got. And the more we liked it. And then…when—" She broke down again and I let her cry, watching her shoulders heave. I put my hand out and rubbed her back.

"It took us a while to get, comfortable with each other. It was hard at first to be naked. And it was weird to touch each other. But then we got into it." Big sigh. "We liked it. And we didn't know what that meant." She stopped. I thought this was the end of the confession. I could see the two girls, playing at being lesbians for the sake of the camera and discovering that it felt good.

"It means that people can give each other pleasure. That if we open ourselves up to it, many of us would discover that some things just feel good no matter who does them to us."

Amanda actually seemed to hear me. She nodded. "We didn't know if it meant we were lesbians or not." The trance was over for the time being. "No boys had ever touched us. We went down on them. They let us do that. But what Simone and I did to each other on the tape, no one did to us. And it felt good. That didn't mean anything, did it?"

"No, sweetheart." I heard myself slip and use the endearment. It didn't matter, all the tenderness in the world wouldn't hurt Amanda right now. "It didn't mean that you were lesbians. Sexuality is very complicated, especially when you're first discovering it. Is that what Simone thought? That's not why she took the pills, is it?"

It couldn't be, I thought. We were living in New York in the twenty-first century. Surely Simone's parents would have been able to cope with a lesbian daughter.

"No. No, that's not why. But it made it weirder. It made the whole thing more of a secret. And then we did it sometimes just us, without the camera. To practice, we said. And then Simone saw the cutter. That's when I got scared. I mean, none of the guys were into that, but Simone liked it. It might have been okay, though…it still might have been okay…"

"Amanda, honey, what happened?"

She closed her eyes. "First you need to promise you won't tell anyone. No one at school knows this is me. Or that it's Simone. You can't show it to anyone at school. I mean the teachers. Timothy knows. But he is the only person who does."

"Okay."

"Do you promise?"

I looked at her solemnly. "Yes. As God is my witness."

"We…we copied what the Web-cam girls were doing and then we sent the movie to Timothy. We didn't tell him then who we were. He showed it to Hugh and Barry. They couldn't recognize us. We were wearing masks, like one of the Web-cam girls. That's where we got the idea. We were going to tell him afterward. First we wanted them to think that these girls were hot. And to want them. But before we had a chance to tell him it was us, after just like two days, we started hearing about it at school. Timothy had e-mailed it to Hugh and Barry and they had e-mailed it to a bunch of other guys. And everyone was passing it around and talking about it. All the guys. Everyone was watching it and trying to guess who the girls were. It got really awful. Someone downloaded it onto one of the computers at school. I don't know how many people finally saw it." She blinked back tears. She was too busy explaining to stop and cry.

"Timothy got suspended for two weeks. So did a few other guys. The headmaster threatened to expel them if they didn't tell who the girls were. But they couldn't tell. We'd never told them. They really didn't know. At least not then."

"What happened next?"

"We were safe. Or we thought we were. But then Simone's mom found the video file on her computer. She recognized her and went crazy. She grounded her and started picking her up at school every day and dropping her off every morning and she took away her phone and her Internet connection. She made her life miserable. She threatened to go to the headmaster if Simone didn't tell her who the other girl was. But she wouldn't. That made her mother even crazier. She saw what we'd done like it was this major crime that we'd—that Simone—had committed against her. Against *her*. Like Simone had done it to her on purpose, and she kept talking to her about how demeaning it was and how pathetic we were…I mean, I know it would have bothered most parents, but she acted as if Simone had done it just to embarrass her. But we didn't. We did it because we wanted to get the guys to pay attention to us. To *us*. Not to those fake girls. We wanted them to know we could do the same stuff."

She swallowed another sob. I could tell from how fast her words were coming that she was almost done and that she needed to get it all out now, as if it was poison rotting her insides. "Dr. Snow, you know about the girls who are getting killed? The Web-cam girls?"

"Yes."

"The ones who got killed…all of them are the girls we copied. The same ones. And in the same order that we copied them in our movie. They've all gotten killed. Except the last one. The fifth one. The girl who wore the mask."

Seventy-Six

Finally, Amanda held out the CD, offering it to me. I took it but she did not let go. "You can't show it to anyone, though. You're the only one who can see it."

"If I am going to help save the last girl, I'm going to have to show it to the police."

"Can't you just tell them about it?"

"I don't think so. Will you let me show it to them?"

She shook her head. "My parents don't know."

"How about this? Let me take it for now. You think about it overnight. Tomorrow morning, I'll call you and get your permission before I do anything."

She was shaking her head. "There's no way it will stay a secret if you give it to the police. Do you know what it would be like if anyone found out this was me? What my parents would do to me?"

The organ music stopped. It wasn't silent right away—the chords lingered—and then it was so quiet in the temple that I could hear Amanda's breathing.

"It's our fault. Simone's fault and mine. If we hadn't made this, Simone wouldn't be dead, and none of those women would be dead now."

"No, it's not your fault. You didn't do this on purpose. You didn't want anyone to get hurt."

"But so many people have been."

She heard the footsteps before I did and was up and walking toward the front doors in seconds. I grabbed my coat and, holding the disk, rushed after her.

"Wait," I said.

"Who's there?" A man's voice echoed from behind me.

I didn't answer as I rushed after Amanda.

"Can I help you?" he called.

Seventy-Seven

❧∼

I'd been with Amanda for fifty-five minutes and only had a few minutes left to get back to the office for my next patient. Not long enough to figure out the ramifications of what Amanda had told me, or even to ask myself what my real obligations were. I wanted to call Noah right then and tell him everything. But could I?

There is nothing more difficult than doing the wrong thing for the right reason. I had an obligation to a human being who had entrusted me with her secret. And I had an obligation to try to save a life if it was in my power to do that.

I didn't get another break until seven that night, at which point I popped some vitamin C pills, hoping they'd do something for my cold, made some tea and sat down in front of my computer with the CD Amanda had given me.

The institute was quiet but not empty; two therapists had group sessions in progress and Nina had patients until nine. I shut my door, returned to my desk, looked for the CD icon on my desktop and then clicked on it.

There's not much about the Web and pornography that those of us at the institute don't know about. We have to understand what stimulates our patients. We need to know what their addictions are. I'm aware that there is film online of every kind of perverse and sadistic fetish known to the human imagination. But of all the porn I've seen, I'd never wept watching it until I viewed Amanda's movie. My heart ached for these two beautiful sixteen-year-old girls who were so confused and desperate for the boys at school to notice them that they'd done this.

There were four segments, each identified simply with a red Roman numeral on a black screen.

Number one had to be Simone because she had blond hair and Amanda's hair was dark, almost as dark as Dulcie's. I couldn't see any of Simone's face because she was wearing a red silk mask over her eyes. Her hand was between her legs and she was using a dildo on herself.

The scene cut and there was Amanda in a blue silk mask, using a dildo.

I had a frightening sense of déjà vu. I focused. What was bothering me?

It was the masks.

I stopped the CD.

Nina once told me there are no coincidences. But this? It couldn't be. There had to be other women online who did their Web cast wearing masks. Blythe couldn't be the only one. As soon as I had watched the whole thing, I'd do a search. There would be dozens of women wearing masks. Besides, Blythe had been very specific, she'd worn a butterfly mask: but these were simple silk eye masks without any anthropomorphic theme.

I hit the play button.

The second segment showed both girls kissing slowly, sensually. It was difficult for me to look at these young women, only a few years older than my daughter. I knew they'd started doing this to entice the boys to look at them, a desperate ploy to get noticed, but it had already turned into something more.

The scene cut and they were massaging each other, smoothing oil over bare backs and long legs, touching each other in intimate places. It was so clear to me that by the time they had made this segment, they were becoming confused by their feelings for each other.

The first segment had been awkward and forced, the girls reminded me in a sick way of Dulcie dressed up in my high-heeled shoes and my pearls, wearing my lipstick, when she was only six. But now there was an authenticity to Amanda and Simone's movements. They had forgotten about the Web cam, they had forgotten about the boys who had never noticed them in the first place. These sex-starved, attention-starved teenagers, who had given boys blowjobs but never been kissed, were kissing each other and experiencing sexual tenderness for the first time.

How could I keep watching?

I was invading their privacy, spying on a moment that should have belonged only to them. That it had been sent out over the Internet by countless high school boys only made it that much more wrenching. That Simone had killed herself over it made it almost impossible to tolerate.

At least they had felt this for each other.

On the screen, they were still touching, their skin glistening in the soft light. A hand on a breast. Fingers grasping fingers. A foot arched against a hip. A neck bent over a stomach. Hair covering a face. Then Simone moaned against Amanda's chest and orgasmed.

The third segment was of Simone cutting herself. The razor blade glinted in the light as she tentatively slid it across the front of her thigh. The first time, she didn't manage to actually make the cut. She didn't manage it the second time, either.

For a second, she looked up into the camera, the masked face placid and inhuman. Except for the mouth. It quivered. It gave her away. It looked like a little girl's mouth.

I hit Stop again.

My fingers dug into my temples. My eyes closed. The image remained. I didn't want to see any more. I didn't want to look at this poor little lost girl.

There were so many of them.

I had treated some, had helped some; others I had failed, the way once upon a time I had failed my mother. With all my heart, I swore my daughter would never be lost like that.

Had Simone's mother felt the same overprotectiveness?

Had Amanda's?

Now there were two girls left to save: Amanda and the last Web-cam girl, who was still alive somewhere.

I hit the play button and let the rest of the cutting scene play out.

Finally, the fourth segment began. I hoped there would be a clue to who this fourth girl was.

Simone appeared again, but now her simple blue mask had been replaced with an elaborate butterfly mask and for the first time she spoke, whispering to the camera as she stood there playing with the buttons of the modest powder-blue men's shirt that was tucked into her tight blue jeans.

"You're watching, aren't you? You're waiting for me to get undressed for you. For me to show you my breasts and my pussy. I know how much you want to see them. To see me naked and with my legs spread for you. For your cock. Well, you're going to have to wait. Oh, I'll get undressed for you. I'll do all kinds of things for you. But you have to be patient."

She undid the top button, and then the next, now revealing a lavender lace bra.

"Are you touching yourself? Are you sitting there and stroking your cock? Is it hard yet? I wish I could see it. I wish I could lean over and put my lips around it."

She smiled a secret smile into the camera. It was the look of a wise and weary hooker. I'd seen it on the women I worked with who were in prison for solicitation, women who know what it is like to give and give and get nothing back.

I didn't think that Simone had figured out this script herself. It must have been what the butterfly girl she and Amanda had copied had said.

Was this what Blythe did online?

I needed to call her. There were other butterfly girls out there, no doubt. But what if I was right? I wouldn't tell Blythe how I knew what she did, I'd just ask her.

Amanda came on the screen and started to strip the same way Simone had. But I didn't need to see anymore. She'd told me they had copied five girls. One who had used a dildo. Two who had used massage oil and made love to each other. Another who had been a cutter. And the last.

The stripper in the butterfly mask.

I dragged the CD icon to the trash, removed it from the drive, and then replaced it in its case. It had been hidden, Amanda had told me. Why hadn't she just destroyed it, I'd asked as I walked her back up Fifth to find a taxi.

"It was all I had left of Simone," she said. "Timothy helped me hide it." Her tears came again. "I couldn't take a chance and keep it on my computer. But I needed to know it was somewhere in case I ever wanted to see it again."

Now I held it the way she had, close to my chest, carefully.

I opened my address book and found Blythe's number. Then dialed it. When the machine answered, I left a message asking her to call me.

I didn't tell her it was urgent.
I wasn't sure it was.
I shouldn't have taken that chance.

Seventy-Eight

$\sim\!\!\!\sim\!\!\!\sim\!\!\!\sim$

Nina wasn't in her office when I went looking for her. The lights were off and her door was closed. I thought she had patients that night until nine. Back at my desk, I called her at home, and then on her cell phone. But she didn't pick up. Restless, I shut off my own office lights and left.

The street lamps cast a soft glow over the snowdrifts. I stood on the steps of the institute and let the freezing air wash over me, breathing it in, letting it dissipate the lingering smell that overheated rooms get in the winter. I knew that I should turn around, check that I wasn't being followed, but I refused to give in to paranoia.

I walked to the corner, not sure what I should do. Go home? Get something to eat? Keep calling Nina? Try Noah?

No. I couldn't see him or talk to him. Not until I knew what to do about the CD. I wouldn't be able to hold back from telling him what I'd found out. One look at me and he'd guess that I was keeping something back. I knew I was going to have to tell him, but I needed Nina to help me figure out how I could do that without risking or compromising Amanda.

I hailed the first cab I found and gave the driver the theater's address. I knew Dulcie was coming home over the weekend, but I needed to see her sooner.

I stood in the back of the theater and watched my daughter up on the stage. *The Secret Garden* was a seemingly innocent story. A child reading it can't guess at the hidden messages that I, as an adult and a psychotherapist, saw so clearly.

Did Dulcie understand the metaphor of the overgrown garden, untended, unruly, abandoned? Did she guess that it represented a woman's sexuality, ignored by all who passed the high, ivy-covered walls?

Dulcie stood inside the garden set, showing it to the young man for the first time. My daughter's face shone with delight—a delight that was not hers but belonged entirely to the character she portrayed. How did she do that? What metamorphosis did she put herself through to become the fictional Mary Lennox?

Against my will and wishes, I wasn't seeing Dulcie on the stage but Amanda and Simone, undergoing their own metamorphosis.

The audience broke out in applause for my daughter and she preened.

What did the boys do for the two girls who stripped down and played at being lovers so well it became true?

Dulcie didn't skip a beat as the applause finally died down, and she returned to the scripted dialogue.

I needed to know I could protect her from what Amanda's and Simone's parents had not been able to protect them from.

Backstage, I wrote my daughter a note, telling her how proud I was of her, how much I loved her performance, how happy I was she was coming home on Sunday, and that I missed her. Beside the note, I laid a bouquet of pink sweetheart roses I'd bought for her at the deli around the corner from the theater.

Seventy-Nine

Dulcie called me from her cell at ten-thirty, on her way back to Mitch's, and thanked me for the flowers.

"Mom?"

"Yes, sweetheart?"

"Are you okay?"

"Sure, why?"

"I don't know. But I keep feeling like something is wrong. It's kind of the way you describe it when something's wrong with me and you feel it, you know?"

I nodded. "Yes, honey, I know."

"So are you okay?"

I decided not to wait until the weekend and told her about my wrist. When I was done, I heard her give a little sigh.

"It was really strange. I kept feeling like something hurt, but it didn't really."

"Oh, baby, I'm sorry. That must have been scary."

"It was, but kind of interesting, too. Could you do it with your mom? I bet you could. I bet it's something else we inherited."

"I don't know." I bit my bottom lip and waited to hear what other amazing thing she was going to say.

"We're here, Mom. I'll talk to you tomorrow. Hope your wrist feels okay." And then before I had a chance to wish her a good night, she clicked off.

I walked into the apartment and played my messages before I even took off my coat. I was expecting calls from Blythe and Nina. There was only one call and it was from Noah, asking me to call him back. I wanted to but I didn't trust myself to talk to him yet.

With nothing to do but wait for Nina to call, I went to the corner of the den where I kept my sculpture. I desperately wanted to chip away at the stone, become lost in the rhythm of the mallet hitting the chisel. But you can't sculpt with only one good hand.

I rotated the piece on its base.

The form escaping was rough and amateurish. That I had less talent than desire for this art form had bothered me once, but not anymore. It had been either accept my limitations or give up the one thing that helped me escape the voices in my head: my patients' fantasies, fetishes, pains, perversions, deep losses and thwarted hopes.

I clicked on the television.

Finally, at twelve-twenty, Nina called.

She'd been at a concert at Lincoln Center and then out to a late supper. I listened to see if she sounded tired. I didn't want to tax her, even though I desperately needed to talk to her. Relieved to hear the energy in her voice, I told her what had happened that afternoon with Amanda and about the CD she'd given me and what was on it.

"Simone?" Nina asked when I finished. "Do you know Simone's last name?"

"Alexander," I said. "I think that's what she told me. Why?"

"Do you have the CD with you?"

"Yes. I didn't want to leave it in the office."

"I'll be there in fifteen minutes."

"Nina, it's after twelve-thirty."

"I have to see it for myself, Morgan. I have to be sure. You don't know whose daughter she is, do you?"

I didn't.

Eighty

Nina didn't waste any time when she walked into my apartment. She didn't stop to take off her coat or drop her bag in the foyer. She tracked snow in on her boots as she walked across the tile floor and into the den, where she sat down in front of my computer.

"Put it on, please," she said.

I pressed the play button and she leaned forward, still in her coat, still holding her bag.

Simone came on the screen in her red butterfly mask and I heard a soft "oh" escape from my mentor's lips. I turned away from the screen and looked at her.

Nina's forehead was pulled tight with tension.

"What is it?"

Nina didn't respond. She was riveted to the screen, watching the action on the computer. After the second segment she turned to me. "You can shut it off, Morgan. I don't need to see any more." Her voice cracked.

I knelt down so that I was on her level and put my good arm around her. We did not embrace often—kisses on the cheek, a hand on an arm, but Nina and I were not physical women. Not touchers. I smelled her spicy perfume and felt her body tremble. "Simone Alexander is Stella Dobson's daughter, Morgan. She died of an accidental overdose last June."

"Based on what Amanda told me, I don't think it was accidental. I think Simone killed herself."

And then I remembered something that couldn't be a coincidence at all. Something both Nina and I had known for weeks, but that hadn't meant anything until now.

Stella Dobson was interviewing Blythe for a book she was working on. A book about women and pornography.

"Blythe—" I started.

Nina had already thought of it. "There has to be a connection. Blythe is in danger and so is Stella. We have to get to them."

I didn't want to question Nina's assumption about Stella Dobson. She was a feminist heroine who still mattered in a postfeminist world.

"How do you know that Stella isn't the one who—"

She shook her head. "You're getting carried away. Stella's a brilliant, driven woman who has devoted her whole life to helping women. What we have to do, Morgan, is *warn* her."

Eighty-One

~~~~~~

While I made coffee, trying to focus on the ratio of grounds to water, Nina called Stella. It was, by then, almost two in the morning and Stella wasn't answering the phone. That wasn't a surprise. Many people let their machines pick up in the middle of the night. My own phone had rung twice since ten-forty-five that night, and while I'd checked the caller ID both times—Noah—I hadn't answered either call.

Nina left a message, asking her old friend to please call whenever she got the message. She left her cell number, even though she told me when she got off the phone that Stella already had it.

I poured the coffee. "We need to talk to the police," I said.

"We can't. You can't. You know you can't."

I sighed. When it came to the police, Nina took the fine line and then doubled and tripled it, so that it wasn't that fine at all, but was thick and much harder to cross. We'd been through this before.

I didn't want to have an old argument with her again. Not that night. Not at two in the morning. "Nina, three women have died. A fourth almost died. How can you justify my keeping silent?"

She waved me off. "Amanda is your patient. You can't call Noah."

"We have to do something."

"As long as you leave Amanda—and the CD—out of it."

"If I don't give them the CD, they won't have anything to go on." My throat hurt, my nose was running. It was late and I was exhausted. But I couldn't give up. There had to be some way to do the right thing without crossing that damn line. "What if we can get Stella to go to the police and tell them about what Amanda and her daughter did?"

"That we can do. When we see her, when we tell her what's happening, we'll advise her to call the police. To tell them about the CD, about Simone, about the Web-cam girls Simone and Amanda copied. All right? Will that work? Isn't that better?"

It was a compromise. One that I thought I could live with.

**Friday
The final day**

next to Dulcie, it on the harder than I expected it to.

Protecting everyone had been all that mattered to me. Dulcie. Nina. Blythe. My patients.

Eighty-Two

━━━◦⟋⟍⟍◦━━━

Noah Jordain had slept like crap. He'd first called Morgan at ten-forty-five and when she didn't pick up he'd had a patrol car in her neighborhood check with her doorman to make sure she was upstairs and safe. When they reported back that the doorman had buzzed her and she was okay, he knew what the unanswered call meant. As a very conscientious therapist, she always checked her messages. So that meant she was avoiding him. But why?

That question had kept him awake long into the night. He really was tired of her disappearing on him. Of how her work kept getting in their way. Fine, if she didn't trust him, he'd accept that. He'd walk away from her. He could take the hint.

A half hour after waking up, he was at the gym, where he worked out for as long as he could stand it, then he took a subway uptown. It was three blocks from the train stop to the station house. He trudged through the snow, kicking at it.

Anyone watching would have thought that he was, like millions of other New Yorkers, sick of the relentless storms, tired of wearing boots and climbing over snowdrifts. But that wasn't it. He was annoyed that Morgan was avoiding his calls, and, beyond the personal disappointment he felt, the way she was acting reinforced his own conviction that Alan Leightman was lying about being the killer.

Damn. What did Morgan know about her patient that she wasn't telling him? Damn her ethics. He needed the information she had.

At the office, Jordain listened to his messages and searched his e-mail at the same time. There were all kinds of reasons a woman might not answer her phone or return his calls. But he knew Morgan, and there was only one reason. She was avoiding him because she had found out something she wasn't at liberty to tell him, and she was not going to give herself the chance to slip.

At that moment he was sure that he never wanted to see her again.

He picked up the yellow pad with his notes on the Web-cam killings and read through them all again. There had to be something there. Something he'd missed. One tiny piece of information that would make a difference.

All the poisons—the one used in the lubricant, the one applied to the Band-Aids and the one mixed into the massage oil—were too easily obtained to be traceable. The Atropine in the lubricant was in eyedrops available in every hospital and by prescription, used by millions of patients. The nicotine on the bandages could have been brewed from a few ordinary cigarettes, or from plants. And the cyanide in the massage oil was used by dozens of professionals, including jewelers and gardeners. The tampered products themselves were all major drugstore brands.

There was nothing there.

All of the items used by the Web-cam girls had been found in their apartments, but the police hadn't been able to find any boxes or envelopes, which might have yielded important information. They must have gotten the gifts weeks or days before and thrown it all out.

Tania, the only one of the girls who'd survived, didn't know anything about the oil ZaZa had used. Yes, a fan had sent it as a gift, but she hadn't asked any specifics. It wasn't the first time that ZaZa had been sent gifts. Many of the girls had post office boxes—in fact, Global Communications recommended it. Clients liked to send presents and photos. It was good business to encourage them. Besides, it wasn't unheard of for women to receive expensive jewelry from the men who'd fallen in lust with them online.

Butler stood in his doorway. "Hey, boss, you busy?"

"What's up?"

"I just got a call. The computer in Leightman's office at NYU is clean. No e-mail to any of the victims' e-mail addresses."

"What the hell? I thought Fisher said—"

She continued: "But we have found the computer the e-mail came from. It's in the NYU library."

"So Leightman used the computer in the library?"

"Either that or someone who found out his password was in the library using his e-mail address."

Eighty-Three

~~~⤜᥍᥍⤛~~~

Dearest,

Happy birthday.

Ironic isn't it? To even use the word *happy?* But truly, soon we will be happy because we'll be together and then we'll know some form of happiness, or if not that, then re-lief—maybe peace, at least peace.

Soon all just punishments will have been meted out and everyone will have been held accountable for the damage that they have done. There isn't anything left that matters to me but this: that you, my sweetest heart, have been avenged.

I can close my eyes and I can see us, not at the end, not when I lost you, but before that.

There was one day at the beach, four, maybe five sum-mers ago. It was hot and you were lying in the sun, soak-ing it up, and I was swimming, and when I got out of the water I stood over you and flicked drops of cold water on your legs and your stomach and your arms, and you laughed.

In my mind, in this memory, you are squinting in the

bright sunlight, and you put your hand up to shield your eyes, and the drops of seawater flying through the air catch the light and shine like broken crystals as they fall onto your skin. Liquid light like your laugh.

I knelt down beside you and leaned over and kissed you, and you laughed again, telling me that my hair was tickling you, but you raised your arms and wrapped them around me, anyway.

It has been my punishment that I cannot remember every time I held you or you reached for me and there must have been thousands. How could I forget any of them? And damn to hell the people who made it so I would have to try to remember them at all. Just damn them to hell.

The bitch witches who thrust and wink and whisper and suck the men deeper, deeper, deeper. They fly through the black ether and weave through the Web, weaving their own web, black night twisted women. I'm helping them get to hell this way. I tried other ways for years and I didn't get anywhere, but then I had something to lose. You. Now that you are lost to me, it doesn't matter anymore.

No, it matters. The truth is it will be a relief to finish and to stop missing you. To give in to the hole in my chest that hurts as badly as if it had been made with a scalpel instead of your absence. Sliced right through, cut open, dripping everything that I tried to do, every bit of good I tried to accomplish, every change I tried to expedite. All discredited, all a giant cosmic joke.

You wrote that it wasn't you I loved, but some idea of you. How could you ever think that? I would kill to show how much I loved you.

Now I have to shower and dress and then pick up your birthday cake, the one you loved the best. A yellow cake with strawberries and whipped cream. Not with one candle for each year, but with only one candle for the year that I have lived without you.

This I do for you.

Eighty-Four

Nina came into my office after both of our ten o'clock patients had left.

"Have you heard from Blythe?" she asked.

I shook my head. "No." I shrugged. "I'm not going to assume that means anything. She's twenty-five years old. There are a million reasons that she might not have checked her machine since last night. But I called her again this morning and left a new message."

"I heard from Stella. She just called. She'd be happy to see me. Well, us. But I didn't mention you over the phone. I'm not sure how to handle that."

"When?"

"One-thirty."

"Where?"

"Eighth Avenue. Forty-fourth Street."

"That's near Dulcie's theater."

Nina nodded. "Stella's part owner of a building there. I guess it's been renovated. That's what she always said they were going to do with it. Tear it down and turn it into offices."

Eighty-Five

─────◆◆◆─────

"I'm so glad you came."

Blythe smiled and extended her hand. The older woman's skin was very cold. But then this whole place was cold. Freezing. Why were they meeting here? It was a strange place for an interview.

Stella Dobson pointed to a chair. There was a single light shining down on it, creating a halo effect around it and painting long shadows on the wall.

Blythe took the proffered seat.

She'd been looking forward to meeting Stella for weeks. Even if it did mean talking about what she'd done and why she'd done it and what it had meant to her. Morgan was helping her with that and one day, she knew, she'd be able to put it completely behind her. Maybe today would even help her purge it.

"Are you comfortable?"

"Yes. But…it's so cold here. Aren't you cold?"

"I know. I'm sorry. The heat hasn't kicked in yet. But it should any second."

Stella walked to the wings of the stage and pulled out a table on wheels that squeaked just a little as she rolled it over.

Blythe was not surprised to see a laptop on it. After all, this was an interview. She'd thought Stella would tape record it, but if she wanted to type notes, that was fine.

The notebook was titanium and looked much more expensive than the used one that Blythe had. But just like her laptop at home, there was a small video camera clipped to the top of this computer. Exactly the same make and model as the one she had worked with.

"That's a coincidence," Blythe said.

"What is?"

"The camera. It's the same one I have."

Stella smiled. "I'm going to film you," she said as she turned on the computer and adjusted the minicamera. "I want to put portions of some of the interviews up on the Web when the book comes out, is that all right with you?"

"Cool."

"Good. I didn't think you'd mind being filmed. You did so much performing online." She smiled. "I hope you don't mind this, either."

Stella reached into a shopping bag. Blythe saw a flash of color and knew what it was instantly. The cobalt-blue feathers had deep purple undertones and were tinged with lavender.

"That's my mask," she said with a combination of wonder and confusion.

Stella smiled. "Well, not your exact mask, but one just like it. So you won't object to wearing it?"

Eighty-Six

Perez and Jordain were talking to Mrs. Johanson, the fifty-something head of the NYU library. It had been a frustrating half hour. There were more than fifty computer terminals in the library, which any student or faculty member could come and use. Plus, there were reciprocal privileges for faculty and grad students from other colleges and universities, as long as the visitor had the right credentials. In addition, there were dozens of carrels where students or faculty could plug in and use their own computers. And while you had to show an ID card to get into the library, you didn't have to sign in.

"So, basically, what you are saying is anyone in the library on these dates could have used either their own or your computers and there won't necessarily be a record of it?"

Mrs. Johanson nodded and her brown curls bobbed. She was wearing a cream-colored turtleneck and a pair of chocolate brown corduroy pants, with heavy snow boots on her feet that gave her otherwise small frame a solid base. "I'm sorry," she said, sounding genuinely distressed.

Jordain smiled at her. "Not your problem, ma'am."

"We appreciate your help," Perez added.

The two detectives went downstairs, and on their way out walked through the high, open space. Jordain thought the library was poorly designed. You needed smaller areas—nooks and friendly alcoves—in a library. Places where you could hole up and study for the afternoon, where you'd be comfortable, have some sense of privacy and at least some semblance of silence.

"Look around," he said to Perez.

"Okay, I'm looking."

"You think you'd come here to indulge your predilection for porn? Nice cozy place to jerk off, don't you think?"

"No."

"Right. The person who sent that e-mail wasn't here to go online and fool around and watch a few Web-cam girls while he had a free half hour. He was here working. Or doing research. Sending the e-mail from here was just convenient."

A few minutes later they were back in Mrs. Johanson's office.

"I'm sorry to bother you again," Jordain said.

"It's no bother." She smiled. "Did you forget something?"

"No, but we do have a new question," Perez said. "Do you think we could look through the call slips from three specific days in the past few weeks?"

"It's a long shot," Jordain said, "but we think that whoever sent the e-mail was here because he was actually using the library."

"Unless you threw out the court order you showed me twenty minutes ago, of course you can. Come with me."

Eighty-Seven

❧❧❧

Blythe couldn't take her eyes off Stella. The woman was a legend. A fearless fighter for women's rights. She'd almost starved to death for her principles. It had given Stella the aura of someone who would stop at nothing. And then she'd taken on Global Communications, hacking into their computer systems so she could contact the women who did Web-cam work and offer to help them get jobs outside of the porn industry. Blythe had gotten one of those letters, as had some of her friends. And Stella had helped some of them. Before she got sued. But even that had made her into more of a cult hero.

So, if Stella wanted Blythe to do the interview in her old costume, she would. But it was still strange. Blythe felt the feathers tickle her behind the ear. The smooth, silky sensation made her blood run hotter. She felt a thrill deep in her stomach. The instant reaction scared her. It was like stepping backward. The way she felt just holding a cigarette, knowing she wanted one but wouldn't have one because she never wanted to go through the pain of quitting again.

"I was hoping you'd indulge me. That you'd return to your character, become the woman you were online. A Venus hiding behind a mask, willing to spread her legs and show her audience anything they asked for."

Blythe didn't know Stella well enough to be sure, but it sounded as if her tone was tinged with contempt. And yet, why would Stella be angry with her? She watched her carefully. Stella's mouth was dry. There were deep circles under her eyes, rings of sweat on her red blouse. Something was wrong. Or was she overreacting?

Morgan had told her more than once that she had strong instincts and that she should trust them and rely on them. That it would help her with patients.

Stella pulled a thermos out of a shopping bag, along with two paper cups. "It's hot chocolate. The theater gets so cold. I thought it would help warm us up."

She handed a cup to Blythe.

Nothing was wrong. It *was* her imagination. It was this spooky old theater. The hot chocolate was delicious.

Stella turned on the Web cam, sat down opposite her and began the interview.

She started with the easy things: how much Blythe made, what hours she worked, when she'd begun.

Blythe answered all three questions and then yawned. "I'm sorry."

Stella smiled. "Did you ever think about what kind of effect your work was having on younger men? On boys who weren't even sexually active yet?"

"Effect? Sure. I was turning them on. It was safe and harmless."

"You were setting up an impossible goal, weren't you?"

That edge was back in Stella's voice. "I'm not sure I understand," Blythe said. She was slumping in her chair, she really was tired.

"You made it so easy for the boys. Just lie back and let me

make you hard. Let me act out your fantasy. You don't have to even think about me. I'm not real. I have no feelings. Do you understand how that affects young men?"

Blythe didn't know what to say. She had talked about these issues with Morgan, but Morgan was her supervisor. She didn't know if she wanted to talk about those things with Stella. Especially if it was going to be in a book. "This isn't what I expected you were going to talk to me about...I thought this had something to do with working my way through school...." Her voice sounded thick in her own ears.

Stella got up and walked around Blythe's chair and stood behind her. Blythe tried to turn, but her body was moving too slowly. Before she knew what was happening, she felt Stella's arms reach around her waist, grab her by the wrists and pull her arms backward.

Eighty-Eight

━━━━━━━━━━◦⊙◦━━━━━━━━━━

"I told Stella that I needed her help with something and she said of course she'd do whatever I needed, but she didn't sound like herself on the phone. Maybe you should wait for me in the lobby and let me go in first and explain who you are and why you're here with me. I'm worried. You know, now that I'm thinking about it, she did look stressed at the funeral last week. I should have called then."

We were stuck in traffic on Forty-ninth Street going west. Somewhere ahead of us, a driver leaned on his horn, adding to the noise pollution. I felt my teeth clench and focused on relaxing. My cold was getting worse and my throat was still sore. I popped a cough drop. "You can't watch out over everyone." I smiled at her. If my issue is saving souls, Nina's is being there for everyone.

"She's had a hard time. First losing the lawsuit, then Simone's death. It's bound to have affected her."

"The lawsuit, right. Did you know Alan Leightman's wife was the lawyer who won that case for the pornography company?"

Nina frowned. "Yes. What a mess that was. Stella was devastated when she lost. I had dinner with her about a week later. She told me it was as if everything she had worked to achieve had been wiped out in one afternoon. It was a huge blow. And then only a month later, Simone died."

"How did she survive it?" I forced myself not to think about Dulcie.

"I don't know if she did."

The traffic opened up and our driver sped ahead; five minutes later we pulled up in front of a building that I recognized well.

"What are we doing here?"

This was the abandoned Playpen Theater, near the theater where Dulcie performed. I hadn't paid much attention to it before Alan had mentioned it, but since then I'd found myself staring at it every time I passed by, wondering why it was still standing, abandoned and forlorn: a memorial to a part of New York that no one wanted to memorialize.

Nina had paid the driver and was waiting for change. "Stella owns this place, along with a group of other feminists she roped into contributing. It was supposed to be turned into a women's center to aid sex workers. There was a zoning problem, but when she told me to meet her here today, I assumed it had been resolved and she'd had the building renovated. I guess not."

I stepped out of the cab, navigating the piles of soot-covered snow. That's when I realized that it hadn't snowed in more than twelve hours. The sky was still overcast but maybe the siege was over.

Nina joined me on the sidewalk and stood with me, staring up at the marquee and the salacious neon figure of a busty woman, sitting with her legs crossed, forming the *P* in Playpen. Some of the neon tubes were broken but you could tell she had blond hair, red lips, pink arms and legs and large pink breasts. I could imagine how it once looked, all lit up, its glaring colors shining down at the men walking by, beckoning.

Nina pulled open the front door.

The lobby was dark, and once the door closed behind us it was almost pitch black inside. The air smelled stale and there was a top note of something that I couldn't quite identify with my stuffed nose.

From somewhere above us, I heard the soft cooing of a pigeon. How many birds had found their way inside over the years? How many rats?

Once my eyes adjusted, I noticed a thin strip of light coming from under double doors, next to what must have originally been the candy and soda concession. That was where Alan had said the X-rated videos and magazines were sold when he'd been here as a teenager. I sensed the ghosts of those men, careful as they walked into the theater, afraid that they might be seen, gulping nervously, feeling the sweat on their palms, wishing they could stay away, already knowing they would be back the next day, or the one after that.

"It will only take a second for me to tell her I brought someone with me. I'll be right back, okay?"

I nodded.

Nina opened the door. The light that came through was weak and flickering. And then she disappeared inside.

Eighty-Nine

❧⤜✧⤛❧

It took Perez and Jordain an hour to look through the lists of people who had requested items from the library or checked out books during the three days in question.

They weren't just looking for Alan's name. They were looking for Kira Rushkoff's, too. And they were also looking for any name that appeared on all three days.

"Here's one," Perez said, pointing. "Familiar, too, but I don't know why."

Perez watched his partner's face running the name through his computer-like brain, searching for the connection. Jordain never let him down. He wasn't as good as some detectives were with hunches, but he more than made up for it with his uncanny ability to absorb everything connected to everyone involved with a case. He only had to see a name once and he never forgot it.

"Something to do with Alan Leightman's wife, Kira Rushkoff. Wait, let me think." Jordain frowned.

Perez waited.

Thirty seconds later, Jordain remembered. "Got it. A civil court case. Last year. In all the papers. Big-time computer hacking of an online porn company. Damn it, Perez. It was Global. All the women who worked for the company got e-mail telling them their boss was exploiting them and that they needed to revolt. Rushkoff defended the slime who owned—" He stopped talking.

The expression on his face was at once elated and chagrined. "Fuck," he growled.

"What?"

"We need to find Ms. Stella Dobson right now."

"Why?"

Jordain was rushing to the car, not even bothering to button his coat. With the windchill it was ten degrees below zero; he didn't even notice.

Ninety

~~~⌒⌒⌒~~~

Before the door shut completely behind Nina, I stuck out my boot to keep it from closing. There wasn't enough space for me to see much: Nina's back, a section of theater seats, an empty patch of old wooden floor, the edge of a threadbare carpet.

"Stella? What's going on?" Nina sounded disturbed. Something was wrong. What was it?

"It's all right. It's all right" came a brittle voice.

Long dark shadows flickered on the wall to Nina's right.

"Stella, what are you doing? I don't understand."

"It meant a lot to me that you called *today*." The emphasis on her last word was strong.

"Today?"

"I thought you knew what today was."

Nina didn't answer right away. She must have been trying to figure out what day it was. When she finally answered, her voice was laced with grief. "Oh, Stella, I'm sorry. Today would have been Simone's birthday."

"Her eighteenth birthday. Look…"

I heard paper rattling, then Stella's voice: "I got her favorite cake. We'll light the candle soon. I'll make a wish for her.

You'll have some cake, won't you? You always came to her parties when she was little. You were always a good friend to me. You can be my witness."

I pushed my foot forward another half an inch and made the opening just a little bit bigger. What was wrong in there?

"Yes, of course. I'd love some cake. But, Stella, why don't you come down off the stage and sit with me, and we can talk first. Why don't we let—"

"I don't need to talk."

I didn't care what Nina had said. Or how fragile Stella might be. They say you can smell trouble. I didn't know what scent I was sniffing, but I knew it was dangerous.

As quietly as I could, I nudged the door farther open.

There was a creak. I froze. I was so still I could feel my own heart beating. My teeth started to chatter. I had to bite down on my cheek to stop them. Leaning forward, I looked into the room.

Nina was standing to the right of the block of theater seats staring up at the stage, where Stella stood looking down at her old friend. It was very dark inside. The stage was lit with only one dim, bare bulb that cast everything in a sallow light.

There didn't seem to be anything wrong after all. Just a distraught woman standing alone in a darkened theater.

And then Stella took a step forward and I could see what her body had been blocking.

Ninety-One

❧~❧~❧

"She's not home and she's not at her office. But she's got an appointment there in an hour which she hasn't called to cancel," Butler reported to Jordain a few minutes later, over the speaker phone in his car.

"What about her cell phone?"

"Her assistant won't give it to me without a subpoena. Want me to work on that from here?"

"Where's the assistant?"

"In the office—1 Washington Square Park North."

"We're still in the neighborhood—we'll go over there and get it ourselves. What does Dobson teach?" Jordain asked as he swung the car around and headed back south.

"Don't you know who she is?"

"Yes, she's a feminist. Noisy one. I just asked what she teaches."

"Women's studies. She's more than just a noisy feminist. She's a brilliant writer who—"

"You ever read her, Butler?" Perez interrupted.

"Is this a real question, or are you giving me shit?"

"Real question. Quick, we need to know as much as you

can tell us. What's happened to her recently? What makes her angry? What's she been fighting lately."

"Her daughter died last June. Overdose."

"Accidental?" Perez asked.

"So the report says, but that's based on Dobson's statement. A few months before that, she lost a large civil court case and was fined six hundred thousand dollars—"

"We're here. Is there anything else I need to know?" Perez picked up the phone and stayed on it while he got out of the car and followed Jordain down the street toward Dobson's office.

"I'm reading…wait…yes…shit…the lawsuit's a little close for comfort," Butler said. "Dobson hired a computer genius to hack into Global Communication's database. She got the e-mail addresses of all the women who worked for them and wrote offering to help them find legitimate work."

"We know that. Stay close by. I'll let you know if we need any backup."

"Perez, you know the lawyer who handled the case for the porn company was Alan Leightman's wife, Kira Rushkoff? That means…"

But he'd already hung up on her.

Ninety-Two

~~~~~

A laptop and a birthday cake sat on a small table in the middle of the stage. The cake was small, frosted with what looked like white buttercream, edged with pink roses, with one pink candle sticking up in the center.

Blythe, wearing a blue butterfly mask, sat two feet from the table. Her wrists were tied together behind her back. Her ankles were tied together beneath the chair. There was a gag in her mouth.

"What is Blythe doing here?" Nina asked.

"She's here for the party, like you are."

"Did Blythe know Simone?"

"No. But Simone knew Blythe. She and her poor friend found Blythe online. She taught these two innocents all she knew. While I was doing everything I could to make sure my daughter grew up to be strong and sure of herself, she was sitting in her bedroom surfing the Internet, learning how to be a slut from a slut like this. I loved her. I loved her so much. And this is what she did. That's what we've raised, Nina. You and me…all of us…despite our efforts and our understanding and our rebelling and our screaming and our marching and getting arrested…we wound up raising a generation of daughters who are so desperate for men's attention that they are willing to debase themselves. Do you know what they did? My daughter and her friend? They turned themselves into New York City Web-cam girls."

Stella had moved to the very edge of the stage and stood staring down at Nina.

"You have it wrong," Nina said, her voice soothing. "It's not the fault of the girls like Blythe. Blythe is a victim, too. She's someone we need to help. Come down, sit here with me, we can talk about how we can help these women. We've spent our whole lives trying to help. We can't give up yet." Nina held her hand up to Stella, offering her support. Her faith took my breath away. She actually believed she could talk her down. Oh, God, I hoped she was right. I was scared for her. And for Blythe.

"You think you can help?" Stella gave a short, ugly laugh. "Think back to when we started. What's changed? It's only gotten worse, hasn't it? Women are more subservient. More accommodating. Men are more abusive than they have ever been. Millions of them involved with pornography now. And what do they want? Women who perform. Who demand nothing. Who accept less than nothing."

I needed to sneeze, but I knew that if I did Stella would realize I was there. And that was dangerous. It hurt to hold it in, but after a few seconds the urge passed.

"Nina, she dressed up like a whore. She and her friend pretended they were lesbians to titillate those boys. They filmed themselves and sent it to the boys, and the boys sent it all over the school. And you know what? Simone didn't care. She loved it. She was thrilled. She had never been happier. She thought they wanted her. I tried to explain to her that what she was doing was only making them want her breasts. Her vagina. Her as a fantasy. As an image. Not to talk to her or share with her or understand her or help her or have her help them, but to have her to masturbate to.

"And you know what she said in her note? She blamed me. She said I only loved her when she agreed to be one kind of daughter. She said I only wanted women to be powerful if they were going to be my kind of powerful—women who didn't need men—who could raise a child without a man, who would rather be single than subservient.

"She was my baby. She didn't think I loved her. Do you know why? Because of these women who are not women, these women who have fangs and claws. She said I was angry with her because she didn't meet my political objectives.

"I watched that movie and I hated her, hated my daughter. I hated her and hated her—until I realized it was all these other women who were to blame. I loved Simone right. I did. I loved her and wanted her to be a woman who had self-esteem and never went on crazy diets and never needed to wear lipstick or to dress to please a man, and she said that I never loved her right."

The whole time she was ranting, Stella was holding something and nervously, anxiously, shifting it from one hand to the next.

The smell I'd noticed when I first came into the theater was stronger here, but I just couldn't tell what it was. It was so rare that I couldn't identify an odor. But my cold was throwing off my sense of smell. But I couldn't worry about that. I had to listen to Stella. I had to keep my eye on Nina. I had to watch out for Blythe. I had to figure out what to do.

"What happened to Simone couldn't go unpunished, don't you see that? What these bitch witch women do has repercussions. Someone has to show them."

"Simone didn't die of an accidental overdose, did she?"

"What does that have to do with it? This is about the women who taught Simone how to be a whore. Who poisoned her." Her voice finally cracked, but her expression remained defiant. "Do you understand? While I was fighting to save girls like this, my own daughter was becoming one. So I hired someone to hack that porn site's servers. Everyone thought I cared about getting caught. That I cared about that trial. I didn't lose. That was a joke. They all thought I lost. No. I won. I needed to get to the girls. I needed to tell them they were throwing their potential away. I didn't lose. That cunt Rushkoff lost. I found out her husband was watching those girls. He used a pseudonym online, but I had the credit card records. Finding him there, now that was sweet. That was something I could use."

Stella laughed. Whatever disaster she'd planned was close to coming to fruition and she was becoming more agitated. Meanwhile, the smell was growing in intensity. I could see that she'd stopped to sniff the air, too. Then she smiled again.

"She didn't know her own precious husband was one of the men who couldn't stay away. Judge fucking Alan Leightman. Paying to watch the same sluts who were ruining Simone. He's in jail. You know that? He's paying for his sins now. For his and his wife's sins. He's my little joke on her. He turned himself in. Can you imagine?"

"None of this will bring Simone back," Nina said.

"No, but it will take me to Simone. I'll go to her offering revenge. She will forgive me then."

I needed to call the police and get them here. But how could I do that without making a sound? Either I backed out and hoped that I could do it quietly enough not to alert Stella, or I tried to dial from where I was.

But how could I say anything without her knowing I was there? Would 911 respond if I didn't talk? No, they couldn't.

This wasn't a land line; they wouldn't know where I was. I was going to have to back out and shut the door. But I couldn't do that until Stella turned around. I couldn't risk her seeing me and panicking.

"Stella, I know how upset you are. I can't imagine how horrible it is when your daughter takes her own life. But Blythe didn't have anything to do with Simone killing herself," Nina said, trying to reason with her old friend.

"She debased herself for those boys, and still they didn't care. They passed the file around and all watched it, and they still didn't want her. When I found out, I did everything I could to make her understand. I wanted to help her cleanse herself. But...but...she didn't listen to me. All she wanted was one of those boys to put his prick in her mouth. That was all that mattered, and if she couldn't have that..."

She was on the verge of losing control. I could see it in her eyes.

"No more explaining. No more. I'm tired. This was all I wanted. To give her this present for her birthday. Every one of those girls she copied has been punished, each of them poisoned by the very act that poisoned Simone. She's the last one...." Stella nodded toward Blythe.

"Now it's time to wish my baby happy birthday. Will you sing with me, Nina? Sing. *Happy birthday to you—*" Her cracked voice was off key.

Nina didn't join in.

"You have to sing with me."

I had seen people break before but it never lost its horror. Stella was angry now. Her eyes were on fire. She fumbled with the thing in her hand. It fell. She bent over to pick it up.

Now I could see what it was.

A box of matches.

Of course, she had to light the candle on the cake.

I don't remember putting it all together.

One second I couldn't tell what the smell was, the next I could suddenly breathe clearly and knew what it was. There was no time think about what needed to be done. Even calling out to Nina wouldn't have accomplished anything. It would have taken me too long to explain.

In one long, slow motion, Stella moved her right foot forward, then her left. She was only two steps away from Blythe and the table and the cake. I saw the tremor in the hand that held the matchbox and heard the sound of the wooden sticks hitting each other so loudly it was as if it had been magnified a hundred times.

I ran forward, taking the steps to the stage two at a time. In my peripheral vision, I saw Nina standing with her mouth in a small astonished O.

Stella had opened the box. She shook out a match. It fell to the floor. She looked at it. Bent to pick it up. Retrieved it. Stood. Held the match to strike it.

I reached her, running right into her, knocking the box and the match out of her hands.

Shocked, she didn't focus on me but looked down at the spilled matches.

"I have to do this. She is the last one. I promised Simone. I have to do this. Get away." She pushed me with enormous force. I wasn't prepared and I felt myself falling, fought to find my balance.

"Nina!" I shouted. "The theater is full of gas. She has matches. She wants to blow the place up. Get out. Call the police."

Stella was coming at me with her hands open and her fingers curled. She tried for my eyes; I ducked. She grabbed my hair and yanked. I heard myself scream and swung my right arm. The flat of my cast made contact with her face. I heard something crack. My wrist? The cast? Stella staggered back, clutching her face. She was screaming. Blood was running through her fingers.

Nina had reached us by then.

Stella's fingers were smeared with blood. Blood was still streaming down her chin and dripping onto her neck and it occurred to me that I had done that to her.

While Nina tied Stella's hands together with my scarf, I pulled the gag out of Blythe's mouth. Clearly drugged, she looked at me with glassy confused eyes.

"You're going to be okay. Just hold on," I told her.

Awkwardly, I pulled my cell phone out of my bag with one hand, dialed 911, gave them the address of the theater and told them to send both the police and an ambulance. "There's a young woman here who I think has been poisoned. Hurry."

Knowing the more information we could give the paramedics, the better the chances for Blythe's survival, I told them all I knew. Once I hung up I turned to Stella.

Sitting in a corner of the stage, she was rocking slightly back and forth as if she could hear music and was moving to its beat. Nina, standing above her, looked down on her old friend with an expression of desperate sadness.

"What did you give her?" I asked Stella.

"She can't hear you, Morgan," Nina said.

I knew what kind of shape Stella was in, I could see it, but I couldn't give up, not yet. "What did you give Blythe?"

Stella didn't even look at me. Staring out into the distance, she was seeing something beyond Nina and me, beyond the stage and the theater, beyond the present.

"What did you give Blythe?" I was screaming now.

Stella started to answer me in a hoarse whisper and I leapt forward to make sure I heard every word.

"Happy birthday to you, happy birthday to you…" she sang in a thin, cracked voice.

"What did you give Blythe?"

As if she'd actually heard the question, she stopped singing and cocked her head toward me and I felt a flutter of hope.

"If only we'd had the cake." Stella's voice was low and without inflection. "It would have made Simone so happy. She would have liked to see all of us so much. If only we'd had the cake. It would have made Simone so happy. She would have liked to see all of us so much…"

Meanwhile, Nina had opened Stella's bag and was rifling through it. "Let's hope this is all she gave Blythe." She held up a prescription bottle of popular sleeping pills.

Even though it was probably pointless, I tried once more. "Did you give her these pills, Stella? How many?"

"If only we'd had the cake. It would have made Simone so happy. She would have liked to see all of us so much. If only we'd had the cake. It would have made Simone so happy. She would have liked to see all of us…"

Her recitation was interrupted by the arrival of the police and the paramedics right behind them.

Ninety-Three

~~~~~~~~

On Sunday, I picked Dulcie up after her three o'clock performance. We were quiet in the car as it pulled away from the curb. We still had to resolve our differences. And I knew, because Mitch had told me, that she still had her heart set on trying out for the television series because they still hadn't cast anyone.

The driver headed west and at Eighth Avenue, turned the corner. The light changed. We'd stopped just a few feet away from the Playpen Theater.

It had only been two days since Stella had almost blown us all up in there.

Blythe was already out of the hospital and home with her parents. She had been given sleeping pills but just enough to sedate her. Stella was in a psychiatric hospital under observation; I doubted she'd ever leave.

A shudder went through me. Inside that theater, I hadn't thought about how much danger I'd been in, but now sitting next to Dulcie, it hit me harder than I expected it to.

Protecting everyone had been all that mattered to me.

Dulcie. Nina. Blythe. My patients.

Long ago, my mother.

I hadn't thought about protecting myself.

It was something, to use the analytic phrase, that I would have to work on.

"What do you want to do this afternoon?" I asked Dulcie when the car started moving again.

She shrugged.

"Nina invited us to go ice-skating with her. Do you want to do that?"

I could see that the suggestion had piqued her interest. Her eyes had widened and she'd almost smiled, but then she'd remembered that she was supposed to be mad at me. "I guess." She managed to keep any expression out of her voice. She really was the consummate actress. I thought of my mother and sighed. There wasn't anything I could do about it.

At Wollman Rink in Central Park, a waltz played, the ice shimmered, and dozens of pairs of silver skates flashed as they raced past. I watched my daughter as Nina must have once watched me. The wind blew her dark hair out behind her and her eyes sparkled as she sped across the rink, skating so fast her feet were a blur.

Nina and I were skating arm in arm, very slowly. She was concerned that with the cast my balance might be off. I didn't think it was, but I didn't mind the contact or the comfort she offered. Despite the cold bite in the air, I kept circling, watching my daughter's agile body flying across the ice, feeling the warmth of Nina's arm against mine. Going around and around. No beginning to the circle, and no end.

Afterward, we went back to Nina's brownstone. I sat in the kitchen while she and Dulcie hovered over the stove, melting chocolate in a double-boiler until it was shiny and soft and then stirring in milk. It wasn't hot cocoa, but hot chocolate, prepared the way they had been making it in Europe for the past three hundred years. The way Dulcie had wanted me to make it two very long weeks ago.

Sitting around the coffee table, sipping the thick, fragrant elixir and munching on cookies, Nina asked Dulcie about the play, and I listened as my daughter launched into a soliloquy about the rewards and frustrations of performing on Broadway. I wasn't surprised when she segued very nicely into how much more exciting it would be to do something different every week. Like be in a television drama.

She managed to shoot me a look but I didn't respond.

I just drank my hot chocolate and wondered how I was going to get my daughter back without giving in to what she wanted.

Ninety-Four

⟨≈⟩

Later that night, I stopped by her room to say goodnight. The door was open and she was in bed, watching a rerun of *The Actor's Studio*.

I walked in, sat down beside her, picked up the clicker and muted the sound. "I know how much the audition means to you, but it's not going to happen no matter how good a job you do of torturing me. I don't know what the right way to deal with this is— I'm sure if it was something one of my patients was going through I'd know just how to advise her, but I'm just being your mother here, and all I can think to tell you is that I don't want you to have to deal with the pressures and stress of doing a television show yet."

"Yeah, yeah. Dr. Sin saves the sinners, but she doesn't know what to do with her own daughter."

"What do you mean saves the sinners?" I was used to her calling me Dr. Sin, but this wasn't just her being cute and clever, she was issuing a new challenge.

She told me what she'd pieced together between the news on TV and what Mitch had told her about the scene at the

Playpen Theater. She'd heard that I'd saved a woman's life and that the woman had been a Web-cam girl—hence, a sinner.

Until that night, I'd tried to shield Dulcie from so much of what I did. I'd always thought she was too young to hear it. But she was only three years younger than Simone and Amanda had been when they'd made their X-rated movie.

So for the next hour, I told Dulcie about the two best friends and how they'd felt about the boys in their school and how hard it was for them to figure out what to do, and I told her what they'd finally done, how it had all turned around and become a nightmare that they never escaped, and how sadly one had taken her own life, but the other was in therapy now and would be getting the best help there was.

When I was done, I brushed a lock of dark hair off my daughter's face and looked into her cornflower-blue eyes. "I know what you want, but I can't let you have it yet. I need to protect you. I promise I'm not going to go crazy and lock you up in the house. You can do the play. And after this play, if you want to do another one, we can talk about that. But I need to keep you with me for a few more years, so I can do everything in my power to help you through this last part of growing up. And so you can help me through it, too."

She hadn't interrupted me once. She still didn't say anything. I hoped I hadn't made a mistake by telling her Amanda and Simone's story.

"Do you want some water before you go to bed?"

She shook her head. "I think I'm really tired, Mom," she said, scooting under the covers, looking so little among all the pillows and the comforter.

I hadn't expected her to acquiesce or to throw her arms around me and tell me that she loved me and would do anything I wanted her to do. This was all I had hoped for. A cease-fire. A willingness to listen to me explain.

I was so grateful.

As long as she would let me sit on the side of her bed and talk to her, as long as she would listen, as long as she took what I said in, that was all I could ask for. It was so much more than so many parents had.

Ninety-Five

Dulcie was still sleeping when I left on Monday morning. I asked Mary, our housekeeper, if she would try to convince her to have more than juice for breakfast for once.

"If she saw you eat something, she'd eat something. She does whatever you do, don't you know that? She wants to be just like you," Mary chided me and was confused when I broke into a smile.

There was enough sidewalk showing for me to walk to work again. Sure, it was cold, but the clean-smelling cold that is refreshing rather than painful.

Twenty minutes later, I was sitting at my desk. I'd just gotten off the phone with Blythe, who had called to tell me she thought she was almost ready to come back to work but thought she could use a few therapy sessions first. I was setting up an appointment when Allison stuck her head in my door.

"Alan Leightman's ready to see you. Are you ready for him?"

I hadn't expected him to keep his standing Monday appointment that first week.

In the first five minutes, he told me that after he'd been released on Friday, he'd moved into a hotel, and had offered to go to therapy with Kira.

"I'd like to have a real relationship. I don't know if it can be with her, but I owe it to both of us to try. You asked me once about the first woman I'd seen naked and I told you how I'd watched her behind the glass in that theater. You knew that all the women are behind glass. The theater glass. The computer screen. Can we figure that out? Will we figure that out?"

I could encourage him, and I did. But no matter how much I wanted to, I couldn't make that promise. The best we could do, the best we can ever do, is try.

At noon, I put on my coat, went downstairs and walked around the corner to the Regency Hotel.

The maître d' showed me to the table. Noah stood up when he saw me. He was smiling, and while he still looked like he could use some more sleep, he clearly had gotten some rest.

"How's your wrist?" he asked after I'd sat down and accepted some of the red wine he'd already ordered.

"Not bad. The doctor said I didn't do any extra damage."

"Didn't do any damage? You smashed her nose. Broke it in two places."

We talked about Blythe and how she was doing and Stella's arraignment, and about the three women who had died because a daughter had not lived up to her mother's expectations. I shifted in my seat, uncomfortable for a minute, thinking about my own expectations for Dulcie. We talked about the past four days, and about how Dulcie was adjusting to being back home with me.

"She's going to be fine."

I nodded, wanting to believe him. "I know I don't have any control over what happens to her. I just want to help her find her way and make it as painless for her as possible. But I may not be able to do even that. No matter what, she'll know I loved her. Not some idea of her."

I was thinking about Stella Dobson and a young woman named Simone whom I'd never met.

"The best you've done with Dulcie has been to show her that she's lovable for who she is. She'll take that with her out into the world, and that will keep her relatively safe, Morgan. It will."

I smiled at him.

"So, this is a little complicated," Noah said, changing the subject.

"Meeting me?"

"Yes, well, what I'm here to talk to you about."

A waiter appeared with a bottle of wine and topped off our glasses. Noah waited until he'd left.

"I think I'm here to offer you a job," he said.

The last time we'd been alone together had been five days ago, on that morning that Noah had dressed me, when we'd made love, and afterward, over breakfast, fought for the second—or was it the third?—time about what I couldn't tell him about Alan Leightman but wanted him to believe me. It wasn't the first time we'd clashed over his profession and mine and I knew each time it happened it took its toll.

It felt like much more time than that had passed, but not this much.

"A job? Is this a joke?"

He shook his head and looked at me a little sadly. He was sitting close enough to me that I could smell his rosemary-and-mint cologne.

"No."

"Okay, shoot. Sorry. Bad choice of words."

He waved away the apology. "The New York Police Department, Special Victims Unit, is looking for a chief forensic psychologist. We have been for more than a month." Noah's voice wavered and he cleared his throat. "You have every qualification. We haven't found the right person to fill the job. Or, I should say we have. You could do it. You'd be perfect. I thought that, at least, I should tell you about it. Not make the decision for you. It seemed to me that you might want a challenge."

"In a million years, I never would have guessed that you would be talking to me about this."

"No, me neither."

The room wasn't conducive to romantic encounters. It was all business. Clean, hard lines, crisp linens. Men and women in business attire. Noah was probably the most casually dressed man there, in his worn leather jacket, a black turtleneck and jeans.

I looked away. At strangers. Out the window. Anywhere but Noah's face. The ragged edge of disappointment I was feeling reminded me that no one lives without regret. A splinter of fear cautioned me that loving someone meant a loss of power, and that even though power was sometimes all that kept me sane, it wasn't always worth holding on to.

A week earlier, I would have thought Noah could read in my eyes all that I was thinking, but when I finally glanced at him, he looked back at me with eyes that were dulled. The electricity was turned off.

"Let me just get this straight," I said. "If I were to take this job, we wouldn't be able to see each other, right?"

"Well, we'd see each other, but not in a personal way anymore." He shrugged. As if that shouldn't matter to either of us.

"We'd finally stop this push-pull thing we have going on. We'd be friends."

"Friends." His New Orleans drawl slowed the word down and turned it into something lesser, something inadequate. "Is that what you want?"

"It would be easier."

"Is it what you want?"

He wasn't going to tell me. He didn't have to. Impulsively, I leaned over, getting as close to him as I could, put my good hand on top of his arm as if to anchor him there, and then I kissed him.

His lips were closed at first.

And they stayed closed.

I'd lost him. I'd waited too long.

And then…then, finally, he moved forward, his hands came up and cupped my face, he pulled me closer to him, as close as we could get in our chairs, and he kissed me back.

Not the way a man would kiss you who offered you a job.

No, not that way at all.

Acknowledgments

To my incomparable agent Loretta Barrett as well as Nick Mullendore and Gabriel Davis at Loretta Barrett Books for all your hard work and great advice.

To my amazing editor, Margaret O'Neill Marbury, for whom I am daily thankful for too many reasons to list.

To Dianne Moggy and Donna Hayes for all your efforts and enthusiasm on my behalf. Thank you.

To MIRA's editorial department, marketing & PR departments, art and production departments and the entire sales force for everything you do and do so well.

To Mara Nathan and Chuck Clayman for your insight, time and creativity. Any errors in this book are because I didn't listen to you two well enough.

To Luci Zahray, the amazing and generous "poison lady." I could never have killed all these poor women without you. You are a novelist's dream.

To every bookseller who works so hard to get books into the hands of readers but especially my hometown booksellers: Jenny Lawton of Just Books Too and Diane Garrett of Diane's Books.

To Lisa Tucker and Douglas Clegg for helping when the words didn't come or this story got stuck.

To all my wonderful friends and colleagues—and those who are both—especially the brilliant and generous ITW gang.

To my wonderful family: Gigi, Jay, Jordan, my father and Ellie.

And always last but also always most important, to Doug Scofield for the laughs, the support, the smarts and the faith.

A new chilling tale by
New York Times bestselling author

HEATHER GRAHAM

The gift of sight comes at a dangerous price.

When Deep Down Salvage begins the hunt for the
Josephine Marie, it seems like any other dive...until
Genevieve Wallace sees the vision of a dead woman in the
water, her vacant eyes boring into Genevieve's very soul.

Genevieve is terrified and confused by what she saw,
and no one—including her diving partner—believes her.
When a dead woman washes ashore, everyone assumes
this is Genevieve's "vision," but Genevieve knows the
truth: the dead woman is not the ghost she saw but
another victim of the same brutal killer....

"Graham...has penned yet another spine-tingling
romantic suspense." —*Booklist* on *Picture Me Dead*

THE VISION

*Available the first
week of July 2006
wherever paperbacks
are sold!*

MIRA®